Evacuation Road

©HM Waugh, 2021

Published by Rhiza Edge, 2021
An imprint of Rhiza Press
PO Box 302
Chinchilla Qld 4413
Australia
www.rhizaedge.com.au

Cover design by Carmen Dougherty
Layout by Rhiza Press

Print ISBN: 978-1-76111-035-1

 A catalogue record for this book is available from the National Library of Australia

All rights reserved. No part of this publication may be reproduced, stored in a retrieval system or transmitted in any form by any means without the prior permission of the copyright owner. Enquiries should be made to the publisher.

EVACUATION ROAD

HM WAUGH

rhiza edge

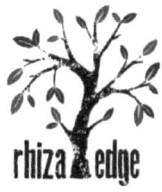

To my parents, for encouraging a much younger me to travel alone to a vast continent, where I could rarely send an email to say I was okay.

Thank you. It was totally worth it.

CHAPTER ONE

Exactly six days before our evacuation flight

Spitting out the gravel was a mistake. It hit the ground in front of my nose, shooting back into my face and eyes. I probably looked like I was crying.

Too far away, dust billowed from the back of several lurid yellow buses as they raced off. Diminishing specks of hope, framed by ochre mountains. It took less than two seconds to comprehend how deep in it I was:

- I was in the middle of South America,
- The world was screwed,
- Someone was firing a gun, and
- My bus just left without me.

You can see why crying might have been an awesome option. Face down on the street. Possibly about to be shot. And all alone.

Almost.

From behind me came Mike Cho's voice, and I was so glad to hear someone familiar I didn't even care that the last time he'd spoken to me had been to ask which op shop reject bin I'd stolen my shirt from. I'd liked that shirt, too.

'What was that noise?' he said. 'Where are the freaking buses?'

Before I could rustle up an answer, I heard Odati Richards reply. 'Careful,' she said, 'it might have been gunshots.'

'Maybe, yeah, everyone's on the ground. Is that Eva Whatzerface eating dirt over there?'

He pronounced my name like everyone back home. *Ee-va*. Not like my old Spanish teacher used to. Not like how they do here. *E-ba*. And for the record, my second name is not Whatzerface. It's Somerville, which I don't actually think is all that hard to remember. I inched up my head. More shots rang out, and I was rewarded with a vision of Odati and Mike's expensive jeans hitting the dust a car length behind me.

My heart was trying to thump a hole through the road. A beat-up ute prowled past, tyres crunching, occupants jeering in Spanish, and I sunk my eyes down.

If this was it for me, then I didn't want to watch.

The shots were so loud I shuddered further into the gravel, wincing against the coming pain. Except there wasn't any.

I hadn't been shot. So who had?

I looked up in time to see the ute backfire, and I groaned.

Unbelievable.

I was cowering in the dust, probably looking like I was crying—which I was 70% sure I wasn't—and all because of a backfiring car.

My evacuation bus left me behind ... because of a backfiring car.

Semi-automatic machine guns having a party might actually have been preferable. At least I would've felt like the bus driver had been saving everyone else's lives when he abandoned me.

They may have been a hideous shade of yellow, but those evac buses were security, safety. Hope. And now ... all gone.

Grit crunched between my teeth. Why had I got off my bus?

So stupid.

I wouldn't normally classify myself as stupid. I don't make mistakes. I don't even make decisions without severe and prolonged investigation into whether it's the right thing for my future, usually involving an A4 piece of paper with PROS and CONS written above two generously wide columns.

I didn't do that before I got off my bus.

If I had it would have looked like this:

PROS	CONS
• Get to go to the loo • Avoid public humiliation of wet pants	• Might get separated from class • Might never get home • Might be marooned with Odati and Mike in the middle of nowhere
UNACCEPTABLE RISK For goodness' sake, Eva, do not get off the bus!	

I felt like kicking myself and was trying hard to stop shaking and to focus on anything that wasn't about how impossible things looked.

Odati hauled herself to her feet with a grunt, squinting after the old ute. 'I wonder if I offered to tune their engine, would they take us to the next town?'

I winced upwards, trying to wipe my face without anyone noticing. It was obvious Odati hadn't understood any of what the guys in the ute had been saying as they drove past. Because if we sponged a lift off them, I had the feeling we'd end up dead in a frozen ditch.

A growing collection of people were watching us, the *gringos* standing around looking lost and terrified, squinting into the lowering sunlight.

Lost and terrified.

At least I was. I can't vouch for the other two.

I shook myself to try and clear my head. It didn't work, so I bluffed instead. I'm an expert at bluffing. Years of pretending I don't care what others think about me.

'We should get out of the middle of the road,' I said to Odati and Mike. 'Wait somewhere safe. Maybe the buses will come back.'

My eyes landed on the stark concrete lines of an eatery, there to cater to the travellers that used to drop in for a brief toilet stop before hopping back on their bus. You know—buses that don't leave without them because drivers don't get freaked out because some car backfiring reminded them of horror stories on last night's news and they decided the end of the world had come.

Which maybe it had, but I still would've preferred to be on my bus while said end played out.

I had to pull myself together. I pointed at the faded Coke signs and plastic tables. 'Let's go in there.'

Mike flared his nose. 'Who asked for your opinion, scab?' He snorted. 'Have you been crying?'

I looked away.

But then Odati huffed. 'Mike! Leave off!' She turned to me and nodded. 'Let's go inside.'

I blinked a few times. I'd never had much to do with Odati— I'd presumed since she and Mike hung out in the same group she'd share his prejudices. I'm happy to be proven wrong on that sort of thing.

The harsh fluoro light inside the eatery transformed us in alien ways as we took places around a precarious table on mismatched plastic chairs. It added a weird ultramarine hue to Odati's skin, and Mike's signature silver streak shone like a beacon above his temple. This close I saw he had dark bags under his eyes. Or maybe it was just the light.

A girl our age inched forward to take our order, and I fingered what remained of my filthy notes. I ordered coca tea—the cheapest item on the menu. It also helps with altitude sickness. Odati and Mike ordered cola.

The three of us looked awkwardly at each other. Well, I felt awkward with them, and they seemed awkward with me, but I suppose they were quite comfortable together.

'Let's start by counting our money,' Odati said.

Cash had become all too precious in the last week or so. Like the entire world had realised it was fine to save money in a bank, but only if the bank could give it back to you when you wanted it.

And we all wanted it now.

I fiddled with my money belt, trying not to make it obvious to any would-be bandits or gun-wielding desperates. Mike rifled through his bag, a shifty look on his face.

We tallied what we had. It was a lot. It was hardly anything. Mike and I had some US dollars, about the same in *bolivianos,* but they were worth so much less. Odati had a lot more of everything. Maybe we could change the foreign notes in a bank in the next big town.

But maybe not.

I hadn't seen a bank with intact windows for days. Banks weren't all that popular since the financial collapse had roared around the globe. Whenever I caught a glimpse of the news, some bank somewhere in the world was being trashed.

Together we held more than an average month's wages in *bolivianos*. But we had a long way to go if we couldn't catch the buses up, and prices kept soaring higher. I wished I'd paid more attention to the map the consulate guy had given Miss C when we'd all been crammed into our already over-full bus.

'Where do you think we are?' I asked.

'Somewhere between Sucre and Potosí,' Mike answered. He sounded confident, his antagonistic edge had even softened. Which was just as well, because I had enough on my plate. He'd dragged a hefty guidebook out of his daypack and was checking a map with fingers that no longer shook. Odati and I huddled closer. We were practically smack bang in the middle of Bolivia, which was kind of smack bang in the middle of South America.

And nowhere at all near Australia.

Winding road, barren mountains, stark and beautiful beneath a cloudless sky; I'd been sketching all day.

We'd been in South America for three weeks already, two and a bit of them our expected class trip, the last three or four days a bizarre messed-up race for a flight home. Not that I expected home to be any better than where we were. The increasingly infrequent news reports made it clear this collapse was happening everywhere.

But still … home, you know?

That day we'd been driving towards the old silver-mining town of Potosí, perched so far above sea level that walking and talking at the same time wasn't going to be an option for coast-huggers like us. The map showed absolutely no towns on the road between Sucre and Potosí. Somehow, looking through the dusty café windows at this withered *pueblo*, I wasn't surprised the cartographer had left it off.

Odati looked up at me, eyes alight. 'We could catch them up! Ask the people here about other buses!'

The waitress came back with our drinks and I ventured to ask her when the next public bus to Potosí might pass through, phrasebook open to the right page. '*¿A qué hora sale el próximo autobús a Potosí?*'

I was pretty sure she told me one would come the next morning.

Not brilliant, but okay. Except then I had a flash memory of my old teacher, explaining how morning and tomorrow were the same word in Spanish. Did the waitress mean morning?

She shook her head. '*Tarde.*'

Oh, heck.

Odati and Mike looked excited. We'd been on a study trip to Brazil, but their super-basic Portuguese wasn't helping here in Spanish-speaking Bolivia.

'She says the next bus to Potosí won't come until tomorrow afternoon,' I said.

Their faces sunk towards the shiny table.

'Miss C will wait for us.' Mike spun fingers through his hair so it morphed back to its normal plastic glory.

But Odati shook her head. 'They won't let her. Remember how the consulate guy left those backpackers at the border? He warned us then that he waits for no one. That's why Miss C told us to carry essentials and stick together.'

Two things I hadn't managed very well.

For the first time, I registered the loss of my backpack, securely crammed in the bus hold. My daypack was piteously small in comparison.

Note to self: in future, pack with the total and absolute worst in mind.

My fleece jacket was around my waist. In my daypack I had:
- deodorant, toothbrush, toothpaste, hair brush and a gaggle of hair ties
- my pencils and sketchbook
- a spare pair of undies—yes, just one
- a pair of hiking socks, toes melted from drying over a fire
- half a block of chocolate (yay)
- a bottle of water, and
- my first aid kit and phone charger.

I felt pretty smug at having remembered to pack the first aid. In my pocket was my cracked and ageing phone, with absolutely no coverage—we'd had no internet or messages for days now. In my money belt was some precious currency, my passport and a freaking useless bankcard.

Oh, and a red pen scribble on the inside cover of my sketchbook.

Santiago, Chile / May 5th, 1830hrs.

Miss C had made us write it down. Just in case.

Salvation, six days hence. The flight details bore no resemblance to our initial arrangements, but then we were never supposed to be in Bolivia either. Everything had to change after the collapse.

Different departure city, in a different country, on a different day, with a different airline.

But the flight would take us home, and that was what counted.

Except we'd lost our bus, and everything had changed. Again.

CHAPTER TWO

6 days until flight
½ block chocolate
US$1560 and Bs2125 between us

Dark falls quickly when there are few streets and even fewer streetlights.

I felt empty, watching the shadows creep over the barren mountains. I wasn't alone, but I wasn't with friends. Things were now on a new scale of bad; I almost couldn't believe it all.

Soup was bubbling in an enormous pot and a few of the locals were in for a meal. Their eyes skittered from us to the street to the aging television in the corner, where blazing static held reign. My stomach rumbled.

'We should eat,' I said.

Mike rolled his eyes, but Odati nodded. I gestured the waitress over and ordered three set menus.

She returned with three piping-hot bowls of comfort, and I inhaled the steam like it could fix all this. Mike poked my arm, and I disjointedly asked her if there was a hostel in the village. She shook her head and her sad smile told me we were out of luck.

As she headed back, I buried my nose in my phrasebook, trying to figure out how on earth to ask if we could sleep in someone's private home. It wasn't in the 'Accommodation' section, so I tried 'Going out'. Maybe that's when people were most likely to need to crash on someone's couch. I did find a way to ask to stay the night, but considering the tone of the phrases all around that section, I wasn't confident it was appropriate for our current situation. As in, a tiny eatery filled with a bunch of strangers.

'Are you blushing?' Mike raised one eyebrow.

'No!'

Heck yeah I was.

I'd never said any of those things to anyone in English, let alone in Spanish. I felt like I'd stumbled onto a steamy romance novel in the middle of a maths book. I slammed the phrasebook shut and concentrated on my soup.

Mike pulled a container of pills out of his bag and chased one down with cold coca tea. 'Vitamins ...'

I nodded. Mike was on the school swim team, and the only way he'd managed to get approval to come on this trip so close to trials was if he took a multitude of vitamins each day.

Noise drenched the air around us and I jumped. Someone was talking, in Spanish. Someone on the verge of panic. I was ready to hit the ground for the second time that day. But no one was pointing a gun in my direction. No one was even looking at me.

Everyone was staring at the TV.

The snowstorm-static had cleared, replaced by a distorted image of walls crumbling, guns firing, people falling. Before I could figure out where it was, the feed changed to show a room filled with prone figures sheeted in white, then again to a mountain harbouring a village of smoking ruins. The voice spoke rapid Spanish, listing numbers dead and danger areas. Then a map came up, showing central South America, covered with flame symbols of varying size. I caught occasional words: 'inside' and 'windows', 'dangerous' and 'take care'. Then it stopped.

The silence was so sudden, so complete; I gasped. The static was back, replacing the horror. The news was gone. Then the whole room started talking. One table of three exited straight away, running down the street.

We had nowhere to run.

I looked at Odati and Mike and it was clear that even though they hadn't understood any of what the reporter had been saying, they'd still got the message. Mike was swearing continuously under his breath, Odati chewing her lip.

Our bus. Our plane flight home. The urgency to get away, to feel some level of safety, had me shaking. What to do?

Three things. There are three things we need. List them out and just don't panic.

'Um. One: We need to find a safe place to sleep tonight. Two: We need to catch that bus tomorrow. And three: We need to work out where to go after that so we can catch up with Miss C and the others.'

Odati nodded at me, but Mike snorted. 'What are you? Freaking crazy? Are you just listing random shit?'

Odati shook her head. 'Get a hold of yourself, Mike! And get that map out again, will you?'

Mike glared at her and the blood pumping in my ears made me woozy. Then he flashed a brittle smile and pulled out his guidebook. This time I could see hand-drawn asterisks next to some of the towns. The route the evac bus was taking, picking up stranded Aussies as it went. I followed his smooth finger as it traced them, trying to overlay the map of flames over this more innocent one. Potosí, Uyuni, across the Chilean border to San Pedro, then straight down the coast to Santiago.

'Not too bad,' I said, surprised.

Just a few more town-hops and we'd be in Chile, barrelling down the Pan-American Highway. Half a continent to cross, sure, but it didn't seem as impossible as I'd feared.

'We can do this!' Odati echoed my new optimism. 'We have enough money to pay people to drive us faster and further. We can absolutely catch the others up!'

We managed to smile at each other. Even Mike, though his was more directed at the map.

In the midst of a meltdown, we had hope.

CHAPTER THREE

6 days until flight
½ block chocolate
US$1560
Bs2100

Looking up, I could see our refuge was emptying, the night chilling like a chest freezer set on high. I slid my jacket on and hugged my emptiness closer. I couldn't blame Miss C for us being all alone, I mean she was the one who stuck around after Mrs Grant did a runner back when this all began. It was easier simply to accept we were on our own, and the solution was to get back—to Miss C and the uncomfortably overcrowded bus the rest of our class were on.

But first, somewhere to sleep.

I re-read my phrasebook and hoped like hell I wasn't about to proposition the waitress. Who had been kind to us but, you know, not that kind. My palms were sweating as I retied my hair on top of my head, doubling the ponytail over so it looked bigger and taller. Sometimes that makes me feel more confident. I needed that now.

The waitress arrived, leading an energetic woman who oozed a level of awesome I could only dream of. She caught my eye and smiled. I smiled back without any thought, that's how open and natural she was. She reminded me of Miss C.

The waitress introduced her as Elena.

'*Mucho gusto, Elena. Me llamo Eva,*' I said.

She smiled, teeth flashing, and responded in Spanish, slow enough for me to understand. 'Hi Eva, pleased to meet you too. I hear you three need to get to Potosí?'

I nodded.

'I have a vehicle. I could drive you there.'

Unbelievable! I turned to the others. 'She can drive us to Potosí!'

Odati sat forward in her seat. 'When?'

I forwarded the question to Elena. 'Tonight, if you wish,' she said.

I couldn't believe our luck. Had I heard that wrong? 'Tonight, tonight?' I asked in Spanish.

She nodded. '*Esta noche.*'

And for the second time in a matter of hours, I forgot I liked to review the PROS and CONS before making a big decision. I was spraining fingers high fiving with Mike and Odati, all of us grinning like we'd won the lottery.

We would catch up with Miss C, and this whole episode would be like a nightmare from which we'd woken up.

I couldn't believe how simple it was going to be.

Elena was like our fairy godmother, except instead of granting free wishes, she was asking for petrol money. But that straight-out honesty just made me trust her even more.

I wanted to trust her.

I wanted to be safe, and she was my ticket to safety.

CHAPTER FOUR

6 days until flight
½ block chocolate
US$1360
Bs2100

It was warm in Elena's dented white ute, three of us crammed in the cramped back seat, speeding through the dark towards Potosí. Someone smelled pretty bad, I hoped it wasn't me. I suspected Elena's friend, next to Odati. He looked the sort to decline a bath or two.

He also looked the sort you'd hope to never meet in a dark alley. Or share a ride with through the dark alpine desert, for that matter. When Elena stopped to pick him up, I got this twisted feeling in my stomach, but I didn't say anything. Nor did Odati or Mike. So there we all were.

Odati was softly snoring, her head on my shoulder. Mike was awake in the passenger seat, watching the moonlit landscape whip past. I kept imagining how surprised everyone would be to see us turning up. The hours since our bus drove off without us seemed like months. I couldn't wait to be secure under Miss C's wing again.

It was going to be worth a few smelly hours.

The car slowed. Elena's dark eyes were watching me in the rear-view mirror and I smiled, but she didn't respond. I looked for the lights of the town, half-fearing to see them because, although I wanted to be back with our classmates so bad my chest constricted when I thought about it, I still didn't want to have to deal with unknown streets in the middle of the night.

But no lights broke the darkness except those of the heavens, and the stuttering headlights of the car. We were simply pulling off the road. In the Middle Of Nowhere.

'Why are we stopping?' Mike asked, his words abrasive in the stuffy warmth. Odati jerked awake.

Elena turned around, a smile stretching her face. 'It's a tough new world we live in,' she said in Spanish, 'you couldn't begin to understand. So just hand over your money.'

I frowned, working through what she'd said, sure I'd got at least half of it wrong. 'We already paid you.'

'You're not very smart, are you? We want more than that.'

Not many people have ever suggested I was dumb. Generally any insults concerning my intellect imply the opposite. But in a way she was right, because I wasn't cottoning on. It wasn't a paltry amount we'd paid her, we'd been so relieved to discover a solution to our problem.

But Odati got it as soon as I relayed what Elena had said. 'They're robbing us!'

I gasped.

Elena snickered, and my heart collapsed. Of course. Of course they were.

Her smelly friend started pawing Odati, checking pockets, feeling for her money belt. I tried the door, unsure what I'd do if it opened, but it didn't. We were trapped. Odati slapped Smelly's hands, and Elena paused from conducting a similar search of Mike to look back at her.

Moonlight flashed off the blade of a knife.

Odati shut up immediately, her fists clenched by her side. Smelly's hands kept searching.

Mike's chin was set as Elena removed a great wad of hard-won notes from his pouch. Hours of desperate queuing at humid ATMs, gone in the flash of a blade. If we lost this money, there was no getting it back. The banks were all shut now, the ATMs broken. At that point, that was the one thing that terrified me. Fragile, dirty paper that it was, money was an endangered species. Once it was gone, it was capital G Gone. And without it, we were doomed. I felt the inevitable hanging in the air.

It smelled of B.O.

Elena turned to talk rapidly in Spanish to her odorous friend, who reached up to Odati's ears and tugged at her earrings. I'd noticed them before. They weren't large by any means, but they sparkled in a way my cubic zirconiums couldn't dream of. Evidently Elena had noticed them too. Odati started to rebel again.

My heart was thumping.

'She takes them off, or he rips them off. Her choice,' Elena crooned in Spanish.

'Take them off, Odati,' I hissed. 'Quickly!'

My head spun. How would we survive with nothing, let alone catch up to the others?

Only one hope. Entwined in my second-hand clothes, my cheap boots, my home-cut hair: Prejudice. Just as I'd immediately decided Mr Stinky was the source of the smell, maybe Elena wouldn't expect anything worthwhile to be wrapped up in my worn package. She'd already figured Mike and Odati were the best bets. Would she accept I was a losing hand?

I reached my sweaty fingers under my jacket and inched open the zip of my money belt. Two separate wads of notes inside. I pulled the first out, US dollars all tightly bundled, and moved my hand down my leg. As slow as I could force myself to move. I tucked the notes into my woollen sock and pulled my cargos back over the lump. Thank goodness for ancient pants. Imagine if I'd been wearing skinny jeans. I'd be so much more fashionable, but with nowhere to stash my cash.

I felt like my movements must've been obvious. I was sweating and cold and my heart was beating so fast, and I fought the stupid urge to grin. But Smelly-dude was still caught up in Odati's jewellery. She was trying to get her nose stud out, shaky fingers making her task difficult.

I delved into my money belt again. Fingers suddenly sure, leaving a few notes behind while collecting the rest. Second pile, second sock. Two strange protuberances hidden by helpful pants. Feeling the rough discomfort against my skin. Feeling a kind of triumph, too.

Hoping that feeling wasn't premature. Hoping robbing us was the sum total of all they had planned for tonight.

I straightened slowly. Just in time.

Because it was my turn.

Mr Stinky leant over Odati to get to me. I could spare her only a moment's pity as she tried to breathe through her mouth. I acted all scared. Actually, it wasn't an act. I pulled out my money belt, elastic strap stretching tight against the skin of my back. He grabbed at the notes I'd left in the belt. I couldn't see how much, but surely not more than Bs50. Nothing really.

He got angry fast, spittle flying, Odati cringing. He talked too quickly for me to follow, but I could tell he was pissed at the puny haul.

Elena turned back to me, her ingratiating smile long gone. 'Where's the rest, *gringa*?' she asked in perfect English. Had watching me struggle to interpret been a game to her?

I didn't have to fake the tremble in my voice. 'I don't have any more.'

Her knife glittered again, cold and silver. 'I don't believe you. Hand it over, or I'll come get it.'

'No, please! I'm not rich, I'm on a scholarship at school. My money ran out days ago. You have to believe me!'

'No. I. Don't.' Danger dwelt in her every syllable.

Then Odati spoke up, voice angry and cynical. 'So she doesn't have any money, why don't you take her diamond earrings instead? Oh, my mistake, they're made of plastic.' Her words, her tone, would have hurt me in any other situation, but her hand was clinging to mine in the dark.

Elena paused, eyes flicking between us. 'I don't believe you,' she said again. But this time she said it differently, and hope sparked in my chest.

Mike snorted. 'Really? What is it about her that makes you think she's worth anything? I'm pissed she has any cash at all—she's been holding out on us.'

Odati's hand gripped mine, crushing my fingers together. Half of me wanted to grab the money out of my socks and throw it at Elena. Because sure, without money, it would be impossible to catch Miss C and we'd get mighty hungry mighty quick. But pissing these two off?

There are worse things than hunger. Worse things than missing a plane.

Elena was a statue gleaming in the moonlight. Then she shook her head at Smelly, who tore my cheap watch off my wrist and shrugged in clear dismissal. We'd convinced them. My hands started shaking. Smelly opened his door and climbed out, gesturing for us to follow.

Which was totally not cool.

It took an icy flicker of Elena's knife to make us move.

I don't know how to explain it. I mean, robbing us was enough. But dumping us out there?

I don't think I was hoping they'd pocket all our cash and then cheerily keep driving and drop us in Potosí with a kiss on the cheek and a kind message for our mothers.

I just think I wasn't thinking.

So. The open door then, was our reality. We were getting discarded on the side of a road in the middle of the night in the freezing Bolivian *altiplano*.

It was more like a death sentence.

CHAPTER FIVE

6 days until flight
½ block chocolate
US$430
Bs410

Mr Stinky opened Mike's passenger door and hauled him out, before hopping in himself. He murmured a thank you, and the car executed a calculated turn, and sped back the way it had come, scattering loose gravel over my shock.

The darkness was darker with their absence. Then my eyes adjusted. But I still couldn't see anything hinting at salvation.

'Tell me you hid your money,' Odati whispered, loud in the silence.

'It's in my socks.'

I was engulfed in her hug. It should have been awkward. It wasn't. She was crying. I was crying. I don't know if it was in sympathy for her having to endure those creeping hands, relief we were all unhurt, or despair at our new hurdle. All I knew was I needed that hug. Extra arms came around me from one side, and I jerked with surprise. Mike had joined in.

Now, that *did* feel awkward.

'Great thinking, Eva,' he said, voice breaking. 'Fat lot of good it might do us, but well done.'

I pulled back to glare at him. It wasn't like I hadn't been thinking our situation had just got a whole lot worse, but hearing it spoken out loud …?

'Fat lot of good? What the hell? We're going to get to Potosí, and we're going to get there before morning, and we'll be on that bus tomorrow with the rest of them!'

He sniffed. 'I want to believe that, but look at the facts.'

'Screw the facts!' I was angry. It's not often I would even think about suggesting anybody screw with facts.

I looked away from his negativity, and I saw it. A soft glow on the horizon.

I smiled. 'No, on second thoughts, let's look at them. Walking will keep us warm. That's got to be Potosí over there, maybe fifteen kilometres away. We can be there in five hours, max. We will make it before morning!'

I didn't wait for an answer. I got the painful bundles out of my socks and roughly divided them into thirds, passing a bundle to Mike and a bundle to Odati. Mike stared at his. Odati put hers away in her belt, all composed and business-like again.

'I have some money in a wallet as well,' she said. 'Ironic. I had it as a sacrificial thing, in case I was ever held up, but they went straight for my belt.'

Mike shivered, put the money I'd given him into his pouch, and then reached into a pocket. 'I managed to hide my watch.'

I grinned. 'We are way better off than we thought!'

'Yeah, we can do this!' Odati was rising in my estimation by the microsecond.

Even Mike smiled. 'Okay, yeah, I'll believe you. So let's get walking, I'm freezing here.'

He wasn't alone.

But the glow was a deceptive thing. It flickered and cooled but didn't get any closer, though we trudged and toiled across the barren landscape, breath fogging our view of the snaking road beneath our feet. Mike's watch counted the hours. We stopped for chocolate every hour. Well, we stopped after the first hour, but it was way too cold, so we started going again immediately, and after that we didn't pause. We just munched on the go.

My feet were aching. I had blisters developing on the side of each little toe, and on my right heel. Don't get me started on my calves. I wanted to ask Mike to check his watch ten times every hour, but more than that I didn't want to hear it wasn't chocolate time again, so I shut my mouth tight. I just wanted to stop and rest, curl up and sleep. But I knew:

Sleep = Freezing to death,

and I found I had the strength to keep going.

The stars were so close and sharp, I felt I could touch them. A couple of times I tried, just to prove I was still on Earth, not wrapped in some jewel-studded black velvet dream among the galaxies.

Occasionally I saw aeroplanes, lights blinking in the vastness. All those people up there. Where were they going? Home? Lucky them.

There among the stars, in the brittle air, I felt close to a truth I can't even describe. Maybe Odati and Mike felt it too, because we all kept walking, and none of us complained. And I caught them reaching for the stars a few times as well.

The sky was pinking before we finally crested a rise that wasn't false like all the others. Beyond it we could see Potosí spread out at the foot of a beaten mountain.

Odati swore. 'That's what I've been wanting to see!'

I was holding her hand and she was holding Mike's as we stood with shaking legs and gazed at the spreadeagled town below, the unnaturally straight mountain towering above its centre.

'You know,' said Mike, 'that mountain's a silver mine. In its day, this town was bigger and richer than London.'

I gazed at the intricate streets, orange-tiled roofs glowing in the morning light, weary wisps of smoke rising. 'And somewhere down there is our bus.'

'Hell, yeah,' Mike said in triumph.

We hobbled down the slope and were soon walking amongst the buildings. Some were dirty shacks, others reminiscent of the mammoth riches of Potosí's heyday, but there was a decided air of neglect.

It was 5am. We'd been walking seven hours straight, but I'd never professed to be an expert at estimating distances. The important thing was—we'd made it!

We passed the dusty bus station as a once-white bus rattled off with bleary-eyed passengers and the bleat of a goat. I caught just a flash of its destination placarded in the front windscreen—UYUNI. It rounded the corner, horn blaring twice.

I opened my mouth to call out, raised my hand towards it, but it was gone.

'What's up?' Odati asked.

'That bus … it's going to Uyuni.'

Our next destination. But that was silly. Our bus, our classmates, were here in Potosí. I shook my head and asked Mike to re-check for the hundredth time the location of the hostel listed as the central point for our classmates.

We toiled up the steep hill through the emaciated air, loose bricks and shattered glass an unwelcome obstacle course. And everywhere the cold smell of smoke. I began to realise what the glow might have been and my heart started stuttering. The few people we saw were furtive as they darted away. The wind wailed down the skinny streets. I jumped at the screech of metal on stone above us.

A wrought iron balcony, flaked like so many others down the street, hung twisted and broken.

When I looked down, dark red clung to the aged cobbles, sticky footprints scattered out from either side, as if a horde had stampeded through. It still looked wet.

Could it be blood? Did people live through that much blood loss?

I crowded in closer to Odati and Mike. My fingers hurt. So cold. Hurrying. I wanted to get off the street, away from the fear hanging like fog over everything.

It was with relief I finally pushed at the door to the hostel. But it wouldn't open. I knocked. No response.

I refused to panic, but started to regardless.

I was shivering. So were the others. Shaking too, from exhaustion. I'd never recognised such a distinct difference between those two types of tremble. Mike shoved me out of the way and started up the most awful din of banging on the door that I was surprised it didn't break. I looked away from his intensity, and caught the edge of a curtain twitching in the window above us. We must have seemed harmless, because finally the door opened a crack and a woman with tired eyes peeked out. She gestured us inside, and we stepped into the welcoming warmth of the hostel.

I hauled in lungfuls of hot-chocolate-scented air.

It was heaven. Different to the one we'd walked under the previous night. But heaven nonetheless …

The woman shut the door, locked it, barred it and then jammed a chair under the handle. She turned. *'Buenos dias,'* she said.

'Buenos dias. ¿Habla inglés?'

She nodded.

I continued in English. 'We're looking for our friends, a school group from Australia? Part of a bigger group? They were here last night.'

She nodded. 'Yes. Of course!' Mike and Odati shared triumphant looks with me, before the lady spoke again. 'I have a note for you, they were hoping you'd follow them.'

The smile fell from Mike's face instantly; it took a little longer to dislodge from Odati's.

'Aren't they here?' he said.

My knees turned to liquid when the *señora* shook her head. 'No, they could not stay.'

'Could you tell us where they are, please?' Odati asked.

The woman went behind the counter, and brought a note back to us. We clustered around to read it, the clear script of Miss C's writing rushing across the paper. The note curled over a few circular blots in one corner, like drops of water had fallen there … I shivered.

29th April
Odati, Eva and Mike—
I am so sorry you got left behind. The bus driver absolutely refused to turn around and the consul staff agreed with him. They've decided to push on to Uyuni tonight because of the unrest here. I can't leave the other students. I'm so sorry.
Stick together please. Keep inside at night, stick to public transport if you can, guard your valuables.
I hope to see you in Uyuni, or if not, at the border.
Take care, Miss C.

At the bottom she'd included the flight details from Santiago, matching those in my diary. Like a mantra.

Santiago, Chile. May 5th, 1830hrs.

And where were we?
Potosí, Bolivia. April 30th, 0539hrs.

I felt like my skull was caving in. I recalled the goat bus rumbling away that morning, and sank into the nearest chair. If only we'd been on it!

It would almost have made that awful trip with Elena worth it. Because now we were abandoned, near broke, with half a continent to cross and no idea how to manage it on our meagre scraps of cash.

I think it was obvious. How tired we were, how lost and alone. The woman ushered us to a polished wood table and brought out three hot chocolates and a plate of crispy *buñuelos,* kind of like donuts but way better. I blinked, fumbled for some money to pay, but she waved my hand away. I rezipped my money belt, relieved. Embarrassed to be relieved.

Hot chocolate and *buñuelos*.

That weary *señora* in the fraying shawl gave me something that, in my exhaustion, seemed precious and joyful out of all proportion.

Unfortunately, hot chocolates don't last forever.

The *señora* returned to take our plates and our effusive thanks. I asked when the next bus went to Uyuni, and the answer was heartening. 12:30pm. Each and every day two buses left. 5am and 12:30pm. It was time to salvage something from the situation, and keep racing. Keep chasing.

We would catch up with them.

We had to.

I didn't want to go back out onto those streets, but more than that I didn't want to miss the next bus. What if it left early? Or another evac bus came through? I dragged my complaining body out of the chair and tottered towards the door. At least the bus station was back down the hill. I imagined I could roll my way there. Mike followed me with heavy eyes and shuffling steps. But Odati paused, thanked the woman again, and handed over some of our treasured currency before herding us out the door to the soft fall of the woman's blushing thanks.

'What did you do that for?' I asked as soon as we were far enough down the cobbled street to not be overheard. 'She didn't want any money.'

Odati didn't look at me, kept moving forward, dodging broken paving and wayward plastic bags. 'She was kind, she fed us what was probably her family's meal, she deserved to be paid something for it.'

'We need all the money we have.'

She stopped, death-sparks firing from her brown eyes. 'Really? Look around you, Eva. You think we need that money more than she does?'

She glared at me, and I got the uncomfortable feeling she was right. Ouch. A lesson in philanthropy from a girl I'd always assumed was spoiled by her wealth, and a woman who'd probably never known any. My eyes dropped to the cobbles, and the heat in my cheeks buzzed against the chill of the morning air.

The moment wasn't passing.

The silence was getting awkward.

I looked back up. Odati's face was set as she watched me. I had nowhere to go to avoid the conversation or try to retain a shred of dignity. Even Mike was staring at me, head to one side like he couldn't figure me out.

I winced. 'I'm sorry. You're totally right. You did the right thing.'

And then Odati started to cry. And she hugged me. Wet cheek icy against my own. I gave her a clumsy pat on the back. When we pulled apart, she rubbed her cheeks and dried her red eyes with the heels of her hands and I found myself echoing her tentative smile.

And I felt warm inside, like I'd just slugged back another hot chocolate. 'We should get going, at least the bus station might be in the sun,' I murmured.

She smiled. 'Yeah, my fingers are so cold they burn.'

We walked forwards together, Mike slinging his arm over Odati's shoulder. My mind was reeling. Our situation was not good. We'd been abandoned and robbed, we'd walked through the night only to find our classmates were well ahead of us still.

And yet, I was happy.

We were a 'we'.

CHAPTER SIX

5 ½ days until flight
No food
US$430
Bs365

Hours later my happiness was heavily diluted by exhaustion. The bus station wasn't comfortable, hard benches surrounded by dusty bitumen, but I'd slept when it was my turn. There I was, keeping watch over the other two and the thankfully docile streets, sketching to keep my mind alert. Mike had collapsed against a dusty corner, hugging his bag. Odati slept with her head on my lap.

A couple of buses had pulled through during the morning, and a truck full of exhausted army guys with blank eyes. Now it was empty enough to be giving me the creeps. Few people, and Big Fat Zero buses. There was a flag pole, a tattered flag flying half-mast. The dry breeze carried the smell of fried street food, ruined by the skunk stink of stale pee and the fester of overflowing bins.

And I'd managed to make an enemy already.

A backpacker, a year or so older than us. He was over the other side of the station, sitting under an umbrella with a girl whose electric blue hair in no way fit the location. It looked like the perfect spot for scoping out desperate tourists to scam.

He'd approached me when I'd gone to buy something to eat from the wary street vendor. Flashed a perfect smile and wanted to know what our story was. And I hadn't told him a thing. *Nada*. I'd made myself walk right past him like he wasn't even there.

I'd been duped by Elena. I wasn't going to mess up again. Except he had still been there when I'd come back juggling three piping hot veg and egg *salteñas*.

'I can see you're waiting near the Uyuni stop,' he'd said, English accent wielded like a devious weapon. 'Is that where you and your friends are going?'

You know what? That was none of his business. I'd attempted to ignore him again, my tired head pounding, but he'd stepped in front of me enough times to stall my forward momentum, dancing an intimate swaying zig-zag in the dusty thin air. He'd looked at me, an uncertain smile playing over mobile lips, his brow creased.

'Because Alice and I are heading that way too, trying to get to Chile. We could all travel together?'

Travel with them? Was he kidding? After how things turned out with Elena? I was done with trusting strangers.

'We're not interested,' I'd said, holding the *salteñas* firmly so my shaking hands wouldn't show.

His smile had fallen away. Face slack like I'd slapped him, and every bit of me was wincing from the bluntness of my words. But, you know, Elena had had a nice smile too, and look where that had got us. We were safer on our own.

I'd walked straight past his shocked face.

'Hey!' he'd called after me. 'Hey! I was only being friendly. No need to be such a …' I'd guessed he wasn't intending on giving a compliment.

And maybe he was just being friendly, and maybe there was a great reason why he wasn't sitting at the proper stop and it had nothing to do with pretending to be going the same place we were, but we didn't need him and we didn't need to risk trusting him. I'd told myself I'd done the right thing.

I'd been avoiding his biting gaze ever since.

The far-off rumble of a plane pulled me back to myself. I found it, flying down to the south, lonely in the huge skies.

I checked Mike's watch, and frowned. It was 12.40. Still no bus. However, Mike's book warned punctuality wasn't always the best in Bolivia. And that was *before* the collapse. So I wasn't that surprised to find the bus to Uyuni hadn't come on time.

But come 1.30, I packed my sketchbook away and woke Mike and Odati. Because I was done talking to myself about all the likely reasons there could be to explain the delay. Blown tyre. Rockfall. Explosion. Extremely long coca tea break. Head-on collision with an alpaca. Whatever.

The bus hadn't come.

Mike and Odati were dry-lipped and bleary-eyed. We decided I should go ask someone what was happening. 'Someone' definitely not being the pissed-off English backpacker sitting under the umbrella.

As I walked through the abrasive dust swirls, I could feel his eyes on me. My gait seemed weird. Was that how my arms normally swung?

CHAPTER SEVEN

5 ½ days until flight
No food
US$430
Bs365

The news I got from the locals hanging nervously around the ticket stall was not good. I was fighting an overwhelming urge to just give in as I walked back towards Mike and Odati. One more blow we didn't need. Not then. What I wanted was some positive karma, please world.

But the universe didn't seem to want to stop throwing crap at me. Because I was once again intercepted by the English guy. The cerulean-haired girl was watching intently from the shade of a dusty red-and-white umbrella no longer in its prime.

English was clearly still annoyed at me, and it was equally clear he was trying his best to be pleasant. But I was
So
Not
In

The
Mood.

Not for creepy strangers. What right did he have to keep stopping me?

'So, what's happening?' he asked when I flustered to a standstill.

'Nothing.'

His laugh was short and dry. 'Funnily enough, I'd already figured that much out. Did they tell you anything about our bus?'

I'd had enough. All I wanted was to sit down and cry, and then sleep for at least a day. 'Our bus? I already told you we're fine without you.'

He cocked his head and ran his fingers through his hair, leaving it standing up in all directions. 'Yeah, but we're waiting for the same bus, remember?'

'Says who?'

'Still just an assumption of mine, based on the fact you three are camped under the Uyuni sign. Or are you just there for fun?' He flashed a humourless smile my way, matching it with a lightning fast eyebrow raise. There and then gone. Lips that expressive shouldn't be allowed.

'Well?'

I tore my eyes away from his intriguing mouth, guts tumbling, drained synapses reigniting. He'd said something to me and I'd been so busy wondering about his lips I hadn't heard. Heat flooded my cheeks, and I wished I could at least pretend not to be embarrassed, rather than always having my face give me away.

He raised that one eyebrow again and I knew I hadn't got away with anything. 'Finished staring?'

I wished myself anywhere but there. Erupting volcano? Sure. Exam where I'd forgotten to study? Or wear pants? Fine. Bus station where I'd just been hypnotised by a dangerous stranger? No way.

I scowled, taking refuge in anger. 'You think you're funny, don't you?'

'Phew, I was starting to wonder if you'd lost the power of speech. Not that I miss your witty remarks … it's only the tiny bit about the bus.'

'Screw you!'

'No thanks.'

I rolled my eyes. 'That's so lame.'

He grinned, eyes dancing. 'C'mon. The bus, and then I promise I'll get out of your way.'

Maybe it was the lack of sleep, but I was about ready to incinerate him with my gaze. 'How about you just get out of my way now!'

'Didn't anyone teach you about polite conversation? I ask a question, you answer, I say thanks. It's pretty easy. How about we try? I'll start—what's happened with the bus to Uyuni?'

I tried to bypass him, but he was too fast. Frustrated, I tried to shove him, and found him to be completely immovable.

'Hey!' His smile dropped and he took a step back from me. 'I've had enough of being threatened lately, okay? Just tell me what they said about the damn bus and I'll gladly leave you alone.' You could almost feel the emphasis on the 'gladly'.

My face went as hot as a bus tailpipe. 'I only …' tried to push him. What was I turning into?

He rubbed his forehead. 'Why is this so impossibly hard? I just want to know about the bus.'

I stared at my dusty boots.

'Eva, what's taking you so long? Were you able to find anything out?' Mike strode over towards me. Then he shot a careful look at the English guy. 'Hi. How're you going?'

English stared at Mike for a moment, as if sizing him up, like I think all guys size each other up. With that dirty streak across his cheek, Mike looked like a model who'd woken up in a nightmare. In contrast, English looked like an ordinary bloke who'd gone out to get milk one lazy Sunday morning and just kept walking. And hadn't slept since.

He nodded at Mike. 'I'm trying to find out from Eva,' he shot me a wicked smile—as if knowing my name was victory dipped in *dulce de leche*—'what's happened to the bus, but she refuses to tell me.'

Mike raised a perfectly shaped eyebrow. 'Have you tried asking nicely?'

'Actually, yes, I have. Eva doesn't seem to do nice.'

Mike made a strangled noise and turned his head away, before finally facing English-guy again. 'Are you going to Uyuni too?'

'Yes, we are.' English waved his hand in the direction of the blue-haired girl who must be Alice.

The pause after was uncomfortable. Mike was studying me like a curious specimen in Biology. Then he shook his head. 'What's happening with the bus, Eva?'

I couldn't find any sane excuse to avoid the question. 'The timetable's changed. They only run the 5am now.'

Mike and English-guy swore in unison, inventively, complete with fist-shakes and dust-kicks.

I left them to it. I needed to sit down.

CHAPTER EIGHT

5 days until flight
No food
3 'new' sleeping bags
US$400
Bs327.50
2 extra travel 'buddies'

The sun was setting over the *altiplano*, but I knew I wouldn't see it finish, wouldn't see the darkness creep in and take control.

I was tired right through.

That day I'd bargained my way through several practically empty stores to procure three halfway decent second-hand sleeping bags. An admission of failure. The sleeping bag I'd left on the bus hadn't been brilliant, but at least it had smelt like me. The new one … well, it did not.

Our money was dwindling, but everything we bought was necessary. What else could we do?

None of us admitted to being frightened by the pressurised streets, but we spent the remainder of the day in the hostel. Come sunset, I'd been avoiding the dorm for a while. Mike had crashed half an hour before. In the nicest sleeping bag. Having still not thanked me for finding one for him. Odati had followed twenty minutes later. And I'd stayed out in the common room, 6B pencil like a lame excuse, fresh piece of paper mocking me, making unsuccessful attempts to draw the building across the road. I rubbed my eyes. The perspective was all wrong. I was more likely to fall asleep right in the booth than ever finish that sketch.

It was time to go in. And hope to hell he wasn't in there. Because, to my chagrin, Brodie (and when he said it in that English accent of his, the name suited him perfectly) and his creatively-haired Welsh companion Alice had been embraced as part of our travelling party. They'd even recommended the hostel. The two of them had stayed there already, hiding from ground-trembling protests that had rolled through the streets, shattering windows and looting shops in response to the collapse of the price of silver.

So all five of us were going to share a dorm like the great pals we were, and I was somehow the only one uncomfortable with this set up.

I think Odati understood—she'd taken my hand while we were walking to the hostel. 'I'm finding it hard to trust after what we went through last night,' she'd said, 'but I'm starting to get the feeling these two are okay. At first I didn't want anything to do with them— you know what I mean?'

Of course I did. Because I was the psycho who'd tried to ignore Brodie's perfectly acceptable attempts at conversation. And Odati knew that. She was just being, well, *nice*.

I was finding Odati was kind, and funny, and smart. I really liked her.

And I was getting a good idea how lucky I actually was. Take, for instance, the young guy who worked at the hostel and had pointed us in the right direction for gear shops. He'd been a silver miner since he was eight, working ten hours a day pushing loaded carts and carrying 60kg sacks, earning a measly Bs30, which is about US$5. But then got silicosis from the foul air and was destined to die painfully.

If the riots didn't get him first.

In contrast I'd been awarded an immense scholarship to a prestigious school that provided me with an education no one could steal. I'd never really gone hungry, my life expectancy was in the mid-eighties (or had been before all this), and even figuring I was trapped in a far-off continent and all the world's financial systems had hit the fan, I was a shed-load better off than him.

I closed my sketchbook with a sigh. The sunset was pouring coral shades through the spattered window. A shadow moved to my right that hadn't been there before, and my heartbeat shot up. A man. Watching me. Vaguely familiar.

'You must be Mike's friend,' he said. And the gears clunked together. Mike had hung out with this *gringo* for ages before he went to bed.

The guy made my skin crawl. No newsflash there. Like, who wasn't making my skin crawl these days? I put on my unscalable face and cringed inside at the fear once again flooding my system. 'I'm actually just leaving.'

He didn't take the hint. Instead he sat on the edge of my table, perfect hair glittering golden in the fading light, expensive brand-name travel gear complementing his new-looking hiking boots. I couldn't get past him, but I assured my primitive reflexes this surely wasn't by design. *Do not overreact again Eva, you fool.*

He flashed a brilliant smile. 'Mike told me you three are down on your luck. Sorry to hear that.'

I wasn't in the mood for a pity party from a perfect Golden Boy like him. Especially today. 'I really do have to go. If you'd please move, your legs are …'

He looked down, then back up at me. 'Blocking your way. I'm so sorry.' Except he didn't move. Instead his eyes conducted a roving examination of my body that had my blood pressure soaring. 'People are calling this the end of the world, you know? The rule book's been thrown out, we're free to do whatever we want. I find that exciting, don't you?'

If only I could get past him. I could actually see the door to our dorm down the short corridor. 'Um, I don't know? Not really.'

He grinned. 'How about I buy you a drink? I know a nice place.'

'I'm underage.'

'No rule book remember? C'mon, it'll be fun. We should take it while we can.'

I was too exhausted, and so confused. 'I'm tired. Can I please just go past?'

I hated how weak that sounded, like I needed his permission to move. I wanted to scream at him, but that would just make another scene. All he'd done was ask me for a drink, surely? My pulse was a series of explosives in my ears. I felt sick. I looked around the room but it was only him and me. Where was the hostel owner? Why hadn't I gone back with Odati?

'Of course you can go past! Another time, maybe.' He flashed his white teeth at me, shuffling to the side, and I was glad I hadn't completely lost it.

I squeezed past, senses still screaming stupid overreactive warnings. Just as I was sure I was free, his hand shot out and caught my elbow, pulling me back towards him. 'Pretty girl like you, I'd hate to see you get hurt. It's only getting worse out there. I could keep you safe, you know?'

Safe was exactly what I wasn't feeling, what I hadn't felt in ages. What he definitely wasn't helping me feel. And I was done ignoring my instincts. 'Let go of me!'

'Why? We're free now. It's a new world.'

A hundred ways to hurt him, escape from him, shot through my head. Which one to try first? I didn't even hear the door opening. But I sure as heck felt Golden Boy's hand drop.

'You okay, Eva?' Alice. Alice in the corridor behind me and even though I barely knew her she was the most wonderful thing I'd ever seen. I was half-tripping towards her before I knew it.

'You think about my offer, sweetheart,' Golden Boy murmured from behind.

I shot a look at him. He was still smiling. Over-confident creep.

'Everything okay?' Alice asked as I reached her.

'It is now. Thanks.'

She watched Golden Boy as he lounged out of the room and down the street. 'You want to talk about it?'

Did I? I shook my head. 'I think I just want to sleep. Today can get in the bin, far as I'm concerned.' I moved through the open dorm door. Alice didn't follow. 'You coming in?' I asked.

'Bathroom.' Only then did I take in the toiletries bag she was holding.

I shot a glance at the common room. 'He might come back.'

She grinned like I'd offered her a full dessert buffet. 'I'd like to see him try. You get some sleep.'

I didn't need further prompting. I slipped through the doorway, the dorm beyond still lit by the setting sun, and a flood of relief threatened to knock my head off its perch. I eased the door closed, leaning back against it, breathing in and out.

What had just happened?

I pushed away from the door. Odati was asleep. Mike too, in the bunk next to hers. And I couldn't stop myself looking to where I knew Brodie's bed was. And he was there, sitting up, dark hair dishevelled from a wash, tablet out. He'd probably been serenely reading a book, but not any more. No, now he was watching me. How much had he heard? I looked away fast, cheeks hot.

No talking. No greetings. I tucked my sketchbook into its special spot in my backpack and wriggled into the musty security of the sleeping bag, fully clothed. A lightning glance at Brodie showed him reading again. I turned over to face the wall, shaking so bad the sleeping bag wouldn't stop rustling.

Mate, I would've loved to have a book, any book, just to divert my mind for a moment. Bloody Brodie. Typical that there wasn't any email or phone coverage, but he could still read his favourite … whatever it was. My book was packed in my main bag on the faraway bus. Possibly never to be read again. And honestly, that was the least of my worries.

Just as I was fading into sleep I heard the door open, snick closed, and then the scrape of the bolt protesting into place. Careful whispering—Alice and then Brodie's lower rumble. Probably talking about me. My cheeks flushed and I fought the tears. I'd been making bad decisions from the moment our bus abandoned us.

Maybe it would all look better in the morning.

It had to.

CHAPTER NINE

4 ½ days until flight
1 packet of cream biscuits
1 block of chocolate
US$400
Bs261.50
+ whatever Alice and Brodie had

Alice and Brodie sat near the back of the bus to Uyuni the next morning and I ended up in a seat opposite them, pressed alongside chickens in cages, an ancient *abuela* with kind eyes, and mountains of knobbly sacks that didn't fit in the hold. It wasn't my idea of awesome, but someone had to be the odd one out and at least I'm well-practised in studied nonchalance. I pulled my sketchbook out of my bag, ready for some isolated drawing time.

I didn't add Alice into the equation. 'What are you drawing?' she asked.

'I'm not sure, to be honest. I kind of use this like a diary, but today my brain is …' I shrugged.

She grinned. 'Elsewhere. I know what you mean. Too early by

far, am I right? Cream biscuit?'

I crunched down on it, crumbs cascading over my paper. Sugar rushing to my head. So exactly what I needed.

'Can I have a look?' Alice nodded at my sketchbook.

I stopped chewing. I normally don't like people to look at my work, but hey—nothing was normal any more, right? Besides, Alice had practically rescued me from Golden Boy, *and* she was sharing her biscuits. What harm could it do?

Yeah, the moment she turned the second page I remembered why it wasn't such a good idea. She snorted, biscuit meteors flying all over the sketch collage I'd done while waiting at the bus station yesterday, unthinkingly titled 'Potosí and the Pissed-off Backpacker'.

'You okay?' Brodie had been staring out the window, but he wasn't any more.

My guts froze as his eyes travelled down towards the paper. I could see the central sketch of him glaring out at me. I'd spent a lot of time perfecting his lips with that one.

This. Wasn't. Happening.

Alice whipped the page over again, back to my terribly exhausted attempt from the hostel and I didn't even care he was seeing something so bad. 'Nothing,' she said, 'just a cool sketch of Eva's. It's a good likeness.' She grinned at me, flashing a cheeky wink and I surprised myself by giggling.

Brodie frowned at us. 'Can I see it?'

'You know what?' said Alice. 'I actually feel a bit carsick. Maybe we should look out the window for a while?'

I couldn't grab hold of my sketchbook fast enough.

Odati and Mike were several seats in front, barely visible past the piles of luggage and certainly too far away to talk to. I hoped things stayed that way the whole bus trip. I'd had a run-in with Mike that morning as we walked to the bus. About Golden Boy.

'Who was that tourist you were talking to yesterday arvo?'

I'd asked. Sleep had made the memory of my fear seem like an overreaction. Maybe a normal girl would've felt like she'd been paid a compliment. Maybe he was just a friendly guy. Mike would know.

But his whole body had stiffened. 'No one. Why?'

'He talked to me before I went to bed. Kind of freaked me out.' I attempted a laugh at myself, but one look at Mike stalled it. Warning bells went off in my head.

He stopped dead, Alice cannoning into him from behind. Her startled apology froze on her lips. Mike's face was working, spasming, his mouth a sharp slash. 'Freaked you out? What a surprise! Is there anyone you don't think is out to get you? Except the obvious? You practically fell in love with Elena, didn't you?'

Blood pounded in my ears. 'Mike, I didn't mean …'

'What did you mean then?'

Tense silence. Three pairs of eyes flickering between me and a Mike whose clenched fists strained at his sides. I ran through what I'd said. I shook my head. 'I just asked about that guy, that's all.'

Mike looked at me with coal-black eyes and gritted teeth. Then, almost imperceptibly, he transformed. 'Sorry. I didn't sleep well last night and I totally misheard. Breakfast is on me, okay?'

Which it technically wasn't, because his money had actually once been my money, and it was more communal money now anyway. But it was a nice gesture and the hot maize drink the locals call *api* was served with sweet *buñuelos* and together they made the morning less icy.

I didn't mention Golden Boy again, and I tried to push away the memory of him and Mike, heads close at a table away from the rest of us. What had they been talking about? Why was Mike so upset about it?

A bus ride away from Mike offered respite. He was like a wild seesaw, swinging from okay to frightening and back again, with a whole heap of surliness in between. I hoped we'd meet up with Miss

C soon, so Mike and I could go back to being completely different people living completely different lives, never destined to talk again.

I knew Miss C and Sarah and the evacuation bus wouldn't be in Uyuni any more. But that didn't stop the jitters. They would have arrived two nights ago, and continued on towards the border while we were languishing at Potosí bus station. Mike reckoned they'd reach the border tomorrow.

All we needed was the fastest driver the world had ever seen.

We *would* catch up with them. And then we'd convince the consulate guy to let Brodie and Alice on the bus too. They'd both heard rumours of a British evacuation, but neither had managed to find anyone to help them get home.

Until they found us.

Alice reached over and touched my arm. 'You must be looking forward to catching up with your class. I can't believe you guys are still at school and you're doing all this cool stuff. I'm so jealous.'

When Alice talked, I felt like the collapse wasn't real. She spoke like she wished she could have been doing exactly what we were doing when she was our age. As in, desperately racing to get home as society disintegrated around you. Except I don't think she saw it like that. I think she saw adventure and freedom.

Alice and Brodie were both on what they called a gap year, at the end of high school. Alice gave Brodie stick for being a kid, because he'd been a year ahead at school, and was only seventeen. But the rest of us were all a year younger again.

I smiled. Her awesomely misguided enthusiasm was infectious. 'What will you do when you get to Santiago?'

'Visit the wineries!'

'Won't you try to go home?'

'Maybe. I dream of just keeping on going. I think my parents would kill me if I did, but they wouldn't be able to reach me!' She flashed a wild grin.

I laughed, but Brodie looked away.

I wasn't sure if they were *together*, or just, you know, together. And with everything going as wrong as it was, it shouldn't have mattered. Didn't stop me wondering, though.

'You think this will just blow over?' I asked Alice.

She looked at me across the crowded aisle, her smile fading, then shook her head. 'No. I think something's changed forever.'

We barely saw Uyuni. The five of us split up; Odati and Brodie scooting to buy heavenly *papas rellenas* and hot, crusty *tucumanas* for lunch, with Mike guarding our gear as Alice and I staggered around the brightly coloured booths, seeking the world's speediest driver.

There were no other tourists.

A wave of evacuations had swept through the country, and we were the flotsam left behind. Desperate drivers made amazing claims on how quickly they could get us to the border. We cut out half the tours using the guidebook's write-ups. Then we chose the one with the newest vehicle.

His name was Onorio and his cruiser was brand new. The poor guy still had his old one parked next to his house with a *'SE VENDE'* sign in the front windscreen. For sale. Good luck with that.

We shook on the deal, but he spent the first hour of the drive trying to sell us extras, like a night's stay in a salt hotel, or a side trip to Fisherman's Island. I was glad when he started focusing on the terrain ahead, rather than smiling back at us.

He was driving a vehicle, after all.

The salt lake was a mind-bendingly vast, dry pan of empty blinding white. It was initially festooned with pyramids of harvested salt that tapered off as we got further from the town. Mike, guidebook open as always, mentioned that below the surface hides one of the richest reserves of lithium in the world. Lithium is in every portable device battery. It could have potentially changed the future of one of the world's poorest countries.

Before everything collapsed, that is.

The *salar* was rimmed by smudges of mountains that never seemed to get closer. White and blue the only two colours in the world. With the altitude, I found myself gasping as I perched in the very back seat of the cruiser with Alice. Odati and the boys simply didn't fit back there. Brodie was super chilled in the passenger seat, one arm on the window and legs lounging in front.

One hill smudge did approach us; Onorio said it was Fisherman's Island. I saw glimpses of jagged volcanic rock and a multitude of prickly cacti as we whipped past. Once Onorio understood we couldn't be swayed from our objective, he worked hard on breaking the land speed record. Which, incidentally, had often been attempted there, because it's so perfectly flat for such a very, very, very long time.

So on second thoughts, maybe Onorio didn't need to keep an eye ahead. There was literally nothing to crash into.

The engine was roaring, and Brodie had bluetoothed his phone, resulting in the addition of some sort of funky mix that meant it wasn't necessary to talk. Mike fell asleep. I felt our communal silence like a sack of silver ore heaved on my back.

Until I got into the groove of the music.

Then I zoned out, watching the salt turn into bare, flat land. Watching the mountains enclose us, classic volcanos rearing impossibly high in a myriad of surreal rainbow hues. I tapped my fingers to the beat, wishing I was brave enough to sing the words to the songs I recognised. Alice excavated a block of dark chocolate from her daypack, and I felt the car relax as it was passed around.

Then an unashamed love ballad I never expected from Brodie's music stash came on, and I turned to Alice in surprise. She raised one perfectly plucked eyebrow and splayed her hands like *I know … what's with his music?*

I cracked up.

Within moments, the two of us were singing our hearts out. As the final chords faded away, I clutched my heart theatrically while Alice pretended to swoon. And I could not help but look at Brodie.

He was watching me.

His broad smile faltered and he looked away, and I felt victorious. Like when someone who doesn't like you catches you doing awesomely fun things with someone they do like, and you know they're wondering whether you're actually cool too and they've made a mistake deciding not to like you in the first place.

I figured he was thinking that, because it's kind of what I was thinking about him.

The afternoon morphed into evening as we manoeuvred around lake after lake, each a different colour. Turquoise-blue, sap-green, pale-pink, sulphur-yellow, all rimmed with the white of salt and swarming with pink flamingos. I hauled out my sketchbook, my pencils recording a colour paradise. We were well above 4,500 metres in a landscape too exquisite to be believed.

And we were making excellent time.

Alice tapped a finger on the side of my sketchpad, pulling me back to reality. 'You're good, you know,' she said.

I shrugged. 'Thanks. I've always liked drawing.'

'You could sell some of those.'

I rolled my eyes.

'I'm serious. This volcano one is beautiful, and you've definitely got a way with portraits.' Her grin spread across her pixie face. 'From what I've seen anyway.'

My cheeks flushed as I thought about that pouty drawing of Brodie. I was going to have to find a way to dispose of it. Permanently. 'Fine then, but seriously, who's going to buy them?'

She looked out the window. At the empty desert. Total isolation. In the middle of a global meltdown. Pursed her lips. 'Good point. Chocolate?' She waved the half-eaten block at me.

I had to grin. 'No thanks. Any more and I think I'll turn into a chocolate.'

'That's actually my nefarious plan for replenishing my stores. Plus, you'd be delicious.'

'What's delicious?' Odati was craning her neck around.

'Eva, absolutely,' said Alice, poker-faced. 'Or she would be. If she were chocolate.'

Odati raised an eyebrow, half laughing. 'We have been stuck in this car too long.'

'You can say that again,' I said.

She grinned. 'We have been stuck—'

Alice threw a balled-up sweater at her, and I laughed so hard I cried on my sketch. Mike tossed the sweater back like he thought he could catch poor fashion sense from it.

Our night stop was Laguna Colorada, a cadmium-red lake. Onorio served us plates of *Pique a lo Macho*, usually a mountain of meat, egg and veg piled over chips and doused in multitudes of spicy sauces. If you can finish a plate of *Pique a lo Macho* you're supposed to be, well, macho. But our plates weren't exactly mountainous. Food shortages? On the bright side, it was way easier to claim macho status. Mike polished his off before I was even halfway through mine. We ate in complete ravenous silence. Until—

'If you girls have lost your bags, do you want to borrow some of my clothes?'

Odati and I stared at Alice. 'Are you serious?' I managed to say. 'Do you have enough to spare?'

'I'd literally kill for a fresh t-shirt,' gasped Odati.

'And we're going to die if you don't wash the one you have on,' Alice deadpanned.

Odati looked appalled, and I surreptitiously sniffed my armpits. Were we that festy? But then I spotted Alice's quirky grin. The thin air rattled with our laughter.

'How long since you guys lost your group?' Alice asked.

I tried to count back on my fingers. 'Two days? It feels like more.'

Odati nodded. 'Yeah, it must be. Last night was Potosí, and the night before … that was Elena.'

I shivered. The dining room seemed poorly lit.

'Where's Elena?' Brodie asked, pushing his food around like he wasn't hungry.

'More like, "Who's Elena".' Mike speared a chunk of pork off Brodie's plate and sank back into his chair.

I still felt weak for letting Elena charm down my defences. Mike and Odati had trusted me. I didn't want to talk about how badly that had turned out. Luckily, or perhaps the memory of Stinky set her off, Odati chose that moment to go and throw up, which was a great reminder that altitude was not our friend.

Though Odati probably didn't think it was lucky. Or great. It put a chilly dampener on our conversation.

In the oppressive dorm, bunks were stacked three high. We were the only ones there. Like sleeping in a ghost town. We all chose a bottom bunk. I knew a metre or so of altitude wouldn't make much difference, but I felt suffocated just looking at the top bunks.

Brodie got out his guitar and started to play as I fluffed out my sleeping bag and clambered in. I'd been preparing myself for this since I first saw his guitar case. Anyone who knew my music collection would know I have a soft spot for boys who play the guitar, and I was absolutely adamant that soft spot was not going to expand to include Brodie.

The music was so beautiful it made my skin quiver, and I found I'd positioned myself so I could peep past the folds of my bag and watch his expression as he played, his total absorption, the way his face softened as his long fingers flew. A different aspect of him, and it didn't gel with the sort of person I'd decided he was. Not much about him did, to be honest.

And then he started to sing.

A dangerous combination. English accent, plays guitar, sings. That was my last thought as his music lulled me to sleep.

I woke often, gasping for air like my lungs weren't big enough in the starved atmosphere. Poor Odati kept throwing up. In the end I curled up with her on her bunk, ignoring the vomit smell and stroking her hair like my mum does when I'm sick, murmuring nonsense to try and keep her mind off the spinning nausea. There's few things worse than heaving your guts up all night.

I allowed myself to hope we might find Miss C at the border the next day. But if not, there would be a record of their passing, and we'd know we were close.

Tomorrow we'd know.

CHAPTER TEN

3 ½ days until flight
½ packet of cream biscuits
¼ block chocolate
US$400
Bs243.80
+ whatever Alice and Brodie had

By the time a pale hint of morning touched the dirty window, we were all up and more than happy to leave that room and Never Return. Mike was stuffing his sleeping bag back into its sack like it was a personal vendetta, like he blamed it for a night spent dreaming of being smothered by a freezer. Odati looked how a reheated bowl of porridge must feel.

Which is what we got for breakfast.

In the cracked toilet mirror my pale face made my eyes look too big. My hairbrush snagged on straggly curls until I gave up and tumbled it up into a messy bun. I shrugged at my reflection. I bet I looked worse now than I had after trekking all the way to Potosí. But inside I was pumped for the border crossing.

Plus, thanks to Alice, I was wearing a clean shirt with, of all things, a rather cheeky unicorn on the front. So I grinned at myself and pushed my shoulders back.

Game face: ON.

Back at the dining room, the others were facing up to their porridge. Brodie was the only one attacking it with any fervour. I caught Odati's eye and she managed a smile, like she was catching my vibe and it was awesome enough to beat back the altitude sickness for a moment. Or maybe it was the unicorn shirt. Odati was wearing one of Alice's shirts too. Studying it, I had to hope the border guards couldn't read English.

But when Onorio entered the room, my joy balloon fizzled out. Something in the way he looked.

'What is it?' asked Alice.

Onorio bit his lip. 'The hostel owners, they've heard rumours the border has closed. No one has come through for a day …'

Total, absolute, tinnitus-in-the-ear silence reigned supreme.

We were so close. So very, very close. Too close to have it ripped away. Odati collapsed with a muted thud on the table, barely missing her pasty porridge. Alice put her arm over her shoulders.

No way.

If it was closed, then Miss C and the others would be on the opposite side. If it was closed, then catching up with them was going to be such a mammoth effort I didn't know how to start thinking about it, didn't know how we'd make our money stretch that far.

Or perhaps it had closed before our bus had crossed, and they'd been turned back, were somewhere in Bolivia still. And that was something terrible I was almost hoping for. Missing the flight might be bearable if I could miss it with my bestie, Sarah, and Miss C. We could be stranded together.

But then none of us would get home. Or would they hold the flight for three entire busloads of citizens?

My mind went blank.

Which doesn't happen often.

'You're mentioning this now, like it's a surprise?' Mike spat out, shaking me out of my fug. Onorio recoiled at the outburst.

'Hey, leave off! It's not Onorio's fault,' I heard myself say.

Mike stared at me. To tell the truth, I was shocked I'd spoken, too. It had to be the altitude messing with my defences.

I breathed in to the count of three. 'I mean, Onorio's just the messenger, yeah?'

Silence. Mike continued to stare at me like I'd grown horns. I ran my fingers over my hair. Nope. Still just my usual.

I wasn't used to this much attention. What I was used to was working through problems and figuring out answers. This wasn't an exam, but still … I cleared my throat. 'I'm thinking we can't tell for sure if the border's open or not unless we go there. And even if it's closed there's a big question we need answered, and that's if the evacuation buses got through first.'

Odati was still huddled over her lumpy breakfast.

So I was glad when Alice piped up, because frankly, the silence was getting uncomfortable. 'I think that's such a sensible idea. We can't make plans until we know for sure the border's closed, am I right?'

'Or open,' Brodie said with an encouraging Play School grin that didn't even come close to clearing the storm clouds around Mike's head. 'It might still be open.'

'We won't know until we find out,' Alice announced.

I took a breath. 'So should we still go?'

Brodie nodded in my direction without meeting my eyes. I think. I'm not so sure because I was avoiding looking straight at him. 'Absolutely. I think we should eat up, pack up and get going.'

The three of us waited for some sort of acknowledgement from my classmates. And I tell you, it wasn't quick in coming. Mike just glared at the tabletop with his fists clenched.

Then Odati reared up, bursting out of her seat, hair flying. 'This is such bull! That border better be bloody open because I can't stand another night up here.' Her cheeks were stained with tears, and then something more desperate entered her face. 'I gotta go hurl!' She dashed from the room in the direction of the toilets, hand clasped to her mouth.

Alice grimaced in a cute pixie way. 'Poor Odati, I hate being sick. You were so good with her last night, Eva. You're a great friend.'

I blinked.

Mere days ago Odati and I were acquaintances at best. Being confused for her friend would have been impossible, but now …?

'I'll go check on her,' I said, 'then I'll pack our stuff. We should get going.' Staring at that porridge, my appetite—not all that ferocious to begin with—withered to nothing. In fact, I felt queasy.

I reached the door before Mike snapped back into life. 'Not waiting for my opinion, Eva?'

I turned, hesitant for a moment. 'Do you think we should do it another way? Rather than heading straight to the border?'

'As if you've ever cared what I think!' he burst out. He turned to the wall and punched his fist through it.

Yes.

Fist. Wall.

Gaping, jagged hole with a view to an empty dorm beyond.

I stumbled backwards. I was aware Alice and Brodie were staring. And Odati was framed in the doorway, frozen in the act of wiping her mouth. I didn't know what to do, except when Mike turned back to face me with that look in his eyes, I was absolutely dead-set against ending up looking like the wall.

I took some hasty backward steps, stumbling over at least two spindly chairs in the process, hands up ready to ward him off.

And Brodie waltzed in between Mike and I with a speed that

made a joke out of the tight squeeze around the dining table. Not a chair was nudged. He was frankly graceful. Mike cradled his hand and glared at Brodie, and I bet he was doing the sizing up thing again, because he still looked like he wanted to hit something. Battles flitted across his face, too fast to grasp. Then Mike simply nodded like we'd agreed something important, stared at the hole in the wall as if he had no idea how it had come to be there, then staggered out the other door.

Brodie watched him go, then pirouetted to face me and Odati. 'Is he normally like that?'

I looked at Odati and Odati looked at me and we shook our heads in bewilderment.

'Altitude sickness …?' I ventured. It was all I could think of. My knees were in danger of knocking each other off course and I was terrified I was going to cry and the hole in the wall was glaring at me.

I escaped into the dorm where I started to pack things. Not easy with the swimming eyes and the shaking hands. Odati came in and tried to help, and she had to take hold of me to stop my mad shoving.

'Let me take over.'

I shook my head, because I didn't want to admit I wasn't doing fine and I didn't want to lose touch with that feeling I'd had before, that maybe I could help Odati, and maybe we could be friends, and it was like packing her bag for her was a critical step in friendship-forming and I was terrified my life was careening off the rails and I'd never get to see my parents again and …

She hauled me into a hug and I bawled. 'You were so wonderful last night. Thanks so much. We're a team. But I have to tell you, you're packing some ancient hanky and what looks like dirty jocks into my bag, so I think you should sit back and relax, and I'll finish off here.'

I pulled away to verify. Sure enough, some manky spider-webbed snot-rag was bundled up with Odati's precious few belongings, and I was holding tightly to a pair of men's undies that did not have that fresh-cleaned look. It was so bad, it was funny. I don't know if I was laughing harder than I was crying, but at least I *was* laughing.

Odati laughed along with me until we had to wipe our eyes—mind you, not with that hanky—or the jocks—and regain lost oxygen, gasping.

Brodie approached from the bunk opposite, holding out his hand despite a nervous look. I had zero idea what he wanted until he nodded his head in the direction of my lap.

No way!

I threw the jocks at him with a speed and accuracy I'd never before managed in any type of sporting activity.

He grinned a magic grin, one eyebrow quirked. 'Cheers.'

And Odati and I dissolved again.

CHAPTER ELEVEN

3 ½ days until flight
½ packet of cream biscuits
¼ block chocolate
US$400
Bs243.80
+ whatever Alice and Brodie had

I didn't have a clue what an open international border in the *altiplano* ought to look like. A guard was wandering around, sporting some sort of automatic weapon. A beaten-up van was parked to the side, its windows frosted white, and beyond it the frozen lines of a tent indicated several people had spent an uncomfortable night out here.

'Crap,' I muttered.

Onorio pulled up at the Bolivian side by a weathered sign that read *INMIGRACIÓN*. A few guards nursed mugs inside the building, but the window was closed and a massive tyre-shredding barrier stretched over the road.

It had already been decided: Onorio and I would do the talking. I figured I didn't really have a choice, but I was so grateful to Onorio for agreeing to help me. And Mike just sat in the passenger seat, staring ahead, nursing a bandaged hand.

His blankness was more frightening than him wigging out.

The dude with the gun was still pacing, shooting glances our way as if he was expecting us to try and charge through the barriers at the slightest provocation. Which, incidentally, was absolutely not a viable option. Odati had checked, and Onorio only had one spare tyre.

I tapped on the immigration office window. The guards inside had been watching us, but they waited for the tap before one of them got up and wandered over to slide up the pane. I imagined some procedure in there for 'Dealing With People Like Us', and 'Step One' was 'Wait for them to tap on the window', because of course, we could have just been there in that godforsaken spot in the middle of a meltdown for aimless sightseeing.

Give me a break.

The guard pinned us with a look merging absolute boredom with brittle despair. I didn't need to understand his rapid Spanish to know what he was saying. The border was closed.

Yeah mate, we'd figured that one out.

Onorio pleaded our case, but the guard was unaffected. The window clicked as its lock hit home.

I jumped when Odati called out, 'Did Miss C and the others get through?'

I couldn't believe I'd forgotten to ask. I stared at Odati a moment, mouth open, hating the requirement to tap-a-tap-tap on the window again.

'You're doing a great job, Eva,' Brodie said. His words held no trace of sarcasm, but as it was clear I was NOT doing a great job, I had to assume he was making fun of me. It's not unheard of, you know.

I scowled, turning back to the guard. He had sulked back to his teacup. I tried to formulate the right question in my head, but couldn't make it come together. I felt like a trapped goldfish with a watching cat.

Onorio cleared his throat. 'I will ask, if you like. You want to know about your friends?'

I nodded, tucking escaping bits of hair behind my ears, and gave him the details. A description of the consulate guy, Miss Cooper's name, whatever might help identify the bus. Then he did 'Step One: Knock-on-the-window'. Again. This time, another guard came forward.

'You cannot go through,' he said in clear and careful English.

'We know, thanks,' I said, taking over from Onorio in my excitement at possibly being understood. 'We were hoping you could tell us if our friends went through. Please.'

We went through the whole explanation, until finally I was watching the guard thumb through the records book on his desk, my heart beating double-time. And then he was shaking his head.

Onorio and I stumbled over each other's words in our haste. Was he sure? Yes, he was certain.

I thanked him, but my head was spinning.

Odati's eyes were glued to me as we returned to the car. 'Did they get through?'

I swallowed. 'No. They didn't even try.'

Her mouth dropped open. 'So where are they, then? Where did they go, if not here?'

And that was the heart of the mystery.

Where could three garishly yellow buses packed full of Aussies, including twenty-four kids and our last-remaining teacher, vanish to?

I looked at Odati, at Brodie and Alice's concerned faces, at Onorio's wide eyes. And then I looked at Mike, still in the passenger seat, all hunched over, shaking like he couldn't get the pain out.

And I didn't know the answer, and I didn't know how to find the answer.

But I did know our task had just become that much more difficult.

Where was our bus?

CHAPTER TWELVE

3 ½ days until flight
Crushed hope
1/8 block chocolate
US$400
Bs243.80
+ whatever Alice and Brodie had

Odati wept as Onorio turned the cruiser around. I didn't know what was going on between Chile and Bolivia to cause the border to close, but I bet it was linked to the financial dominos going down everywhere. Money's kind of key to everything, and when it disintegrates to pixels on a screen, people get upset. People get scared. People like Onorio. He was driving even faster back to his family than the blistering speeds he'd managed getting us out there.

We had been running the wrong way. Somehow, we'd missed a signpost.

I cradled Odati's head in my lap. Poor Odati. We still faced days of high altitude before we could descend. The back of my seat bulged and I guessed Brodie was trying to get comfortable behind me. We couldn't get Odati into the rear seat, and Mike was still catatonic in the front. So Brodie had to sardine himself in the back with Alice. He barely grimaced.

I suppose he could have sat where I was and had Odati's head in his lap, but that option wasn't really considered. I mean, I sort of thought of it, but I didn't mention it.

Though, from Odati's point of view, at least we knew Brodie was wearing clean underwear.

We whipped past some geysers steaming murky grey amid the white, and it was so excruciatingly cold I almost wanted to jump in. I didn't have a death wish. I knew I'd be parboiled in about half a second and that would be the end of me. It was the first quarter of a second, where I might actually feel warm all the way through, that beckoned.

Once we'd made it back to Uyuni, Onorio dropped us off at a hostel run by a guy he knew, who seemed to have an unusual idea of the tariff he could charge. I tried a tentative type of bargaining, and I was talked down so completely I'm glad the others couldn't understand what was going on. Even if it was more than we would have chosen to pay, it was at least cheery and clean.

Unlike us.

My cargo pants looked like they could, at any moment, stalk off on their own in search of a wash. The hostel guy must have noticed because he offered us free use of the laundry facilities, barely offsetting the pain of how much he was charging for the beds.

We hauled ourselves into the cosy bunkroom. Mike was dismal and uncommunicative. Odati was listless and smelled of spew. Alice's drawn face didn't match her usual carefree attitude.

And Brodie? He looked as filthy as the rest of us, but he was whistling as he puffed out his sleeping bag. I could almost admire his ability to adapt and keep smiling.

But we'd lost our bus and wasted days, and the world was going down the toilet. I couldn't dredge up the heart to whistle. In fact I can't even whistle. But if I could, I wouldn't. You get what I mean?

It was pure joy when I finally attacked myself with some of Alice's shower gel until I was as red as a strawberry and smelt like one too. I walked into the dorm feeling more human. And delightfully fruity.

In stark contrast, Mike glowered on his bunk. I kept as far away from him as I could. Odati was asleep, curled up against the wall. But Brodie set his tablet down as soon as I walked in. I was knocked completely off course by his sudden undivided attention. Literally. I hit my knee on a bed end, face turning red hot. No way to hide that.

'Eva.' His eyes flicked to my knee and back, and his lips twitched. 'Hi. I've been thinking we should search for a sign of your missing bus.'

I forced myself to nod in what I hoped was a natural fashion. 'Good idea.' I wondered who the 'we' could be. I took one look at Mike's vacant face, and frowned. I turned back to Brodie. 'Where's Alice?'

'Here.' Alice strode through the door. 'Pile up whatever you want washed, I'm hitting the laundry for some therapy.'

That confused me. 'Therapy?'

She smiled. 'I wash them, they get clean, I feel great. It's a win-win.'

Soon the three of us were grouped around an ancient cement basin filled with a modest array of clothing, watching the frothy water dance under the tap and turn murky. I turned to Alice. 'I'll help you transfer them to the machine.'

'It's all good, I'm finding my happy here. You go hunting with Brodie.'

My brain stalled. Icy streets. Desperate people. Lost buses. And Brodie, whom I seemed to embarrass myself in front of with regularity. The laundry looked inviting in comparison.

Alice looked at me funny. 'Hey Brodie, can Eva and I have a girl moment, please?'

I listened to his footsteps walk away, my face burning.

Alice took my hand. 'I don't know all that went down back at Potosí with that dude, and Mike is honestly a bit scary, am I right?'

I nodded, looking at my feet.

She squeezed my hand. 'But trust me when I say you're safe with Brodie. He's a good guy.'

I shot a look to where he was waiting, a shadow across the courtyard. I sighed. 'I think I've figured that out, it's just … we've never really got on very well.'

Alice grinned. 'That's an understatement. Give it another go, hey?' and she prodded me out the door.

I trailed after Brodie towards the street. Just before we reached the gate a thought grabbed me. 'Wait, we should go tell Mike. He might want to come.'

The way Mike had looked, I hoped he didn't, but I didn't want him believing he'd been left out either. And having him along almost seemed better than just being the two of us.

Brodie put up his hands, shaking his head. 'Not happening. Alice and I already asked Mike while you were in the shower. He refused to have anything to do with it. Like, really refused.'

I hoped all four walls of the dorm were still intact. 'Maybe he wanted to stay and make sure Odati was okay?'

Brodie shrugged. 'Maybe you're right. Anyway, he's not coming. We should get going.'

I dropped my eyes to the pavement, feeling the heat in my cheeks again. 'So. Then …?'

'It's just you and me.'

'Oh.' Fabulous. Just what I needed.

'Don't sound so excited.'

'No, I am! I mean, of course I'm not. Not like that …' I shut my mouth.

His lips danced. 'Too tired? Or are you scared?'

I forgot my fluster and rolled my eyes. 'Tired doesn't come into it. And why should I be scared? Apparently I have big bad you to protect me.'

One half of his mouth quirked up and he inclined his head towards me. He hadn't dropped his gaze, so there was no way I would either. If he was looking for weakness, he wasn't going to find it. Finally, he looked away, towards the grim street.

'Alright then, shall we?' Was he blushing?

'Lead on,' I said.

Barring our first argument, it was the longest conversation we'd ever had by a statistically significant margin, and certainly the most civil, and yet now we were heading out alone together for an evening's sleuthing. I was in uncharted territory.

CHAPTER THIRTEEN

3 days until flight
US$350
Bs156.90
+ whatever Alice and Brodie had

For the first half a block we enjoyed silence.

'How well do you know Mike?' Brodie finally asked.

That's what you get when you don't take charge of the conversation. An awkward topic. I grimaced. I was walking down a street half a world away from school, wearing Alice's offbeat clothes and feeling vastly different to the girl I'd been even days before. And I liked that. But it was time to pop the bubble.

'Not well. We weren't really friends at school.' In the same way machine guns weren't really ice creams.

Brodie frowned. 'He seems a little … how to say? … Unpredictable?'

I scrubbed tired eyes with snap-frozen fingers. 'He's probably just stressed. Aren't we all?'

Brodie pursed his lips and we walked up to our first hostel, asking the grimy-faced woman behind the counter whether she'd seen a few busloads of *turistas* come through. She hadn't. I wasn't surprised.

Re-emerging from the dimly-lit foyer, the street was even darker than it had been moments before. I hugged my jacket to me. One hostel down …

Brodie cleared his throat. 'Any idea where your teacher and friends would have stayed?'

'Nope. They hadn't planned to stay here at all.' Suddenly the town seemed enormous. I wanted a hug from my mum.

'But they would've been thinking of you three? Surely they'd stay somewhere you'd look?'

I stared at Brodie, mouth open. 'You're right! But where?' I felt better just knowing there might be a simpler way to solve the puzzle.

We'd reached another hostel, and that went the same way as the first, except this time the person behind the desk was wispy and worried and looked like the breeze from opening the door might knock him over.

Back on the street, we launched right into deconstructing the thought processes of the occupants of a yellow bus or three.

'Australia's the obvious first choice,' Brodie said. 'Are there any places named after Australian things around here?'

'Or maybe near something kind of Australian? Like a eucalypt or something?'

'A hostel owned by an Australian?'

I chewed my lip. 'Mike would probably know, he knows everything in that book of his.'

Brodie hauled something out of the small backpack he wore, lips wide with a grin. 'You mean this book?'

He was holding the guidebook. 'Brilliant! I could hug you!'

He shot me a quick look, eyes wide. Okay, so we might have moved from arguing to polite conversation, but evidently we were nowhere near hugging. Why had I even said that? I snapped my mouth shut, feeling my cheeks warm in the dark air.

I looked around for something—anything—to say. 'Oh, look, another hostel.'

I marched up the steps, but found as much luck as in the first two. The day had faded now. Barely half the streetlights were working, casting deep and sinister shadows across the cobbles, where it seemed anyone might hide. I suppressed a shiver.

Brodie was struggling to read the guidebook in the dim light, and I felt silly for even asking at the hostel. Random questioning wasn't going to help us, we needed a plan. I dug in my jacket pocket and pulled out a piece of paper torn from my sketchpad, and a trusty 2B pencil. I always carry something like that for impromptu sketching or note-taking. And I started to make a list of things we could look into. Dot point one: To do with Australia. I thought hard, but I couldn't come up with any second dot point. Which was making for a pretty poor list, if I'm honest.

'Nice, a plan.' Brodie's voice at my shoulder made me jump and I flailed a frightened fist in his direction.

'Whoa, sorry. You scared me.'

He was rubbing his arm. 'I see that now. Sorry.'

I looked at the pitifully short list. The buzz of electricity in the nearby streetlight seemed loud in the stillness. 'So, did you find anything in the guidebook?' I asked.

'Not so far.'

'I'm surprised Mike let you borrow it.'

'The guidebook? Ah, yeah, about that. He probably doesn't know I've got it.'

'You just took it?' I stared at Brodie.

'He didn't seem to want to talk.'

'Dude, he'll be pissed when he finds out.'

Brodie frowned and looked away. 'Yeah, probably. This thing

with Mike, it worries me. Does he do drugs?'

I blinked at the change of conversation, bringing the memory of Mike's rage and my fear back to mingle in the murky darkness. Was there something behind his weird behaviour? 'No, I don't think so. He's on the swim team, they'd be looking for that sort of thing …'

I thought of Mike, safe and snug back at the dorm. Odati too. How was it that I didn't get a choice about creeping around a post-apocalyptic nightscape?

I scowled at the stuttering streetlight. 'Screw this. We're never going to get anywhere. I'm going back.'

Brodie stared at me. 'Where did that come from?'

I kicked at a piece of shattered brick. 'It just sucks!'

'What?'

'This. That I'm out here, and I've got no choice in it, and they're back there, safe. But if something goes wrong, it's going to be my fault again.'

'What else was your fault?'

'Forget it.' I began to walk away, knowing it was stupid because I couldn't walk alone. Hating that, too.

'Eva. Wait. Is this about Elena? Who's Elena?'

Hearing that name made my insides do the chicken dance and I stopped so fast one boot slipped on a smooth cobble and I had to windmill my arms to stop from falling. 'Look, I'm grateful for your help, but that doesn't mean you get to ask all these questions!'

'Eva, the world is collapsing around us. The five of us need to pull together or I'm worried we'll die out here. But it's hard when you're keeping so many secrets!'

That stung, because it's one of my family's mantras—No Secrets.

I swung around to face him, pale in the fake light, his eyes intent on me.

He took a step forward. 'I chose to be here.'

'What?'

'Maybe you didn't have a choice about coming out tonight. You speak the language, Eva. That's gold. We need you. But you're not alone. I'm here. I didn't have to be, I chose to be. So cut me some slack.'

It was the grain of salt that broke the flamingo's back. I sat on the icy step and cried, hiding in my arms. Hating that Brodie was there to see me so low. He hovered like he didn't know what to do—who does when someone starts blubbing? He murmured a few things about how it was all going to turn out alright. He vowed we would find Miss C.

Then he sat down next to me, head in his hands. 'Oh, this is screwed!' Finally, some truth.

We sat until my butt went numb and I remembered all those warnings about getting haemorrhoids. I looked up, tears crisping into ice down my cheeks, and Brodie stood so fast I gasped. He held out his hand to me. I regarded it like I might regard an alpaca: cute, but likely to spit without provocation.

'C'mon.'

I shook my head. 'No. No more hostels. Not tonight.'

He kept his hand there. 'No hostels, I promise. Something better.'

'What?'

'A cup of tea! The standard English solution to any problem, be it large or small!' He smiled in a way that could have made whatever he suggested seem like a great idea.

But some tea? In the freezing darkness, that sounded like an awesome idea. Hoping it wasn't a bad mistake, I put my hand in his. His fingers were colder than his palm, but warmer than me. I let him pull me up.

CHAPTER FOURTEEN

3 days until flight
Pot of coca tea
US$350
Bs156.90
+ whatever Alice and Brodie had

We found a quaint place behind an angular white archway, serving damn fine coca tea, despite being totally, achingly empty except for us. I sculled half a cup, staring out the window at the beautiful clock tower gleaming in pale gold splendour, before I had the guts to look at Brodie. He was leaning forward, intent on me, a slight furrow in his brow.

    I was so tired.

    His eyes were luminous in the lamplight.

    My resolve broke.

    I told him. About Elena. About trusting when I shouldn't have trusted, about losing our hard-won money and our hope of home, and how I felt responsible for it all. We sat in the brilliantly-lit cocoon, and I talked like I could make everything fine again just by saying it out loud. When I wasn't talking I was biting my nails. Once I'd finished, the silence stretched, making me aware of how much of a psycho I must have just sounded. I shrank back into my chair.

Brodie cleared his throat. 'I just want to say, after hearing all you guys have been through, getting robbed and all … Well, I understand why you didn't want to talk to me at the bus station. And, well, I'd love to start afresh, try to be friends.'

I stared at him. Brain. Not. Working.

He laughed, sounding nervous. 'Don't tell me it was actually my inherently untrustworthy face that put you off …'

I snorted. My English Lit teacher used to hate it when I snorted. She was big on etiquette. Snorting is, apparently, exceedingly unladylike. Probably so is wearing my undies from two days before, turned inside out so they're fresh like new. I giggled.

Brodie's eyes widened. 'Something funny?'

Oh embarrassment, he was probably thinking I was the weirdest weirdo to ever walk the earth. I fumbled for something to say to explain my snorty-laugh.

'Yeah, um, don't worry about me, I was thinking about my undies …' Despite my requirement to suffer complete and utter mortification at saying that out loud, I giggled again. 'That came out wrong. Altitude …'

His brow furrowed and his lips quirked and I wanted to touch them to see if they were as soft as they looked. 'So, can we please start again and try for friends?'

I made myself be serious. I don't get offers of friendship often enough to giggle one away. 'I'd like that. Thanks Brodie.' I stumbled over his name. It was the first time I'd said it out loud. It felt delicious, and being with him in that moment seemed like Tim Tams dipped in Milo on a stormy night. My cheeks heated, his closeness tingling the nerves in my belly.

It was an inconvenient time for a crush.

I'm personally of the opinion there is no such thing as a convenient time, so I guess what I'm trying to convey is, this was Very Inconvenient.

I stared out the window, at anything but him. A few deep breaths. 'Sorry for the verbal vomit …'

'No, don't be. I'm glad you told me, things make more sense now.'

'Nah,' I said softly, 'nothing makes sense anymore.'

The clock outside struck nine, reminding me I was hungry. That clock tower told us we were smack bang in the centre of town, but I was still feeling lost.

'How's about some good old fried chicken?' I asked with an attempt at a normal smile. *Picante de pollo* was like a national dish in Bolivia.

He grimaced. 'Well, firstly we could probably find a cheaper meal away from here, somewhere not so … scenic …'

'You came here for the scenery?'

'I thought you might appreciate a nice outlook. And it got a great rating in the guidebook.'

I looked again at the glowing clock tower, then back to him. We studied each other over the plastic-topped table, tentative. Brodie didn't drop his gaze. A smile grew on his lips, spreading so his eyes warmed too. The hairs on my arms stood on end.

My excuses for perceiving him negatively were gone, and I had to make sure I didn't make a total fool of myself. We were just going to be friends. *Got that, Eva?*

I clawed my way back to the conversation. 'What was the second thing?'

'Huh?'

'You said "firstly" we could find a cheaper place. What's "secondly"?'

'Oh. I'm vegetarian.'

Ouch. That had to be tough. There wasn't a heck of a lot of choice when it came to vegetarian food in Bolivia. Hang on … 'But you ate the *Pique a lo Macho* Onorio served us …?'

He gave me a despairing look. 'How could I not? They'd put so much effort into it, hadn't they?'

I didn't know what to say.

And then he laughed. 'Your face!'

My laugh is all on the intake, and that's great I suppose, because it sounds so funny it makes other people laugh, and a weird laugh is still heaps better than no laugh. But Brodie's laugh leapt from him, and crinkled the corners of his eyes and made me feel all warm, like everything in that moment was fabulous.

'Let's get out of here,' he said. And he bounded up, offering his hand to me like a challenge.

I took it without hesitation. Because I'm up for challenges when they laugh like he does.

We slipped out of the hot tea atmosphere and into the freezing night, making me shiver from toes to ears. I've met some cold places, but the *altiplano* takes the cake, and of the *altiplano* nowhere had felt colder than Uyuni with a breeze gusting down that dark and cobbled street. Which is why I think neither of us tried to reclaim our joined hands. I knew it wasn't anything goo-gah or lovey-dove, though a rebellious portion of myself insisted on theorising it *could* be. We were simply on an adventure. And it was butt-crunchingly cold.

I spotted the eatery first, behind a greasy doorway spilling merry firelight and sporting bubbling 44-gallon drums on open fires. Filled with locals, and cheap as … well … chips! Which is what we had. Chips and crusty cheese *buñuelos*.

Once we weren't so damned hungry, we started a Conference Of War: how could we find out whether Miss C had come through here, and if she had, where she'd got to? Knocking on every hostel door was a pointless mission. Uyuni wasn't big, but before everything collapsed it had been a hive of tourism, and every second door seemed to offer some sort of accommodation. Now the tourists were gone, barring some ragged few who seemed content to dream their way through life in the hope that when they woke, the world would be normal again. And the money had gone with the tourists, so desperation was cranking up in the town.

If we kept walking those streets in a dazed fug, we'd be lucky to only be robbed once.

We needed a plan. But nothing was leaping out. We couldn't find any Aussie references in the guidebook, and I screwed up my very short and equally useless list before throwing it into one of the cooking fires.

Brodie finally jumped as if electrified. 'Let's go to a club!'

My mouth dropped open. It wasn't a clubbing sort of moment. We had priorities. When I told him so, he rolled his eyes.

'This time of night, that's where people will be if they're anywhere. Drowning their sorrows. Tourists are getting rare, surely a busload of them would have caused some talk? And surely that talk would filter through to the bartender?'

Ah … I finally understood his thought process. As ideas went, it scored points for originality, and then won outright by the simple expedient of now being the Only Idea We Had.

Thus I found myself in a huge, dusty underground room with flashback strobe lights, a lot of out-of-luck tour drivers, and the occasional head-in-the-clouds tourist. Brodie's lean strength beside me felt like a personal bodyguard. We strode straight up to the bar and Brodie beckoned the bartender over, putting up two fingers.

The nice way. Luckily.

'*Dos Inca Kolas, por favor.*' His expressive lips challenged me with a smile. 'See, you're not the only one who can speak Spanish around here …'

'Brodie!' I hissed. 'We don't have money to waste on drinks!'

He grinned. 'In all the movies, they have to butter up the bartender by buying stuff.'

I rolled my eyes.

'At least we're not ordering whatever he's got,' Brodie whispered.

I looked where he was indicating, only to find a shambling tourist dancing on the spot, mumbling lyrics, eyes closed, contents of his bottle dribbling with every step. I snorted, glad for something to break the tension.

Our drinks chose that moment to arrive, gleaming highlighter yellow under the bright lights of the bar. My chest lurched as Brodie handed over a precious orange note. He waited with his hand outstretched.

And so did the bartender. Eventually the bartender rattled an explanation to Brodie, who turned to me in confusion.

'Okay, I admit my Spanish is crap. What did he say?'

'You gave him twenty. He needs fourteen more.'

'Thirty-four? For two bottles of pop? I could buy half a store for that!'

I flicked a glance at the bartender before answering. 'Maybe you could, before … but I don't think you can … anymore.'

He swore. The two of us pooled the coins from our pockets until the bartender was finally happy. I made sure to grin at him the entire time, because the whole point of this was to make that guy like us. Right?

Brodie shook his head. 'That's a miscalculation I won't make again. Sorry.' Then a wicked grin surfaced as he picked up his bottle. 'We better make it worthwhile!'

I sniffed at mine. It smelt like pineapples and sugar. 'What is this stuff?'

'Only the best pop in South America. You haven't tried it? This is your lucky day. Plus, it's yellow, and your buses are yellow, so I thought it might bring us some good luck.'

I couldn't not smile. 'Are you sure?'

He laughed. 'We could be safe in the hostel right now, but instead we're out here, crusading for truth. We deserve a few perks. And believe me, this stuff is a definite perk.'

He raised his bottle, and one devastating eyebrow.

We were close to broke, along with every other person, country and entity on the planet. We didn't know how to get home, we didn't know what we'd find at home. All we had left was each other.

And, I hasten to add, that wasn't the Brodie-and-me each other, it was the all-five-of-us each other. It just so happened it was only Brodie and I out there at that moment. And we'd already paid for these weird yellow soft drinks …

I grinned and tapped his bottle with mine. '*Salud.*'

His second eyebrow came up to join the first. '*Salud.*'

The sweetness fizzed onto my tastebuds and up my nose, making my saliva glands hurt, and giving me an instant urge to grin. The feeling was freaky, especially in a weirded-out sixties underground time machine on top of the world, with a boy I probably liked too much next to me. I put my bottle on the countertop again.

'Verdict?' asked Brodie.

'Um, interesting flavour. I hope it's worth it.'

Brodie's laugh boomed out again. 'You ready to find out?'

I nodded and waved over the bartender. I asked the questions I'd been perfecting all evening, and watched his leathery face with a hope that began dying before I'd finished speaking.

No, he hadn't heard anything about three busloads of Aussies. But he'd ask around and get back to us.

I looked at Brodie, and for the first time I seriously contemplated the possibility the buses never made it here. That somewhere between Potosí and Uyuni, painfully yellow smashed shells of dead hope lay on the side of the road.

'Nothing?' he guessed.

I shook my head. 'He's going to ask a few people … if we wait here he'll …' I stared at the strobe lights gleaming through the cola in front of me. Reminiscent of stars on the lake the night before, when I'd still held hope we'd be across the border and heading to the coast.

How a day could change things.

And our situation could change just as much again. So why worry?

Fear, I suddenly understood, killed life. Fear was what consumed you while possibilities passed you by.

Screw fear.

I spun to face Brodie, who almost fell off his stool. 'We're going to find them, Brodie. They're okay, and they're thinking of us, and they would've done their best to leave a message we could find. And we're going to find it!'

I lifted up my bottle and took a swig. Brodie watched me with wide eyes.

I grinned. 'I think this stuff is growing on me.'

He laughed and picked up his own drink. 'You crack me up.'

We drank until our bodies buzzed with a potent mix of sugar and caffeine. We danced to a unique blend of modern pop and Bob Marley, until our feet ached and my hair fought free of its bun to tangle sweatily down my back.

We laughed. A lot. At our bad dance moves. At the shambling *turista* who tried to hug Brodie and missed, embracing a pillar instead. At life.

At one point Brodie leant forward to speak in my ear, his fingers electric as they tucked a stray lock of hair back and then slid down to the ends. 'Alice will be so pissed she missed this!'

My head-spin at his lips so close to my skin was doused. Of course. I tried to act normal. 'How long have you two been together?'

He threw his head back and laughed, before grabbing my hand

and twirling me around in a mad dance. The song ended and I staggered against him. He was grinning. His head came back to my ear again, this time with no music to muffle his words. 'We're not together.'

I'd thought I was dizzy before. I'd been wrong.

Then he spoke again. 'Alice and I are just friends.'

Wait—settle down Eva, I thought. *That's just-friends, like what he said he wanted with you. Do not be the fool here.*

I could have hugged the bartender for choosing that moment to find us through the medley of lights, sporting a grin. Someone knew someone who'd heard from someone who knew the proprietor of a hostel who'd been delighted when three yellow buses had turned up on his doorstep three nights ago, filling his hostel for the night, as well as those on either side.

We'd found the trail!

I translated for Brodie, amid thanking the bartender and encouraging him to scribble down directions on a musty serviette. Sore feet were forgotten as Brodie and I surfed up the stairs and out the door on a wave of fist-pumping joy. Even the severe chill of the night couldn't shake us, though it definitely cleared my head. I scrambled into my jacket as we set off down the street. The memory of the music was still thumping in my ears.

CHAPTER FIFTEEN

2 ½ ish days until flight
US$350
Bs140
+ whatever Alice and Brodie had (minus 2 unexpectedly expensive drinks)

It was dark and I bet it was dodgy, but I didn't feel unsafe. I had Brodie, and we'd finally found evidence that Miss C and the others had been here. I felt bullet-proof.

It didn't take long to reach the bus station, which definitely wasn't the sort of place you'd choose to hang out at nearly midnight in a town with intermittent lighting and rapidly soaring unemployment. But there, right in our face, was the hostel they'd stayed at.

It was the first place you'd see getting off a bus at the station. Why hadn't we thought of something so simple? If we hadn't been so desperate to get out to the border, if the 12:30 bus had still been running and we'd turned up in the dark, then we probably would've tried that hostel. Except we'd arrived at midday and dashed straight to the salt lakes.

And our haste had cost us an entire day. But I couldn't regret. It was the smartest thing we could think of at the time.

Now we threw caution to the wind and knocked on the closed hostel door. My heart was beating a mile a minute and I held onto Brodie's hand like it was the rail on an overcrowded bus negotiating the potholes on the way into Uyuni. It took a few minutes, then the door opened a crack.

An eye surveyed us, then evidently made a choice on language. 'Can I help you?'

'We're looking for some friends, a busload of schoolkids about our age, and one teacher, with a bigger group. We think …'

I leant back in surprise, my shoulder hitting Brodie's arm. The eye had vanished. The door shut with a thud.

I blinked, but then heard bolts being drawn back. The door opened again, fully this time. The eye reappeared, now in possession of the face and body of a middle-aged man. 'Yes, your friends stayed here. Come in, quickly, the streets are not safe, especially now.' We followed him into a frigid foyer. 'You're late. We expected you a few days ago.'

My mouth hung open, but Brodie interceded. 'Did our group leave a message?'

The man nodded and headed to the desk behind him. 'They wanted you to know there's been a change of plans. They are heading to Lima now.'

'Lima? As in Peru?' I was stunned.

The man nodded and handed me a folded copy of our original school trip itinerary. I was confused until I opened it and saw Miss C's handwriting inside.

'When did they leave?' Brodie asked.

'Two days ago.'

Lima. I couldn't imagine a single reason why the bus would now be heading to Lima. Except, of course, up was down, and weird was normal these days.

I jumped when Brodie leant closer. 'What does it say?'

Of course. *Focus, Eva.* I held the note with tremulous fingers.

> 30th *April*
> *Odati, Eva and Mike,*
> *I hope you'll get my text messages and find this note in time. We've had a setback, we can't fly from Santiago anymore. We only got the notification today. Our new flight is from Lima. Same day—May 5th, but at 1510 hrs. I've made sure they keep three seats open for you. It's vital you make this flight.* <u>*Absolutely vital.*</u> *This is the last Australian evac out of South America. There aren't any others scheduled.*
> *Stick together. Be careful.*
> *Miss C.*

Brodie whistled under his breath.

My mind was spinning like a whirlwind down a freezing side street. I looked at the calendar hanging behind the desk and counted days on my fingers. It was the second of May. Probably even the third, considering the time of night.

We had less than three days.

'How do we get to Lima in three days?'

Perhaps I should have asked, where the heck *is* Lima? I've never won awards for South American geography, but I was pretty sure Lima was the capital of Peru, and I had a good idea Peru was west of us. But I had the uncomfortable feeling an extensive stretch of ancient mountains hulked in between that had managed to hide the jewel in the Incan crown from the gold-hungry Spaniards for centuries.

Santiago had seemed simple. Find the coast, hail a bus, make sure it's heading south.

Lima on the other hand ... I looked at Brodie, who was running his forefinger across the continent map in the guidebook. He was frowning.

The hostel owner spoke. 'You should stay here tonight. Where is the third person? A girl?'

I shook my head, not even bothering to explain that Brodie wasn't Mike. 'No, thank you. We're staying elsewhere.'

The man's face fell. And like that, I understood why it was so cold in there. He couldn't afford to heat the place.

There was too much going wrong. I couldn't help everyone. But I still delved into my pocket for a few coins and handed them across. 'Thank you for your help.' I blinked hard. I wasn't going to cry twice in one night.

He pleaded with us to take care, even offered to walk us home, but that would only leave him alone on his way back. His advice echoed in my head as we walked out into the lonely dark of the bus station. I zipped my jacket to the max and stuck close to Brodie, my hand creeping into his again.

'So many buses,' I whispered.

Brodie raised an eyebrow. Probably because the bus station was completely empty.

'Between here and Lima,' I explained. 'So many connections to make, so many schedules that might've changed.'

Brodie's hand dropped mine, but before I could lament, his arm came across my shoulder, heavy and comforting. I let myself be drawn into his warmth, even if it made normal walking difficult.

'If we don't make this flight,' I said, 'I don't know what we'll do.'

Brodie gave a rueful snort. 'At least you *have* a flight.'

I winced, remembering Alice and Brodie were just running with a whiff of hope and nothing else. 'Sorry. I didn't think …'

A dark figure came down the street towards us, and Brodie's arm tightened, drawing us further to the side. He didn't speak again until the person had vanished into the ink behind us.

'It's fine. Why do you think we're sticking with you lot? Not just for your good company. We'll hitch a ride on your flight. Australia isn't England, but it's more like home than here.' He squeezed my shoulder. 'We're going to make it, Eva. Mere hours ago we had no idea what was going on, but now we have a destination and a deadline.'

I nodded, mind windmilling. The evacuation buses were at an obvious advantage—they didn't have to wait for departure times or connections and they were already days ahead of us. I brutally culled any hope we'd catch them before they reached Lima. But Brodie was right: we could make the flight. We'd catch them at the airport.

Then I gasped. 'Why don't we hire a bus and driver, like they did?'

We were all smiles until we started trying to imagine how much it might cost.

He sighed. 'It'd certainly be faster than relying on the bus services.' Then he dragged me to a halt so I was staring into his shadowed face. 'Onorio's cruiser!'

Of course! 'That would work … we'd all fit …' Then my face fell. 'But it would cost a lot, it's practically new, and Onorio has his family here … would he want to come?'

'That's what I mean!'

'What?'

'His cruiser's new! Remember he was trying to sell the old one!'

I danced around the cobbles. 'What? Drive it ourselves?'

'Yes! He told me he was almost giving it away, but no one wants it, because there's no work anymore.'

I smiled, stretching my freezing cheeks until they felt like they were splitting. 'Like a road trip?'

'Exactly like a road trip!'

I whooped, he laughed, and I tried to say something about how awesome his idea was, and he picked me up to whirl me around, and then we were both dizzy, and I was clinging to him for balance.

And before you could say *what was that about just-friends?*

he had a warm hand curled into the back of my neck and I was tilting my face up towards his. His breath played over my cheeks for a delicious moment, then his lips met mine, gentle, icy, hesitant. Pulling him closer I arched myself up to deepen the kiss. It felt surprisingly natural, totally right.

The attack came as an unwelcome surprise.

They came for me first. I felt their hands at my hips, creeping forwards, searching for pockets. I cried out, disengaging from Brodie's shoulders to scratch and slap at those phantoms.

It was so dark. So quick.

Brodie pulled me behind him and his warmth was gone. I heard cursing and the sound of fists contacting flesh—horrible thuds as moon-kissed figures grappled.

Then someone—a shard of fear until I knew it was Brodie—grabbed my hand and we scampered down the street as fast as the thin air could allow, barely slowing until we'd made it through the gate of our hostel and into the relative safety of the courtyard beyond. Both puffing. In the dim light I could see he was bleeding.

'Your nose …?'

He shook his head, dabbing with his sleeve. 'It's nothing. I can't believe I was so stupid.'

Heart pumping, head spinning, mind confused.

'Are you okay?' he asked, whipping his bag off his back to check it was still intact.

I nodded and checked for my all-important money belt. 'I'm fine, they didn't get anything. You?'

'Nothing. Just as well. I'm so sorry. That was one of the dumbest things I've ever done.'

Our kiss? Or being attacked? I desperately needed to know, but there was no way I could ask. I'd practically thrown myself at him. At 'just-friends' Brodie. I bit my lip.

'Me too. Without you there …' I didn't want to think what

might have happened.

'Without me, you wouldn't have been there,' he said.

Maybe he was looking at me, I don't know, I was too scared to look. I wanted to reach out to him. Instead I dug my hands into my pockets. The silence stretched.

'Hell,' he said. 'I'm sorry. It's late, and we have a lot to do tomorrow.'

He hesitated a moment more, before turning and making his way into the dorm. I tilted my face up to the cold slice of moon and took two deep breaths, then crept after him.

We slunk into our individual bunks, across the room from each other, set up when we were each still thinking the other wasn't a particularly nice person. And because we didn't manage to discuss privately between ourselves the fact we'd ended up pashing in the middle of an Uyuni side street, neither of us knew how to approach it the next morning with all the others around.

So we didn't allude to it at all.

Like the kiss that never was.

But the memory of it wouldn't go away.

CHAPTER SIXTEEN

57 hours until flight
5 hot mugs of api
Not enough sleep
US$350
Bs115
+ whatever Alice and Brodie had

The next morning was a riot of confusion. I was woken by Alice squealing at my bed.

'You're back! You guys were out so late, I gave up waiting and went to bed to nightmares of you dying in a gutter.'

I lifted my head, noted the barely risen sun and groaned. It was, simply put, Way Too Early to be woken. In response to my muffled query, Alice told me it was 6:45, in the kind of voice you might use to tell someone they've won a year's supply of rocky road ice cream, or a genuine Namatjira painting.

On a scale of one to ten of acceptable wake-ups following an attempted mugging in the freezing dark in the teeny weeny hours, where a ten is you're allowed to sleep as long as you wish, and a one is you get woken after five minutes, 6:45am scored about a two-point-three. And pulling an all-nighter would have been a two-point-four for me.

As in—preferable.

I felt beaten-up.

Brodie was sleeping like the dead across the room, one arm flung across his pillow. And he really *was* beaten-up, which trumped me. I remembered his lips on mine. And then I remembered he said he'd been stupid. And of course, we'd earlier agreed to be just-friends, and I reckoned just-friends forget when they get kissed by other just-friends at the end of a long night, just like that sleepover at Sarah's house in Year Nine. Never. Spoken. Of. Again. So I decided to focus on all the other cool things we'd done, and forget that anomalous kiss.

I thought all of this through at a blistering mental pace, but since I hadn't woken up properly, I guess I lay there like a stunned mullet.

'Eva, are you okay?' Alice's voice brought me closer to reality.

I blinked. Someone laughed, but it wasn't unkind. I squinted and saw Odati, looking much brighter than the night before, holding two steaming mugs of *api*. I reached for mine, giving her a smile.

I drank two mouthfuls before my synapses started sparking at anywhere near the required rate. And by that time, I was too late to stop Odati waking Brodie.

I mean—really? I knew we were in a hurry but—really? It was early and freezing, and he was asleep.

He groaned and I looked away from him in confusion, cheeks burning, and for the first time I spotted Mike, prickly on a bunk across from me. I made sure to concentrate on my *api*. *Api* can't read anything into your facial expression. And even if it could, you'd drink it anyway so it wouldn't be able to share what it learnt, would it?

When in doubt, look at your *api*.

Alice jumped in excitement. 'C'mon you guys! You were out practically all night! What happened? Brodie is that *blood* on your pillow?'

It was far too early for this sort of mental effort.

I could think of nothing to say except yelling WE KISSED! and running around the room collecting high fives, and I'd already determined that was wholly inappropriate, especially because we probably shouldn't have kissed.

Brodie wasn't saying anything either. Did he really wish we hadn't? I shuffled position to wake up more, and something crinkled in the pocket of my pants. The pants I hadn't had the energy to remove before bed.

Miss C's note.

Saviour from relationship confusion.

Rescuer from awkward conversation.

'We found where Miss C and the others got to,' I blurted. And it had the required effect. Everyone had Eyes On Eva. 'We need to get to Lima.'

The responses were varied, from 'Where the hell is Lima?' (this from Odati, and I admit, I felt her pain), to a rather coarse expletive that doesn't need to be repeated (but I get how Mike was feeling too). I explained about Miss C's note, and you could feel the chill descending. We'd been isolated for a while now, away from the big cities, still no internet or phone coverage. I suppose we were all starting to appreciate some nasty stuff might be going down around the world. And to get home, we had to stop hiding from it.

In fact, to get home we had to walk right up to it, and say g'day, and ask it how it was going.

Mike was studying his guidebook, the pages trembling, and I happened to be watching him because I still wasn't sure if he knew we'd nicked the book last night. Nothing to do with avoiding looking at Brodie all sleep-mussed and rumpled on his bed. My mug paused halfway to my mouth and hovered.

Nothing about Mike was still.

Everything was twitching or shaking, like a little kid who needs the toilet but doesn't want to admit it. An uncomfortable sensation gripped my chest.

Fear.

Then Mike jumped up, making me leap back until the chill wall slammed against my spine and a slug of *api* catapulted onto my sleeping bag. 'It's impossible!' he said. 'We'd have to catch, like, eight different buses or something!'

His face was all blotchy, so I quickly mentioned our plan.

'Buy a car?' Mike's eyebrows merged with his hairline and his voice cracked. 'We're worried about having enough money to freaking eat, and you want to buy a car?'

Odati made a calming gesture. 'Let's start by looking at how much we have. Include anything we might have of value.'

The rest of us reached for money belts and wallets, but Mike whipped around, grabbed his bag and marched out of the room. A flurry of wind made me shiver before the door slammed closed. I blinked after him, mouth open and heart hammering.

Odati frowned. 'That's weird. He's being very weird. Do you think he's hiding money?'

Brodie shrugged. 'He's hiding something. And now you mention it, on the drive back yesterday I realised I was missing cash.'

I gasped, and Brodie's eyes met mine for the first time that morning. Narrowed in thought, I couldn't read a thing in them. 'You think he might have …?'

'I'm missing money too, this morning I noticed it, when I checked my bag,' Alice said.

Odati was busy counting, and then she punched her mattress. 'I can't be sure but I think I'm short too. What about you, Eva?'

I shook my head. 'Do you seriously think he's stealing from us?'

It was Alice who answered. 'The bigger question is—why? And I have a bad feeling I know the answer.'

I had an equally bad feeling that I didn't want to know what Alice thought she knew. So, perhaps it was lucky that Mike waltzed back in at that point, all dusty air and dishevelled hair. He was met by an impenetrable wall of uncomfortable silence he didn't seem to notice, and sat down like nothing had happened. Casually started tallying his suspiciously small number of notes.

Not a note shook.

His hands were as steady as a solid armchair on the back porch, the kind that collects redback spiders that crawl out to scare the heck out of you when you decide to move the chair to catch the breeze. And watching those smooth brown fingers, a chill ran down my back.

Because I knew something was not right.

And maybe I had known for a while.

I hid my fluster by counting my own stash. Nothing missing. But when it came to buying even a beaten-up old landcruiser, my contribution could be neatly summarised as Abso Nothing. So I bent my mind to Odati's other request—anything I might have of value. Plastic earrings. Pencils it would break my heart to lose. Some well-worn second-hand clothes …

Hmmm.

Things weren't looking good for us if my net worth was anything to base things on. No wonder Mike hadn't bothered stealing from me.

Odati looked gorgeously scary, fists clenched and a vein pulsing in her forehead. 'How much have you got, Mike?' she asked.

He took one look at her and hunched in on himself. He had quite a bit less than me, even taking into account my rough thirds-ing after we got robbed.

'Where's it going?' Odati asked, steely and cold.

He fiddled with his fingernails. 'Where's what going?'

'Don't play dumb. Your money, and the money we're missing, too.'

'I don't know where yours is, but I've been buying things we need.'

'Like?' Odati asked.

His mouth worked. 'Y'know. Things. Food.'

I shook my head. 'You bought breakfast at Potosí, but that was less than seventy *bolivianos*.'

Mike rounded on me, nostrils flared. 'What are you? Some kind of freaking memory-machine?'

I stared back at him, though my heart was thumping like the rising wind outside. 'The prices had gone up since the day before, I remember being worried by that.'

He scowled. 'Don't listen to her! She hates me!'

Odati came to stand by my bunk. 'That's how I remember it too, Mike. C'mon. You and I have been friends for years, don't lie to me.'

'I don't know where it's gone. And it's your fault if you've lost yours! I haven't stolen anything!'

Brodie's voice was calm. 'I'm missing fifty dollars. You want to tell me anything about that?'

Mike exploded. His guidebook hurtled through the air. Brodie dodged to the side and it smashed against the wall, one torn page fluttering free.

'Mike!' Odati cried. 'Stop this!'

He collapsed back like a blow-up mattress with the plug out. And began to cry.

It was Alice who emptied his bag. I expected the swim team vitamins. But not the other two packs, lacklustre white labels with miniscule writing. Alice nodded as she picked them up, reading cursorily.

'These aren't yours.'

Mike shook his head without looking up.

Alice turned to us. 'They're a stimulant, they help you focus. But they're prescription-only. They're addictive and cause liver damage, shit like that.'

I shuddered.

'How long, Mike?' Odati said.

Mike's voice was muffled. 'Couple of months. I usually buy it off a guy at school. And the second pack I got from a tourist in Potosí. I was running out …'

A memory of golden hair and a slippery white smile came to me, and I was fairly certain I now knew what Mike and the horrible Golden Boy had been discussing in our Potosí hostel.

'Pills, stealing … almost smashing Eva in the head!' Odati cried. 'Why would you take these things? You don't need them!'

Mike cradled his head in his hands. 'I failed English last term, they were threatening to expel me. I was told these would help my grades.'

'Who told you?' Odati still looked angry, but like it wasn't just at Mike anymore.

He froze. Then he looked up, straightened his back, pulled up his chin. 'I'm not supposed to say, but who cares? We'll probably never make it home anyway. My coach told me to get them. He didn't want to lose me off the team.'

There was an awestruck silence, and then everyone acted at once. Outcries, swear words, pillow punching.

Odati strode across to Mike and hauled him into a hug. 'That coach is an arsehole!'

Mike was still crying but he started laughing too. 'Man, it feels good to actually tell you. And here's something else while I'm at it. I freaking hate swimming! I hate the early mornings, I hate the constant testing and pressure. But they keep telling me I'm "the next big thing". Well, who gives? I just want to be me.'

I noticed Alice pocketing the two offending containers. She headed out the door after whipping a look my way, so I followed her into the icy morning wind, bleary in the dusty air.

'Thought those two might appreciate some alone time,' she murmured.

I heard a sound behind me and turned to see Brodie. A quiver passed down my spine.

I spun back to Alice. 'You got them? Should we flush them or something?'

She shook her head, rereading the labels. 'No, he'll need to be weaned off them. At least we have more than enough to get him to the plane.'

We sat on the step outside our room, huddled away from the rising wind. Warm in the sun, frigid in the shadows, Brodie and I related the excitement of the previous night. In highly edited fashion. No mention of me blubbing (thanks to Brodie who was narrating that bit), and no mention of getting busy before the thugs arrived (thanks to my narration). When we'd finished, I heard some shuffling behind me. Mike and Odati. Mike was hunched into his black blazer, cheeks flaming, but he didn't drop his eyes. 'Yeah. Like. I've been an idiot. I'm sorry.'

Odati smiled at him and grabbed one of the drug containers from Alice. It rattled, it must have been the new one.

The full one.

'No thanks to this.' Her face twisted, and in one motion she unscrewed the top and flung the contents down the festy drain beside her.

It was a frozen tableau.

Alice reaching out to stop Odati, Mike's face contorting as he yelled 'No!', Brodie pale with his mouth hanging open.

There was nothing we could do. The moment passed and there was Mike, scrabbling his fingers through the scummy water, trying to find any surviving pills.

'You don't need them!' Odati was trying to drag him back up.

He was crying again, huge painful racking sobs.

Alice spoke then. 'Yeah, he kind of did.'

I felt like hurling. The wind shifted direction, flapping at a sheet of roofing and spearing through my jacket. I shivered. I didn't like Mike, but I didn't want him going cold turkey in the middle of a meltdown, either.

What would you give to turn back time?

But it was done now. It was all done, and my stomach churned as Alice counted the few pills that remained in the second container.

Odati's face crumpled. This time it was Mike comforting her.

Alice chewed her lip. 'How many a day, Mike?'

He wouldn't meet her eyes. 'I dunno. Three? Maybe four? More? It's been pretty stressful, you know?'

I stared at Alice's face. 'How many are left?' I whispered.

'Four.'

I winced. Four pills. Three days until the flight. I was out of my depth—what happened to someone when they halved their drug intake?

Alice swore. 'I wish I could access the internet!'

I put my hand on her shoulder. 'You seem pretty knowledgeable about this already …'

Her blue eyes sent a death beam my way. 'I'm not a druggie, Eva.'

'No! I wasn't … I meant you were really smart to recognise what was happening. I meant, I would trust you to do the best by Mike even without Dr Google.'

Brodie put a hand on Alice's arm. 'Eva wasn't being nasty, Al. And you're doing great, okay?'

She blushed at me. 'Sorry, I guess I'm just so used to being judged. I'm going to study medicine when I get home …' She paused, grimacing. 'Or I was.'

'Medicine. Wow! Well, I'm glad we have you around.' I paused, then smiled. 'And there's only one thing you have to be sorry about today.'

'What's that?'

'Waking us up so damn early!'

Odati did a snort-laugh through her tears and Alice smiled, but her hand was still rattling that last pill container in an echo of the loose roofing, and her eyes were worried. The sound of four pills was pretty lonely.

Mike looked up, wet cheeks red from the cold. 'You know what? It's done, and I'm actually glad. I really am. I know this isn't going to be a hug-and-it's-all-okay thing, because I've tried to go off these before, and I'm not a nice person when I do. I'm sorry for that. In advance.'

'We might be able to find more here,' Alice said.

But Mike shook his head. 'I went out looking while you were in the laundry last night. Nothing.'

Brodie stared at him, mouth hard. 'So, who was watching over Odati, then?'

Mike's nose flared and he shot a glance at Odati. 'No one was going to come in and get you!'

I kind of wanted to point out Brodie's swollen face as evidence that maybe Odati could've done with more than an unlocked door to keep her safe, but Odati caught my eye and shook her head.

The conversation stuttered along until Brodie cleared his throat. 'Okay, so can we get back to the issue of buying Onorio's old cruiser? How much have we actually got?'

Short answer was not much. Long answer was not enough. We still had to budget for food and fuel. But I'd been thinking, on the back burner so to speak.

I spoke up. 'The same creep who sold Mike his drugs was all

at me about how everything was changing, how the old rules don't apply anymore.'

Alice's eyes raked my face. 'Was he now?'

'Yeah, and it's got me thinking. Maybe he was right?'

'Absolutely not,' Alice said. 'What I saw was not right.'

Odati was looking back and forth between us. 'What did I miss?'

I grimaced. 'Nothing. Look, I'm explaining this badly. I mean, what Golden Boy said about the rules changing might've been right. Like, maybe we have things that are just as precious as cash? Something we can offer Onorio to make up for not having as much to pay him?'

Odati clapped her hands. 'Yes! That's a great idea.'

'Things like what?' Alice asked.

We all looked at each other. Honestly, I hadn't got that far in my thinking. And it looked like no one else had, either.

Brodie stood up. 'I think this requires a pot of tea.'

'A mega one, am I right?' grinned Alice.

I shivered again as the sun ducked behind a sprinting reddish cloud. 'How about inside, out of this wind?'

And we sat wrapped in our sleeping bags and drank hot, black tea and brainstormed ideas on a fresh page in my sketchbook.

It felt almost normal.

CHAPTER SEVENTEEN

55 hours until flight
US$1,130
Bs1,280
4 nasty pills
A few useful skills

The wind was a wild thing, all too willing to play. By the time we'd walked to Onorio's stall, there was dust in my eyes and grit in my mouth, and don't even start on my hair. He was happy to see us, until he heard we now had to make it to Lima. I could see him assimilating the news, and then he said something that stung my eyes.

'You would be wisest to drive yourselves. I will give you my old landcruiser. It may be old, but it is solid. It will get you there.'

I didn't know what to say. There was Onorio ... I knew he had a family to care for and probably no income for some time, and maybe about to face potential starvation (hey, worst case scenarios and all). And yet he wanted to gift us a vehicle? I blinked hard. We couldn't do that to him ... just take it.

Could we?

Brodie looked around at us, his head shaking. 'Thanks Onorio, honestly. But we'd like to pay something for the car.'

Onorio smiled. 'No, you will need everything to get to Lima in time. I do not need the money.'

'But your new cruiser … this'll help to pay it off.'

Onorio shrugged. 'The savings in banks, they are lost. But so is my debt. My bank chased it up once, but now I hear no more from them. I don't think they'll come asking again.'

I'd never thought of that before. A silver lining to this cloud of collapse. My parent's meagre savings had vanished, numbers on a screen that they couldn't even use to buy me a new ticket home, desperately trying to hide their fear through that last phone call way back in Brazil. Apparently the bank had lent their money to others, but house prices had collapsed and food costs skyrocketed and now it seemed no one had any money. But if my parents' savings were gone, perhaps so was their mortgage?

'Please,' said Onorio, 'understand that I would like to do this for you. This is my gift.'

Brodie looked at me, and I gestured at the sketchbook in my hands with all our plans. He nodded and turned back to Onorio. 'We really appreciate your offer, really. Because we know this is going to be hard for us. That money will be so helpful. So thank you, we accept. But we'd still like to help you in some way, please.'

I cleared my throat. Which wasn't easy—the dust was getting thicker on the wind. 'We thought you might like some help with some things. If you've got paint, I could repaint your sign so that if—I mean when—tourists come back, your business will look really awesome.'

Alice grinned. 'And I could give your family all a hair treatment and cut.'

Onorio was staring at us, and my guts were sinking. Maybe we truly didn't have anything of value?

Mike stepped forward, hands full of bottles. 'Yeah, and I've got all these vitamins that I honestly don't even want. You can have them, too.'

Silence. Onorio was still staring. Then his face broke into a smile. 'You kids are too good. That all sounds wonderful. Let's go get you a car.'

I could have hugged him. I wanted to bawl. He drove us to his house, me jammed in the back next to Mike.

Who swivelled to look at me. 'Seriously Eva, are you crying again?'

I wiped my cheeks. 'It's the dust,' I muttered. But this time I was 90% sure I was wrong on that.

Thank goodness we arrived quickly, right in front of the most beaten-up landcruiser you could ever imagine. Onorio handed over the keys, and there was this truly awkward moment as we all looked at them.

'Right,' said Mike eventually, all sardonic with a notable shake to his hands, 'now we have this car, someone tell me they can drive, because I sure as hell can't.'

Nor could I. Needing to maintain grades for my scholarship meant I had deferred learning to drive until the next summer holidays at the earliest. My heart sank.

But then Alice smiled. 'I have my licence.'

'And I'm on my provisional,' said Brodie.

Odati split her face with a grin. 'And I learnt to drive when I was eight. I can take this baby places you'd never dreamed it could go.'

Yeah, it was road trip time!

Well, almost.

First we needed to fuel up and buy supplies. Onorio offered to go with Brodie and Odati, saying the fuel station might not sell us diesel at the 'local' price, which was still likely to be eye-wateringly high—triple the normal according to Onorio. He waved at his wife—already helping Alice wash the youngest child with rose-smelling shampoo—and turned the key.

Nothing.

Like, I'm no expert on cars, but I think usually the engine is supposed to at least make a noise at that point.

Onorio rolled his eyes and Odati grimaced. 'Battery?' she asked.

He nodded. 'No worries. I will jump start you.'

Odati swivelled to look at Brodie. 'Have we got money for a new battery, do you think?'

Brodie shrugged. 'Depends on the price.'

Odati pulled a face. 'Only an idiot would do what we're planning to do, on a dodgy battery.'

Onorio pulled his new cruiser up closer. 'Let us see,' he said. 'Maybe it is just flat from sitting so long.'

A jump start later, our battered vehicle was finally growling off, Brodie waving from the back. I settled in to repaint one of Onorio's old signs. Renewing his business details was the easy—and boring—bit. But the picture I put underneath was my thanks to Onorio and I put my heart into it. He didn't have many different colours—white, black, blue and red—but when painting the salt lakes there's not much else you need.

My stomach was reminding me I'd only had a half-spilt *api* for breakfast when I finally stepped back to admire my work. Alice clapped her hand on my shoulder, making me squeak.

'Great stuff,' she said. 'I'd definitely go on that tour, am I right?'

I grinned at her. 'How are you going?'

'Finished fifteen minutes ago. Been watching you ever since. It's fascinating how you make something from nothing.'

I looked around, only just taking in the darker skies, gloomed in red dust. The rising wind. 'Are the others back yet?'

'Nope. They better be soon, though. I'd like to get going.'

'I don't know. This weather doesn't look good.'

'Missing a plane's not good either.'

I nodded. She had a fine point there. I stepped out to look down the road, and stopped in surprise. 'Mike?'

He was leaning on the side of the house, staring down the street. He glanced at me with a face of perfectly arranged boredom, before turning back again.

I nipped back in the house. 'Mike is out there?' I whispered to Alice.

'Yeah, weird right? I asked him to help out earlier and you should have seen his face.'

'I think I just did. So he's been sitting there the whole morning doing nothing?'

Alice's eyebrow quirked. 'That boy takes brooding to the next level. But he's going through a lot. I figured I'd let him be.'

My thoughts on that matter were interrupted by the roar of a returning engine. Alice and I tore outside to see how the shoppers had gone.

Brodie grinned at us. 'Filled both tanks and two spare five-gallon containers, plus we bought a few cartons of water bottles and as many cans as we could manage.'

'How much did that cost?' Alice asked.

Odati emerged, a streak of oil across her cheek, shooting a careful glance at Onorio, who was admiring his family's shiny new hairdos. 'Let's just say,' she murmured, 'our stash of cash is now less like comfortable padding and more like worrying dregs, even without paying for the car.'

Brodie came in close, his grin diminished. 'Everything cost more than we thought. If Onorio hadn't been there …'

Onorio came up then, face serious. 'You should get going. This weather … sometimes there are dust storms. Sometimes they stay for days. You don't want to be caught.'

I shivered, shooting another glance at the red clouds devouring the horizon to the west. 'Is that why you left the car running?'

'Yeah, about that,' said Odati. 'We couldn't afford a new battery, but this one looks like it'll be fine once it charges up.'

I looked at her and I looked at Brodie and it was like their eyes were pleading with me not to say a thing. So I didn't. But it was clear we were quite literally putting everything on the line to get to that plane. Because if we missed it …

CHAPTER EIGHTEEN

48 hours until flight
2 boxes water
3 bags food
2 full tanks + 2 full containers fuel
US$535
Bs201.20
4 nasty pills

We quickly said goodbye to Onorio.

'Remember,' he said, 'drive on the right-hand side.'

Alice jingled the keys at him with a smile. She opened the car door with a confident swagger and half-launched herself into the seat before registering the lack of a steering wheel. Swearing, she hopped back out, skirting around the car to the driver's side. Brodie pretended to be choking on something, but Odati just grinned.

Onorio shook his head and pointed to a small piece of lined paper stuck to the steering wheel with black electrical tape. 'That's why I put that there—to remind you of the second thing.'

In careful jagged letters he'd written SOUND HORN

AROUND CORNERS. A myriad of road rules, but Onorio figured those two were the important ones. Drive on the right and, when in doubt, blast the horn for good measure. Alice pressed the horn twice as we chugged off, waving at Onorio and shouting our thanks.

We hit the road to Oruro, our first stop on the way to Lima. We saw far fewer cars than we expected. In fact we saw less of everything. The dust got thicker and the wind more malevolent, until we were surrounded by ruddy gloom. The roar of the engine was offset by the hail of grit and pebbles pinging against the side of the car. Alice blew that horn diligently, driving north as fast as was safe.

Which was way slower than we'd have liked.

I was in the very back seat. In front of me were Brodie and Mike. If there had ever been seatbelts back here, they were long gone. I eyed the storm. No one spoke for what seemed like hours. The storm was catching at the car. If we didn't escape it, we could kiss goodbye to our flight out. And there was absolutely nothing I could do about that. I felt so useless, staring out the window into the red nothing.

Suddenly I shot upright. Squinted my eyes. Grinned. 'I can see!'

'And this is news why?' muttered Mike.

But I didn't care what he thought. I could see mountains. And maybe sky. The dust storm was thinning!

There were celebrations and the passing around of biscuits as the road in front began to appear. And with every extra stretch we could see, Alice sped up that little bit more.

By the time the sun returned, low in the sky now, our Trucko was roaring. Desert sands and stark mountains whipping past my window. I sketched until it got too dark to see the paper.

And woke to muttered conversations and an annoying squeak. The seat in front of me was screeching, that sort of irritating noise made when someone is uncontrollably fidgeting. I peeked through my eyelashes at Brodie and Mike in front.

'C'mon, just one,' Mike pleaded.

'Alice has already said you need to try and stretch it out, Mike,' Brodie responded.

'I don't want to stretch it out. I need one and I need it now.' His voice was rising with every word. 'I've been stuck in this stupid car for hours! Give me a damn pill!' He seemed to erupt then, and there was a terrible crunch of broken plastic.

Struggling bodies. Yelling. Swerving tyres. I'm not ashamed to admit I scooted to the opposite side of the vehicle to Mike, and tried to hide. Mike wasn't going to see me anyway, he appeared too focused on disembowelling Brodie with his teeth. But Alice spotted me, having rotated out of the driving position a few hours before. She tossed me something I could barely see in the dimming light but instantly recognised when I caught it—the remaining pill container.

'One half!' she yelled over the noise.

Was she serious? How would I go about getting half a pill into Mike's mouth with him like this? I unscrewed the cap and grabbed the half we'd split at lunch, hoping some grand plan would come to me before I was done.

I was to be disappointed.

Brodie's forearms bulged as they protruded above the top of the seat, holding Mike in something closely resembling a headlock. Which actually turned out to be a headlock, I'd just never seen one in action before. Without a shred of prior planning I scuffled across and tried to shove the half between Mike's clenched teeth. It totally didn't work. His head thrashed and I nearly lost the pill.

'Hold him steady!' I yelled.

'What do you think I'm trying to do?'

'Try harder!'

Brodie swore, let's face it, probably at me, and it looked like he was going to pop a blood vessel. Mike's head stilled, and I judged it was going to be the best I'd get. I tried to pop the pill in again, but perversely Mike closed his mouth tight, fighting against what his body was crying out for. So I did what they always do in the movies, and held his nose. The movies never show how slippery and sweaty a nose can be. The colour of Mike's face soon resembled Alice's hair, but then his mouth gasped open and I shoved the pill in down the side of his cheek, crushing it against his gums with my palm.

He fought like a wild thing at first, violent in the gathering darkness, but after what felt like forever the tension drained out of him as the drug soothed his system.

Finally he spoke, muffled by my hands. 'I'm feeling better now.'

I pulled my hands away, but Brodie held on.

'Can I trust you're not going to do anything stupid?' he said.

Mike sniffed. 'Of course. If you'd given me what I wanted when I asked for it, this never would have happened, you know.'

Alice shrugged and Brodie released him slowly. Mike slumped away and against the window, breathing hard. Odati clambered back and wrapped her arms around him, snapping me out of my trance like a slap to the face. I looked wildly about. We were pulled to the side of the road. Which, considering Odati had been driving, was just as well.

'What broke?' Alice asked.

The seat in front creaked as Brodie moved forward. 'The cover for the rear aircon vent. No real loss, the aircon didn't work anyway.'

My heart was still thumping a mile a minute and I felt lightheaded. I pulled out my water bottle and swigged a big drink, which made me think, and …

'I need to pee.'

All of us piled out, boys to the front of Trucko, girls to the back. The heavens were speckled with stars, the inky blackness had lost any hint of evening light. Shades of our walk to Potosí. How much life had changed since then. And it was still changing.

Our future was unlikely to be anything like the one we had

been taught to expect.

Brodie took the wheel for the last leg of the journey to Oruro. I don't know how. I was simply and totally knackered, and Brodie had barely had a minute's more sleep than I the night before. I felt I had to stay awake in homage to the driver. Or at least so I didn't seem piss-weak in comparison.

And also with the vague idea that if he fell asleep, I could wake him up before he drove us into a canyon or something.

Road trips weren't supposed to be this hard. Where were the cans of cola and the laughter? Soft drinks were near the top of our Too Expensive list, but laughter was free. Wasn't it?

Mike and Odati fell swiftly asleep, his head on her shoulder. Slow breathing. Rhythmic.

Soporific.

I woke up as Trucko creaked to a stop in front of some beautifully carved façade with a fearfully faded hostel sign out the front. Oruro. As I cursed my weakness, I noted Alice was driving and Brodie was looking haggard in shotgun. It made me wonder how the decision had been made to swap drivers. A casual, intelligent discourse? Or had we almost driven off the road and I'd slept through the lot?

I wouldn't be surprised if it was the latter. I felt like a steamroller had run me over. Bleary eyes checked the glowing dashboard. It was barely 10pm. Still, hours later than we'd planned on getting here.

Alice looked at me over the still-sleeping figures of Odati and Mike. 'Are you okay to get us some beds for the night? I don't think we're up to driving through.'

I snorted. That was about the biggest understatement I'd heard. Ever. It's like someone saying 'the ATMs have been a bit unreliable lately' or 'the back seat of an ancient landcruiser with a broken aircon system can get a tad chilly at night'.

Alice spoke again, voice strained from long hours of driving. 'I'm sorry, I don't speak Snort. Can you check for rooms or not?'

'Whoa!' I shook my head to try and clear it, with marginally successful results. I yawned. 'Calm down. Yes, I'll go ask, just give me a moment to figure out my name, what continent I'm on and what year it is.'

I ignored the snigger, which I think came from Brodie since Alice then punched him on the arm. I peered at the sleeping cherubs in front of me. How to get out? Then I grinned, collapsed my backrest and opened the boot. I think I managed a fairly dignified exit, but I did stumble on the first step leading up to the hostel door.

It mustn't have been level.

By the time I got to the door, I felt someone behind me. Relief warred with disappointment when I saw it was Alice. Her smile was crooked, dark smudges under each eye.

The door took an age to be answered, and the amount of money the proprietor was asking for was well beyond our means. We had no idea how much diesel would cost in Peru, but it was likely to be eye-wateringly high. We would need to purchase more before we made it to Lima, so preserving our cash was paramount. We'd set a maximum of US$6 each for the night, and the owner wanted US$30—like Bs210. Each. I tried an uninspiring bargain, then conferred with Alice before walking away. The owner tried to entice us back with another offer, but it was still above our means and I felt like bawling.

The next place we walked into was bare in the extreme, in everything but price—Bs140 each. I tried the same bargaining—'*¿Es posible más barata?*'—and of course cheaper was indeed possible, but not cheap enough. I was defeated.

'We could sleep in Trucko?' Alice whispered.

I shook my head. Trucko was already freezing. I turned to leave, then whirled back.

'Do you have many guests tonight?' I asked in Spanish.

He was hesitant. 'No.'

I explained we had our own sleeping bags and he wouldn't even need to have sheets on the beds if he didn't want to wash them afterwards, but we wouldn't pay a *centimo* more than Bs40 each. In the time-honoured fashion of bargaining, he offered a little less than his original price, but I set my shoulders. Screw bargaining protocols. He'd get us for my price, or nothing at all.

I was about to turn around again when he nodded. And we shook hands on the cheapest beds we'd seen all trip by a long shot. I was smiling, but he was too. He had money coming in when he had ceased to hope for anything that night.

Alice grabbed my forearm as we exited the door. 'What price did you agree on?'

'Forty b's each.'

'Wow, I heard that and I thought I'd got my numbers mixed up. That's awesome! When you put your mind to it, you can be quite intimidating, am I right?'

She laughed and I joined in, because I had a bed waiting for me, and everything seemed brighter.

Alice and I shot out onto the street to tell the team the good news. It was terrible to have to wake Odati and Mike, and we all shuffled like some zombie revival up the steps, through the door, down the hall and into our room. We just zipped Mike into his sleeping bag and he was out for the count, but the rest of us tried to hold onto a shred of dignity and protocol by brushing teeth and changing into whatever constituted pyjamas. I looked at what I had on offer. A luxuriously clean singlet and fresh undies seemed the winning bet, and all at once I could feel how grimy I was. Grime beat fatigue, and I marched back out and into the showers.

It was like torture. The hot water was so hot I had to turn it down and wind up the cold, but if I did that enough to make the temperature pleasant, it was insufficient to run the heater and the water would turn frigid, so I'd turn down the cold and increase the hot and the whole process would restart.

It was one of the best showers I've ever experienced.

Back in the dorm, I was asleep in about 1.3 seconds, engulfed by dismembered dreams where Golden Boy was leering at me as my yellow bus drove away ever so slowly. But I could never ever catch it.

I was relieved when the beeping woke me. Like some zany alarm clock that started in one corner of the room and travelled to the other and back again, and played different tunes each time until the whole room was a chorus of bings and thrums.

I frowned. Half-forgotten sounds of technology. I recognised one of them.

My phone. My message notification.

I hadn't got a message since Brazil.

CHAPTER NINETEEN

38 hours until flight
2 boxes water
3 bags food
1 full sub tank + 2 full containers fuel
2/3 full main tank
US$535
Bs1.20
3 nasty pills

All five of us were electrified. We'd been charging our phones every chance we had, but only in the way babies have their comforters, and just their presence is enough. I'd almost ceased to believe my phone was anything more than a glorified camera.

Yet suddenly we were receiving messages.

I got three. I scrolled through them with trembling fingers.

Mum and Dad Mobile
Eva, take care. We're thinking of you. We love you. We've heard about the plane home. We're so glad. See you soon. XX

That could have been sent anytime. But they evidently didn't know we'd lost Miss C. I wondered how they'd taken that news, or if they'd even get it before we arrived home safe and sound anyway.

Sarah Yeo Mobile
Crap J! Were those gunshots? Ru ok? Plz don't b dead. Can't believe they wont go back 2 get u. Crying. XX Sez

Probably that was sent four or so days ago, just after the bus drove off without us.

Miss Cooper
Flight changed. Now leaving from Lima International Airport. May 5th 15:10. DON'T CROSS INTO CHILE! Miss C/ April 30 @ Uyuni.

At least I didn't have to guess when that one was sent. Miss C was so smart.

Odati let out a groan and I looked up. 'I've one from my brother,' she said. 'Someone stole blasting gear from one of Mum's mines and blew up the airport.'

Brodie was looking pale. 'I've two messages from my dad, one saying I've got to get out of South America because it looks bad on the news, and another saying they've declared martial law at home, and to bunker down somewhere safe. I don't know what to do.'

He bit his lip, pressed a few buttons, and held the phone to his ear. I gasped. Like, I'd kind of forgotten that's something phones could do. Could I call home? Call Miss C? Which was more important? Would they even have coverage at the same time as us?

Brodie groaned, and I was saved from further agonised thought over who to phone. He was staring at his screen.

'It's down again.'

'What?' I poked my screen, determined not to believe what I saw. But there it was, the 'x' again. Our brief flash of connection had vanished once more. And I hadn't managed to contact anyone.

Or had I?

My fingers shook as I accessed my sent items. Three new messages gone. Three? I'd almost forgotten I'd ever tried to send them. One to Sarah saying we were in Potosí. One to Sarah saying we were in Uyuni heading to the border. And thank goodness, one to my parents saying I loved them. I was glad. I'm learning that's something you can't say too often.

But my phone didn't manage to send what was possibly the most important one—the one to Sarah I wrote the previous morning, saying we were heading to Lima.

She'd be so confused. And worried too, thinking we were still trying for Santiago, that we'd never learnt of the change of plans.

I frowned, went into that pending message and updated it to show where we were, where we were going next, the names of everyone with me, that we were well, and the date. And I vowed that each day I would update it so that if we got coverage again, the right message would get through.

Coverage was so brief. That night I discovered you have to grab it with both hands and use it for all it's worth.

CHAPTER TWENTY

32 hours until flight

1 ½ boxes water

3 bags food

1 full sub tank + 2 full containers fuel

2/3 full main tank

US$535

Bs1.20

3 nasty pills

The next morning saw us up early and bleary-eyed, but all the better for a night in a bed. I fought my way out of my twisted sleeping bag like a butterfly emerging from her crinkly chrysalis. A butterfly in some rather scanty clothes. I almost died when I looked down and registered how much of me was on display. I hauled the bag over my thighs and did a quick scout of the room to see if anyone had noticed.

Brodie had noticed.

He was watching me, eyes warm behind their livid bruising.

'If I wasn't awake before, I am now,' he murmured, before hauling himself to the showers with a grin. Wearing less than I was.

He was right. It was certainly a way to get the blood pumping. I didn't know what to think about his reaction, but my face kept insisting on a goofy grin for half the morning.

Our three drivers were looking far more roadworthy than they had the previous night. We raced through breakfast. Porridge made with water. It could grow on me. It needed to, there wasn't much choice.

That day's itinerary was onto La Paz, 225km by the map, and then a dramatic left turn towards Lake Titicaca and the border with Peru, maybe about the same distance again. So hopefully by late afternoon, we'd be driving through the mountains towards the old monastery town of Arequipa, which we would hit about 8pm if we Didn't Stop and Nothing Went Wrong. And from there we still had about fourteen more hours of driving, so I couldn't see us stopping for the night again.

But it was, after all, South America. And we were, after all, living through chaos. So the idea Nothing Would Go Wrong was like a fairy tale we enjoyed, though we knew it was pure fantasy.

It was 7am. The next day, at 3:10pm, a plane would take off from Lima International Airport with my schoolmates, my tireless teacher, and my hope. We had to be on that plane. No ifs. No buts. No discussion entered into.

So while the cobbled streets of Oruro were still slick from the night's chill, we piled into our battered lifeline, the freeze of vinyl seats soaking through the fabric of my pants, and waited with bated dragon-plumed breath for the engine to catch.

Phew. It did.

Eventually.

Trucko was like an icebox.

The *altiplano* had an aspect of sameness about it, a curious unreality that made me forget we were on top of the world. The air so cold and thin it burnt my nose as I breathed in. Towering hills embraced Oruro as we spilled out of the town into a pure land of perfect snow-capped peaks, lakes and fertile flatlands far greener than Uyuni had boasted. The scenery felt like we were somewhere near the sea. But I don't think we could have been further from the sea if we'd tried. We were still 3,800 metres above sea level, in the centre of South America.

And racing a deadline made for nerves.

But this was a road trip, dammit!

I started out in the rear seat again, isolated and shivering. This car needed an injection of soul.

I leant forwards onto the seat in front. 'Okay peeps. Worst trip in a car ever, not counting Elena, because we can't have three answers the same. What would it be for you?'

A moment of silence stretched that bit too long and I was thinking no one wanted to play, or perhaps it was still too soon to joke about Mr Smelly and the road to Potosí.

But then Mike spoke from just in front of me, and you could have knocked me over with an alpaca's tail. I'd thought he was drifting in a drug-induced daze. 'Driving to a swim meet in Albany,' he said. 'This chick behind me kept leaning on the back of my seat …'

Exactly what I was doing! I sat back with such force the seatback collapsed and my momentum combined precipitously with a bump in the road and I was on my head in the boot with my feet against the rear window before I knew what was happening.

A moment's shock.

Then I almost wet myself laughing, which considering I was upside down would not have been a good look. A head appeared above my butt, I could barely believe it was Mike's. He was trying very hard not to laugh, which was another surprise. He hadn't laughed much this trip. At all, maybe.

My eyes met his, and we both lost it. He grabbed my arms and tried to pull me out, but I was wedged and we were cackling too much to be strong.

In the end Odati had to clamber over and help, and then all three of us were sprawled across the now fully flat back seat, wiping our eyes.

'Everything okay back there?' Brodie's voice drifted back from the passenger seat.

I hauled myself up. Amazed to see Alice was still driving, tussock and sky whipping past. She'd taken to heart the requirement to Not Stop Today. I grinned at the look on Brodie's face, at the stabbing glances Alice was flashing us in the rear-view mirror. 'Yeah, we're fine, the seat just kind of collapsed.'

When I'd catapulted out of the boot the night before I must have haemorrhaged something vital, because the seatback refused to stay upright after that. Thus was born the Nap Seat. More comfortable than you'd expect, actually. A far better bed than it had ever been a seat.

Odati, Mike and I hauled ourselves into the middle seat, and there we snugly sat, all three in a line, smiling as if something special had happened.

Because it had.

CHAPTER TWENTY-ONE

31 hours until flight
1 ½ boxes water
2 ½ bags food
1 full sub tank + 2 full containers fuel
2/3 full main tank
US$535
Bs1.20
2 ½ nasty pills

'So, as I was saying, before I was rudely interrupted,' Mike said with a mock stern look at me, 'we were driving to Albany, which for you Brits is five or so hours, and this girl behind me was hanging over my seat and talking all the time, and I just wished she'd shut up, and then she did, but it was because she was getting carsick, and then she threw up all over me, and the smell was something else, and it was about forty degrees outside and the aircon broke, and we had to drive sixty k's before we got to a place we could clean up. And then I found the vom had got into my player, and it never worked again.

So there—Worst Car Trip Ever.'

We all mulled over that one. Hard to beat.

Alice piped up. 'Late last year I took this bus from Marrakech to Fez in Morocco, and this guy next to me smelt like he bathed in camel dung, and he started asking my name and then he wanted to know if I was married, and then he wanted to know if I had any sisters. So I decided, a little late I know, to pretend I was German, and my English wasn't good enough to understand him. But it turned out he spoke perfect German, and I think invited me to his place, or proposed, but of course I couldn't understand him, and I had to pretend I spoke some weird dialect.' She swore. 'I couldn't wait for it to be over.'

Odati reached forward to pat Alice on the shoulder. 'That sounds like a really "Fez"-ty ride, Alice.'

We all groaned as the pun sank in.

Before we knew it, we were swapping tales and sympathising with each other, and it truly felt like a road trip. Except for Odati and Mike, we were all virtual strangers, so everything was new and interesting. The hours whipped past, and the fear always dwelling in the background receded, replaced by laughter.

Eventually we partook of the textbook What Do You Want To Be When You Grow Up discussion. Alice, of course, wanted to be a doctor. Odati felt she was destined to follow her mum into geology, but the price of iron ore was making her think twice.

'In an ideal world, Odati,' said Brodie. 'What would it be?'

'Geologist.'

He smiled. 'Geologist it is, then!'

'You?'

He nodded. 'Agricultural science. Then I'll buy a farm and make goat's cheese. I like goats.'

Odati clapped. 'I love goats, I think they're so clever.'

Brodie's eyes lit up, his face transforming as he spun to face her. 'They have attitude, don't they!'

And I don't know why—I certainly didn't ask it to—but my mouth opened. And it started to speak. 'Goat's cheese is great. What a great idea. That's … um …' I shut my mouth before I said 'great' again.

Brodie turned his bright smile to me. 'Yeah? You like it? Some people think the taste is too strong.'

'Too strong? No way. It's like …' Like eating essence of curdled woolly jumper. A memory surged to the front of my brain, of the one and only time I'd tasted goat's cheese. I'd wanted to spit it out. My cheeks flamed.

Brodie's lips quirked. 'You hated it, didn't you?'

My hand was grasping the side of the seat, like it was searching for a patent-pending Trucko Emergency Ejector Button. Which was more likely to be found than anything I could say to make this less embarrassing.

I gulped. 'Actually, yes. Sorry. I, ah, forgot. That I didn't like it. But I bet I could learn to love it.'

If I needed confirmation that was the wrong thing to say, I got it with Mike's smothered guffaw. Now, rather than just thinking I was an idiot with a poor memory, Brodie probably thought I was a stalker with a poor memory. I might as well have started planning curtain material for his dream farmhouse. He was staring at me, lips twitching at the corners, and I wanted to die.

I could have hugged Odati when she asked Mike what his projected path in life was. That made him drop the sniggering.

Then suddenly he yelled, 'Not a swimmer!'

'Good for you, Mike,' said Odati, resting her head on his shoulder and tucking her hand in his elbow until his shaking settled.

Which left just me. Barely recovered from my last mortifying gaffe. And everyone else waiting.

'Ummm. Maybe a doctor or a lawyer?'

Alice peered back, grinning. 'I didn't know you wanted to be a doctor as well!'

I scratched my nose. Want didn't come into it. It was what I gathered was expected of me as a scholarship recipient. I remember telling our Career Advisor I'd like to study Art or History. He choked on his perfectly-brewed skim soy latte and handed me a few brochures he thought would be 'more appropriate' for someone with my marks. Medicine and Law. Hence my answer.

Money was king, I'd learnt that the hard way.

Or at least, it had been king. I didn't know what would rule the new future.

A kind of madness brewed deep inside me. Everything had changed. Golden Boy had been right in one way—this was a new world. 'Actually, I'll change my answer,' I said. 'I'd like to be an artist. If I was free to choose, you know. Or work in a museum. Maybe both.'

There. I'd said it. Three heartbeats passed and, you know, no one laughed. Odati seized my hand and squeezed it. 'That sounds so awesome.'

I grinned.

I won't say I was itching to fill in the blanks when it came to Brodie, because that would just sound sad. But something made me ask the next question.

'So, favourite sports played?' I asked.

'Hey Mike, you're not going to include swimming on your list, am I right?' Alice grinned into the rear-view at him, and he shook his head slowly, like a dog leaving a sea of jelly. Odati laughed.

'What's yours?' Brodie asked Alice.

'Hard to pick … it's a fight between lawn bowls, tennis and squash. And if you count chess, I was school champ.'

'Do we count chess?' Brodie roared the question back to us.

Enough yeah's were sounded to accept chess as a sport, but my grin was wobbly. When I was agonising about whether to initiate the topic, I'd hoped Alice might be more on my side when it came to sporting pursuits.

'What's your pick, Odati?' asked Alice.

'Cricket. Definitely.'

'What are you?'

'Fast bowler.'

Mike piped up. 'She's in the state team. She's awesome.'

I let out an 'Ah', because now a few things made sense. Alice spotted my face and said I simply *had* to share my epiphany.

I felt my cheeks heating up. 'It's just that the only time Odati hasn't bowled me out playing cricket in PE was when I hit it straight back at her and she caught me instead. I don't feel quite so bad if she's on the state team.'

Alice grinned. 'Yeah, I'm no good at cricket either.'

'Who said I was no good?'

Odati pummelled her hands on her thighs in delight. 'You're no good, Eva. I'm sorry.'

I don't know what my face looked like, but it made the rest of Trucko rock with laughter.

'So, what about you, Eva?' asked Alice.

I grimaced. 'I spend a lot of time studying, you know?'

'Surely not all of it?' She rolled her eyes into the rear-view.

'I'd say "all of it" is pretty accurate.'

'Don't you have any life?'

My cheeks were burning. There was this silence, thick enough to cut and eat for morning tea.

Again I could have kissed Odati as she smoothed over the awkwardness and finally moved things to where I'd really wanted them from the start. 'Do you play a sport, Brodie?'

Brodie nodded. 'Yeah, I do. If you didn't guess from my array of shirts, I play rugby. Union. Fullback, mainly.'

'So, you must be pretty fast then?' Mike asked.

'I'm one of the fastest in my team.'

Alice grinned. 'Does it feel awesome to score a try?'

He grinned back. 'Every time.'

She nodded. 'I often dream about doing that.'

Their laughter was cut short by Trucko swerving to the side with a brain-sloshing lurch. It wasn't enough to avoid a deep pothole, and my teeth jangled in time with the broken aircon vent.

Alice gasped an apology, Brodie yelped a warning about an abandoned tyre on the road, and my head slammed against the window as I tried to look outside.

We were approaching La Paz.

The road ahead was littered with burnt cars and abandoned household goods. My head ached. By the time we were amid the sprawl of the mud brick shanties that marked the poorer outer areas, our banter had died. La Paz is built on a canyon. It must be the only city I know where the rich live down the bottom and the poor up the top. Nice view up there, but it's a whammy about the altitude. We were back up around 4,000 metres and I could feel it. Odati was staring fixedly at the horizon. There was no more laughter.

The sun was harsh, the sky a dangerous blue. An angular mountain topped with brittle white loomed above. And the land had been transformed into a sea of buildings the colour of the desert. People milled everywhere, women with their distinctive bowler hats and multitudes of *pollera* skirts, colours abundant and varied.

Eyes watching us with deep suspicion.

Plumes of black smoke marring the perfect blue.

'A barbeque?' Mike asked.

Alice frowned. 'Lots of barbeques?'

I think we all knew the smoke wasn't from a casual barbie lunch. But to take the turn towards Peru, we had no choice but to go further in.

It's hard to explain how wrong that felt.

CHAPTER TWENTY-TWO

28 ½ hours until flight

1 ¼ boxes water

2 bags food

1 full sub tank + 2 full containers fuel

1/8 main tank

US$535

Bs1.20

2 ½ nasty pills

The further into La Paz we got, the harder it became to negotiate past the cars and trucks littering the road. Burnt-out hulks, some still smoking. There were shattered windows on every floor of the roadside buildings. A sense of desperation permeated the scene, coiled-up violence, just waiting to spring forth. Our broken aircon started leaking a stench of prehistoric proportions, equal mix of blocked drains and burnt hair.

We sobered right up in the back.

Mike clung to the insufficient map in his guidebook. I scoured every street sign we went past. Alice's hands were white on the wheel as we crawled through the destroyed streets. It felt like a war zone.

A shiver ran through me.

It was a war zone.

Things had morphed from bad to unimaginable only two weeks before, and two weeks was long enough for hunger to bring out the worst in people. I wished Alice's hair wasn't so blue in the front seat, that Odati was driving instead, or me, even though I couldn't even drive, so it wasn't so obvious we were *gringos*. We were nearing the end of our money and our food, but I could bet we had more than some of the people we were passing.

It was with intense relief we found the turn we needed, and began our painful passage out of the city. I was gripping the door so hard my fingers ached, sweat trickling from the crease at my elbow. Every vehicle moving on that road—and there were frighteningly few—made my insides clench. I got the feeling our fuel canisters alone would make us a prime target.

And then it happened.

You could hear it, the swishy sound that boded ill. And you could feel it, the sluggishness, the pull to the right. Brodie dared to hang his head out the side, and he swore. I choked back the urge to hurl.

Alice started hyperventilating in the driver's seat. She'd driven like a trooper, but the pressure was now too much. 'What do I do? What do I do?'

'We can't stop,' said Brodie.

'But surely we have to?' she wailed.

Odati stirred beside me, emerging from an altitude nightmare. 'What's wrong?'

'Flat tyre, right-hand rear,' Brodie said.

'Why aren't we stopping?'

'We can't! Haven't you noticed the thousands of desperate people dotted around the smashed-in burnt-out cars?'

Odati looked around and gasped. She was silent as we crept on, then whispered, 'This is madness!'

I wasn't sure if she was talking about the state of the city, or us driving on the flat, or life in general.

'What other choice do we have?' moaned Alice. Trucko started to slow down, veering to the right as Alice took her hands off the steering wheel to cradle her head.

'Brodie!' I hissed, and he looked straight at me, jaw tight. 'Take over from Alice. Can you do that while we're still moving?'

He nodded, and they managed a beautifully smooth transition, only hitting the horn once. Alice was shaking, and we all helped her into the middle of the back seat, shuffling places before I climbed into the front, trying not to kick anyone by mistake. I glanced back at the three behind me. Odati was frowning out the window. I hoped she was thinking hard. I hoped it was about how to get us out of this. Alice was curled up, talking to herself, trying to wind down from the strain of all she'd driven through, especially this past hour.

And Mike was sweating and looking like he could start throwing punches any moment. I caught his eye, wished I hadn't.

'I'm fine,' he said, through a sheen of sweat and gritted teeth.

Yeah, and our tyre will magically re-inflate. 'Alice?' She looked up, startled. 'Can you help Mike, please?' I smiled to take the sting out of it, and Mike's lips twisted.

Alice took a hold of his hand, and the two of them sat there together, knuckles white against each other's.

Odati looked up, eyes alight. 'We can't keep driving on the rim forever, but it can get us far enough to be safe changing it. What have we to lose? We only need this car for another day and a half, if we ruin that rim, who gives a damn!'

Brodie's smile was a grim line. 'That's the spirit. I just hope we have a full spare.'

She stared at him, one eyebrow raised. 'Yes we have a spare, and it's fully inflated too. What exactly did *you* look for when we got this thing?'

Brodie was silent for so long I thought he hadn't heard. Finally, 'Yeah, I suppose I just looked for four wheels and an engine that started.'

I expected a biting reply from Odati, but it didn't come. I was glad. I was feeling pretty stupid myself. I hadn't checked a single thing when we got Trucko. Surveying a broken, burning metropolis, I only had space for thankfulness that Odati had.

Oh, and fear. There was fear too.

'Brodie, there's an orange van behind us … quite a way back, but it's been following for a while,' I whispered, not wanting to disturb the others.

'Yeah, I've seen it,' he murmured. 'I'm trying to go faster, but I think we're losing the rubber on that wheel.'

'Is it just me or is it getting louder?'

'Yeah, I was thinking that too.'

I risked my head out the window to look at the wheel, catching a glimpse of a group of men in ponchos with machetes staring at us from beside a burnt-out building. Sure enough, not only was the rim bare to the metal and making an awful din, it was also starting to make …

'Sparks,' I said.

'What?' Odati's head popped between Brodie and I.

'The rim is sparking. And there's a van following us.'

Brodie grunted. 'But otherwise, all is fluffy kittens, hey?'

My laugh sounded a bit hysterical. Odati was too busy thinking.

'Ever changed a tyre, Brodie?' she asked, and I didn't bother feeling miffed she hadn't asked me. The answer, in my case, was kind of obvious.

'Once,' Brodie said, 'in my driving course.'

Odati nodded. 'Cool. I've changed plenty. So I'm going to lead this, okay? You're stronger than me, so you'll be quicker, but you'll need to follow my directions.'

'Sure thing.' Brodie sounded calmer now.

I checked behind. The orange van was still there. Was it drawing closer? It might just be a legitimate person driving on the road, scared stiff like we were.

But maybe it wasn't.

Odati hauled herself into the Nap Seat, and returned with what I presumed was a tool kit and jack. And for the first time, I was chest-crushingly happy Odati's dad was a tea magnate and her mum a mining mogul, and she'd spent her childhood tearing around the wild north and all through the subcontinent. I'd always been jealous, but as we curtained sparks out the side of Trucko, I was grateful Odati had had all those experiences I'd only dreamed of.

Because they obviously included *lots* of tyre changes.

Rapidly but clearly, she detailed what she and Brodie would do as soon as Brodie stopped Trucko. Brodie nodded his head every now and then. And I watched the orange van closing the gap between us, my heart beating like it wanted to bust out of me.

We were making a dreadful noise by the time Odati told Brodie to pull over, and when we ground to a standstill the sudden silence was overwhelming. We must have heralded our passage for blocks all around. The two of them jumped out like coiled springs, and I sat tight in my seat like I'd been told to.

And watched the van come closer.

Odati was on her back placing the jack while Brodie ran around chocking wheels and then he was winding that wincy little jack winder like there was no tomorrow.

I could see the van closing the gap.

Brodie kicked the tyre wrench to loosen the nuts, strain showing in his face. Odati paused to throw up before disappearing behind Trucko to get the spare off the back.

And the van came closer. I could make out the hulking shapes of men through its partially shattered windscreen.

People were watching from neighbouring buildings, expressions lost in the shadows cast by their hats. They were pointing, talking. Lots of them. Watching.

And the van was even closer. We weren't going to manage the tyre change in time.

One of the watchers lit up a paper-wrapped package, and the sweet yet revolting smoke wafted to us.

'Pachamama,' Mike said, like it meant everything. Maybe it did.

'What?'

'I think they're burning an offering to Pachamama, the Earth Mother, herbs and dried llama foetuses and stuff. For luck. I read it in the guidebook.' He swallowed twice, throat bobbing, then grabbed his phone and focused on it.

My stomach churned. Mike and Alice looked terrified. I probably looked the same. And yet we were in the relative safety of Trucko. How must Brodie and Odati be feeling?

Movement teased the corner of my eye, our ruined rim wobbling across the smoky road. Odati had rolled the spare over to Brodie and the two of them were lining it up. I had my first taste of hope. Maybe Pachamama was helping us.

Maybe we could do this.

But one look back crushed me. The van was too close, slowing now as it neared us. We needed more time.

CHAPTER TWENTY-THREE

28 hours until flight

1 ¼ boxes water

2 bags food

1 full sub tank + 2 full containers fuel

1/8 main tank

US$535

Bs1.20

2 nasty pills

No opportunity to ruminate on PROS and CONS. I opened my door and jumped out to stand between Trucko and the now stationary van. Holding nothing but mad courage. The orange van's occupants bared their teeth at me in horrifying parodies of grins.

I hadn't been over-analysing our situation.

They really were after us.

Two men got out and swaggered towards me. One was carrying a knife. My heart was yammering, but my head was composed.

One of the men began to speak, and despite focusing on him

hard, all I could make out was the *Hola* at the start. He spoke fast, words dribbling together. I got the sick feeling he was drunk. His teeth were yellow and blunt, not sharp and feral. But his eyes were those of a predator. Their gleam reminded me of Golden Boy.

'Please leave us alone,' I said in Spanish, as soon as he stopped speaking.

The men just kept on grinning, ambling closer.

My darting eyes spotted more people beyond the orange van, and most of them looked a whole deal more decent than the guys coming for us. On impulse I called out to them to help us. Some moved restlessly. Some slunk away. No one came forward.

The only person to approach was knife-guy. I heard a warning call of *¡Ojo!* from an onlooker, barely had time to spin away before I was engulfed by his rough arm. His breath stank like he had rotting shreds of durian between his teeth.

I was screwed.

But maybe the others could zoom away in Trucko while attention was all on me. If only they could change the tyre in time.

Except then I heard this terrible thwumping sound, and I had more than just attention on me. There was blood too.

Whose blood?

Not mine. Knife-guy's. And the reason for all that blood was pulling me back towards him. Brodie, with a set jaw and a tyre wrench, and if Knife-guy hadn't been so damned angry I would have hugged Brodie, because I've never been happier to see someone in all my life, including the pompous chap who awarded me my scholarship.

But Knife-guy *was* angry. Angry and terrifying with blood oozing from his forehead and the knife still in his hand and Brodie was yelling at me to get away, except I was searching around for something—anything—I could use as a weapon.

Until a monster *crack* made a mockery of the tyre wrench

thump. Loud and sharp and clear.

I froze.

My heart raced.

And Knife-guy fell like a rag doll. Brodie scuttled back out of his way. Blood bloomed like fluid acrylic across the back of Knife-guy's shirt.

Knife-guy had been shot.

From behind.

Who had shot him?

And who would be next? Ears ringing, I searched the scattering onlookers. Behind the orange van a small group of people had emerged, several carrying what looked like rifles. The other van-dude roared into life, running at this new threat. A man in the centre of the group raised his gun and shot that guy, too. That was enough. The orange van spluttered into life and raced away, spewing black smog.

Which left Brodie and I in the middle of the road with two dead bodies and a group of strangers wielding lethal weapons. I wasn't sure whether to be relieved or terrified.

Brodie was standing in front of me, so close I could feel the breath heaving in his chest. My head was spinning with one thought. Keep them away from the others in Trucko.

Then the man lowered his rifle and made a calming gesture with his hand. In Spanish he asked us if we were okay. And for the first time, I entertained the hope he and his group of friends might actually have saved us.

I forced myself to nod, to say we were okay, and to add a *gracias* at the end.

The man with the gun gave a grim smile, eyes flicking up and down the now empty street. He said something that I didn't understand and my face must have shown it. '*El neumático,*' he repeated, pointing past me to Trucko. '*Rápido.*'

Rápido I understood. 'Brodie, we need to finish up fast.' I grabbed Brodie's waist from behind and tried to steer him around towards where poor Odati was struggling to tighten bolts with something that didn't look like it had ever been designed with bolts in mind.

Brodie was still holding the bloodied wrench.

And he was impossible to budge.

'Quick Brodie, please! That guy's scared of something, and I don't want to meet anything he's scared of.' I caught Brodie's eye, and finally he nodded. And loped back to Odati.

I was left staring at the group of people who had come to our aid. Men and women of all ages now moved to encircle Trucko. My eyes prickled, these perfect strangers were willing to protect us. Many of the figures that had been watching before had run away, but I remained on edge.

Finally I heard Odati. 'It's done, Eva. Let's get out of here!'

I looked at the man with the gun, not sure if I should thank him for murdering two people, even if they had been potential murderers with knives. He made a shooing gesture and said '*Rápido*' again.

I made my decision. '*Muchas gracias.*'

'*De nada*,' he responded. You're welcome.

Brodie called urgently, and I turned and ran. I hauled myself into the passenger seat and Brodie sped off with a screeching likely to test the new tyre. I felt bad to be leaving those people, but so relieved to be moving again.

Silence lasted for at least five dreadful minutes. Like we couldn't figure out anything to say. I wet an old rag I found in the glovebox and tried to wipe the sticky blood off my face and neck. Impossible to get it off my shirt. It would be a good look for when we crossed the border into Peru in a few hours' time.

Not.

The shacks and shanties began to thin, and I greeted the

increasing tussock with relief. I found myself constantly twisting my head to check the side mirror. After about the tenth check, Brodie's hand snaked out to catch mine, taking me so much by surprise I jumped and almost brained myself on the roof.

'Stop checking the mirror. You're putting me on edge.'

'Sorry. I keep thinking I'm going to see that orange van.'

Odati sat forward, face tight. 'That was something back there. What the hell really happened?'

'If you want to know,' Mike said, 'I got it on my phone.'

Odati frowned. 'I think I'd like to see that … one day … but not now.'

'Me too. I was too scared to watch,' said Alice. Plastic bags rustled and she passed around a packet of biscuits and some wet wipes.

I shuddered. 'I never want to see it.'

Odati took a wipe with a grimace, but passed on the biscuits.

'You will one day, you'll show your grandkids,' said Alice.

I shook my head.

'Why not?'

'Because two people are dead back there.' The words burst out of me. 'And I don't want to see how stupid I was in getting them killed.'

Brodie almost drove off the road. 'Whoa! No way! What you did was brave. *They* came after *us*, remember. They chose to do that.'

I shook my head, too grimed with blood and sweat and ash to believe. I grabbed one of the wipes and cleaned my hands, like that would make it better. It didn't. I ignored the biscuits, but Alice kept shoving them in my face until I took one.

Brodie went on. 'If you hadn't done what you did, they still would've attacked us but I wouldn't have been able to say whatever you said to get help. And if we'd been helped anyway, I wouldn't have been able to understand they meant us no harm. We would've been a lot longer trying to change that tyre. If we *had* managed to change it. So don't you dare say you think you were stupid. I think you were a hero.'

I thought he was a hero as well, for clanging that guy over the head to save me. I wanted to say that, but my throat wouldn't work, and instead I made sure I didn't bawl by crunching the Monte Carlo in my hand.

In a way I was glad when Odati opened the side window and hurled. Not glad for her, definitely not, but for the respite it gave my mind, in having someone else to focus on.

I think we'd all been heroes.

Brodie had put himself in danger to help me. Odati had worked right through her altitude sickness. Alice had driven like a pro for as long as she possibly could. And Mike, well he'd kept a hold of himself, which may just have been the hardest task any of us had that morning.

Odati being sick put a dampener on the drive, if you can excuse the pun. She crawled into the Nap Seat and we didn't hear anything from her until the border. Alice crashed, occasional snores all I heard from her, and Mike zoned out, staring through the window.

Me? I grabbed a packet of crisps and developed a surreptitious way to keep an eye on the side mirror for suspicious vehicles without raising Brodie's hackles. Not one appeared, either in front or behind.

And that struck me as very, very unsettling.

We were on the major road between the largest city in Bolivia and the coast in Peru. How were we the only people driving it that morning?

My guts clenched. The only answer I could come up with was that while we'd been amid the isolated beauty of the Uyuni Salt Flats, the real world had undergone a far greater and more violent change than even La Paz had taught me.

The thought made me shiver.

'Stop it, Eva.' Brodie's voice was soft against the engine's roar.

'Stop what?' I whispered.

'Watching for that orange van. You're going to make yourself ill.'

I looked across at him, his face hardened with the focus of driving, and my heart fluttered like a butterfly's wings. I was starting to know that face. The straight nose, the curved jaw, the mobile lips. That face was like light on a dark night. I let out a breath and reached out to grip his shoulder before relaxing back into the seat.

He glanced at me quickly. Nothing like those deep and meaningful looks in movies that go on and on, until you feel like screaming at the driver to look where they're going. It was a brief peek, a lightning flash that went right through to my centre. And at the end of it he smiled.

When he turned his attention back to the road, I was left with a hot face and light head. I wished I could call up my past self and tell her not to be a wimp back in Uyuni. Instead, past-me should take a chance, be brave, grab hold of Brodie and show him that though I made a lot of mistakes the night we were mugged, kissing him was not one of them.

Brodie eventually broke my musings. 'Your shirt is not a good look when it comes to international borders.'

I looked down and grimaced. 'Nor is yours. It's covered with blood. Have you got something to change into?'

A welcome grin spread over his face. 'Are you trying to get me to strip off?'

I paused, wanting to be brave. 'Well, evidently you think I should …'

His shoulders shook with silent laughter. 'Sure, but that would just be a fringe benefit. You honestly do need to change.'

I checked for my daypack. It was out of reach, behind sleeping bodies. I turned back to Brodie and shrugged. 'Later.'

His smile widened.

I settled back against my seat, which was luxuriously comfortable compared with the rear seats, and finally allowed myself to smile. I was glowing, which was so weird after all we'd been through.

And it might have lasted, except at that point Brodie switched to the sub tank. We weren't even halfway to Lima.

CHAPTER TWENTY-FOUR

27 hours until flight
10 bottles water
1 ½ bags food
1 full sub tank + 2 full containers
Empty main tank
US$535
Bs1.20
2 nasty pills

The scenery ahead flattened out, hinting at the approach of the fabled Lake Titicaca. The world's highest navigable water body. A lake that looks like a sea, except it's 3,800 metres above sea level. The lake that birthed the Incas.

I couldn't believe I was heading there.

Mainly because Lake Titicaca had 'holiday' connotations and what we were doing was more 'desperate survival'. Burnt-out cars kept cropping up on the side of the road as we headed west. Occasionally, human bodies too, ravaged by freezing nights, alpine sun and animals.

I stopped smiling after I saw the first one.

And started stressing about the border in a way no exam stress could ever have got close to. I couldn't forget the last border. If this one was shut too …

Well, we'd cross this border if we had to swim the entire lake.

I grabbed my phrasebook from the pocket of my cargo pants to work out what to say. Our first attempt to cross would be crucial. I couldn't let my mates down.

Brodie sighed and I looked up. We were approaching a major crossroads, with a big sign pointing right that read COPACABANA. Agriculture was all around. We were near another town, smudges of smoke darkening the blue sky. Thankfully, we seemed to be bypassing the smoke this time.

Brodie flashed me a grim smile. 'I always wanted to go to Copacabana.'

'This one?' I asked, thinking of the bronzed volleyballers our class had seen at the famous Rio beach.

'Both, really. But I'd definitely planned to take a tour through here. See the Isla del Sol and all that.'

But he drove past the turn-off without hesitation, heading instead on the direct route to the Peruvian border. And I spared a thought for the amazing Incas, a civilisation so grand, so advanced, yet extinguished so rapidly. Had they felt like we did now? At that point when their empire began to collapse?

I sighed. 'Well, I went to the other one. It was pretty cool.'

'Yeah? Tell me, please.'

So I did. I talked about the balmy weather, temperatures in the high twenties and skies so blue. The taste of the coconuts people would walk around selling, straws sticking out and delight inside. How the hills leapt up from the sea, how meaty and sweet the papayas were, and all the interesting and glowing people I watched as I sat in the sand.

Brodie nodded when I finished, lips pursed. 'It sounds awesome. It sounds like things were all still normal then.'

'No. Not when I look back. But we were still pretending they were.'

We looked around at the stark landscape, flat and unwelcoming, and maybe Brodie was seeing all the dead bodies again too. The time for pretence was well past. Things were most definitely not normal any more.

In point of fact, things were screwed.

All of a sudden we came around a small hill and there, on our right, was water. Blue and vibrant and impossibly, mind-bendingly far-reaching. I had to remind myself this was Not The Sea.

'Time for clean clothes,' I said, heart thumping.

He nodded and Trucko bumped onto the shoulder of the road. You know, in case the first car in several hundred kilometres just happened to choose that moment to come past.

That woke Mike. 'What's happening?'

'Toilet break. We need to make ourselves suitable for a border crossing,' Brodie responded. 'Can you wake Alice, please? They might want to see a licence, and despite me being an undeniably superb driver, I'm still only on my provisionals.'

I hauled myself out the door. A chill wind was blowing. Heavy clouds coiled above. Mike woke Alice, who chucked my frayed daypack at me before creaking out to stretch her legs. I dragged out my original t-shirt, clean thanks to her efforts in Uyuni. Just then, Brodie popped up at the opposite door to get to his own backpack. And the look he gave me was wicked.

I burst out laughing, and after a moment of pretending to remain aloof, Brodie joined in.

'What's going on?' Mike asked, reappearing at the side of Trucko.

'We're trying to look less unsavoury,' I said.

Mike grimaced. 'Yeah, I see what you mean. Have you got anything clean?'

I waved my old shirt, and Brodie brandished some heavily embroidered long-sleeved get-up he must have bought in the Amazon. Mike nodded. He didn't leave, though, rummaging instead through the food bags.

'Do you mind?'

He jumped. 'Oh, you're changing *now*? Sorry.' He turned to leave, then noticed Brodie wasn't moving. 'Mate, do *you* mind?'

Brodie flaunted his wicked grin. 'Not in the slightest. In fact, I'm looking forward to it.'

I turned away, suppressing a grin, and changed as rapidly as I could. When I was done, I cocked a challenging eyebrow at Brodie and he responded by flexing off his own shirt. And he didn't bother turning away.

Way to make a girl blush. It made Mike pause, too, plastic spoon laden with tuna halfway to his mouth.

Brodie swivelled to get his fresh shirt, muscles rippling under his pale skin. Thank goodness for the bulk of Trucko separating us. The urge came to touch those muscles, follow their curves, verify they were as smooth as they looked, which was pretty damn smooth, I can tell you. With supreme self-control I made myself close my mouth and walk away, thus denying him the satisfaction of knowing I'd been glued to his performance. Fleeing to where Alice was doing vague yoga moves, I twisted my tangled hair into a bun. Straightened out my fresh shirt. And dusted off my cargos.

I was about as neat as I was going to get.

Alice stopped mid-downward dog, peering at me from between her legs. 'I love your hair. I could style it for you, if you like.'

I looked at her blue pixie mop hanging upside down, and shook my head. How could she be thinking about hairstyles? 'Maybe later.

I don't think hair is going to be big on their immigration checklist.'

'I promise I won't make it blue. Mainly because I think I've run out of dye.'

'Thanks, but no, really. I'm fine.'

Alice grinned. 'Your loss.'

I smiled, but I was thinking about the border ahead, going over all the words and phrases I'd been reading up on. My heart was pounding.

The border. The border. What would it be like?

In not much more than fifteen minutes, we found out. The town of Desaguadero was small and grim under a threatening sky. There were enough people hanging around and looking desperate to have my pulse up, and we quickly became the most interesting thing in the entire *pueblo*.

It didn't take long for a multihued cape of people to gather, trailing behind Trucko. Alice was sweating up front, trying to avoid stopping or running anyone over. Hands began banging on the side of the car, faces pressed against the windows, jars of dried frogs and swathes of bright fabric were offered. Voices were raised, calling, pleading, snarling.

'What do they want?' Mike asked from next to me.

I swallowed. 'Food, money. Or to sell us stuff.'

He nodded, pale-faced. 'The frogs bring good luck, something we could do with.'

I smiled. 'We're not stopping to buy dead frogs, Mike. Or llama foetuses.'

He shrugged, managing a small smile back.

Our forward pace was becoming painfully slow. Too slow.

'Lock your doors!' I cried.

I went to lock mine. Just a moment too late. It opened as my hands reached for the lock.

And desperate hands were reaching for me.

My connection to the seat was lost. I screamed. I kicked out, succeeding only in having my foot grabbed by someone else, and I began crowd surfing out the open door of our still-moving vehicle, just without any good music or pumping atmosphere. Only pumping adrenaline.

I could feel someone, probably Mike, trying to hold onto me from around my waist. Odati was yelling at Alice to speed up, which she did with horn blaring, and some of my attackers fell off.

But they were taking me with them.

Trucko went over a pothole that jolted me hard, and people outside were screaming and Alice was screaming, but all I could register was that the guy hauling at my hands had finally let go. I fell sideways, knee twisting, Mike's hands slipping. Hard impact against the open door, the force pulling my foot free of my last assailant. I was grateful. I've never been able to do the splits and I didn't want to start trying.

Then I was falling.

I had nothing to grab, and the pressure of hands around my hips seemed too tenuous. I hung. Just below my head, sharp gravel rushed by, snapping at my hair.

I heard objects impacting the side of the car, I felt something hit me, although I didn't feel any pain. And the roaring of the crowd seemed to grow louder with every second. All I could see was the blurred ground, so close beneath me, the jumbled underside of Trucko. I hoped Mike could hold on.

I should also have been hoping that the door didn't shut with me in it. Which it did right then, like a rusty guillotine across my back. Pain seared and I winced at the road base racing past my forehead.

The vice of the door swung open again, and hands grabbed me by the back of my shirt, hauling me in. It was the most welcome feeling ever. Blood rushed from my head back to my extremities with reeling force and I sprawled against the seat, gasping, clutching my middle. Mike had his arms around me. Odati was leaning over from the Nap Seat, locking the door as it slammed itself closed again. Brodie was curled around from the passenger seat, hands still clenched in my shirt fabric, face sheened with sweat.

Evidently, saving me had been a major team effort.

'Eva? Holy hell! You're bleeding!'

I looked at Mike dumbly before I noticed a wetness under my right arm. And recalled the sound of something hitting me.

Like an internet clip with buffering issues, my pain ran a race to catch up with my hearing.

Wham.

Yeah, I hurt.

I could barely focus my eyes as something was pressed against my side to stem the bleeding. A rag. An old shirt. A unicorn.

The bloodied shirt I'd taken off before the border.

'Oh, crap,' I moaned. I looked like a crim again, just in time for the border.

'You'll be fine.' Brodie's voice was tight.

I couldn't block the unhappy roar of the people still outside, even over the sound of the engine. We were practically inciting a riot.

Then gunshots rang out, sustained firing like I'd never heard before. Alice swerved with fright, barely missing an old lady carrying a small child.

'Police!' Mike cried, ecstatic.

I wanted to be ecstatic too. Police. Only I wasn't sure if that was good or bad.

CHAPTER TWENTY-FIVE

26 hours until flight
10 bottles water
1 ¼ bags food
1 full sub tank + 2 full containers
US$535
Bs1.20
2 nasty pills

The officer ahead of us blocked our way, and he was not budging. His gun was aimed at us now, rather than the dull clouds. Alice hit the brakes with such force Mike and I ended up sprawled on the floor, and by the sounds of it, Odati had suffered a similar fate behind us and become entangled in Brodie's guitar.

'¡*Pare!*' came an authoritative cry from ahead of us. '¡*Policía! ¡Pare!*'

'Stop, Alice. He's saying stop,' I managed to gasp as I struggled to get myself back up on the seat. Every part of me felt busted.

'Oh, I'm stopping alright. Something about not wanting to be shot.'

I took one look at the stern policeman, one look at the swarming street behind, and launched myself out the door towards him, holding my door-crushed middle, not entirely sure everything was going to keep together without help. Thank goodness the roiling crowd were keeping a healthy distance from his gun.

'¡Pare!' he cried again, and I stopped mid-stride, arms raised above my head.

Something bumped against my elbow. Brodie.

I took a deep breath. I called out that we were students from Australia and Britain. We were trying to get home. We had to catch a plane out of Lima the very next day.

Mate. Talking to this intense man with his business-like gun, wearing a shirt drenched in my own blood, and with an ugly *manifestación* behind me … the next day felt impossible.

'Show me your passport,' he ordered in Spanish.

I removed it from my money belt, holding it out with a trembling hand. He gestured for us to come closer, and I did, only with the greatest of self-control. Running back to the car and hiding behind the passenger seat was a more attractive option. He checked the identification page, then my Bolivian visa stamp. And he nodded.

He looked no less severe than before, but I felt myself relax. He was doing his job. Amidst chaos and collapse, he was holding tight. He looked me in the eye, sharp as a sparking wheel rim.

He spoke again then, considering. 'Eva Somerville. I have been expecting you and two other Australian students, though not the others. Your teacher came through three days ago.'

I gasped to hear word of them, and also because they were so far ahead. Three days?! I asked if they'd been well, and he said they had, but that we needed to move onto formalities. He told me normally passports were stamped in the adjacent building, and people had to walk across the border via the bridge ahead, but he suggested for the sake of time and safety we get our stamps right where we were and drive across the bridge.

I risked a glance at the angry crowd behind us. They were creeping closer now the officer was focused on Brodie and I. And then I saw one of the other immigration guards glaring through the window at us, and I was head-spinningly glad he had not been the one to come out and investigate.

I thought getting our stamps and getting out of there was the best option, but I had to check first.

'What do you think?' I asked Brodie.

I got a blank look. 'Are you talking to me?'

I nodded, confused.

'Okay, well, you were speaking Spanish.'

My eyes widened. That was the first time that had ever happened. I repeated my question in English, but the look was still blank.

'He was speaking Spanish too, you know,' said Brodie, with an exasperated smile.

Later I would probably have time to be proud I knew enough Spanish to not be able to recognise if I was understanding Spanish poorly, or being spoken to in poor English. But right then, I didn't have any time at all. The officer was back to training his gun on the hungry crowd, so I quickly explained our options to Brodie, and together we asked the others for their passports.

The policeman took a lightning look at our documents and faces. In less time than I could ever have hoped, he handed back our passports and gestured us towards the bridge. The chaos was growing, there were cries for others to be let through, for food, for far worse. I chose not to interpret for the others.

The man told us to go, urgently this time, and Brodie and I bundled ourselves back into the car.

Alice leant across, jangling coins into my palm. 'It's not much, but it's not like we'll need these anymore …'

I looked at my hand. One silver boliviano and two copper ten *centavos*. Alice was right, it really wasn't much at all. Then I looked at the officer, too embarrassed to even offer such a tiny … what? Bribe? Thank you? Was it even legal to give?

He gestured for us to go again, then rolled his eyes and grabbed the three coins.

'Muchas gracias, Señor. Lo siento.' I gestured behind me at the mess we'd stirred up in our passing.

He nodded, eyes on mine. *'Tenga cuidado.'*

Alice got Trucko moving, passing under a massive blue sign that read *BIENVENIDOS AL PERU / WELCOME TO PERU.* I sank back and exhaled. We crawled onto the bridge, spanning a river that was technically part of Lake Titicaca, and crossing a border at the same time.

Halfway across, Alice flashed me a look. 'What was that about at the end?'

'I thanked him and said sorry, and he said to take care.'

Gunshots rang out behind us and I ducked, but they weren't coming our way. Alice sped up. I thought of that officer's eyes as he pushed us to leave. My fingers came away from my cheeks wet with tears.

'Why was he so nice?' Odati asked.

'The evac buses came through three days ago and Miss C asked him to watch out for us.'

Mike was hunched back in his seat, shaking. I wasn't sure if it was a reaction to the morning, or drug withdrawal. Both?

'At least they got this far then … I started wondering after La Paz …' he said.

I nodded. 'They got all the way. We have to believe that. Just look at us! We're over the border.'

'Don't speak too soon,' Alice said from the front. 'Here comes the other half.'

I looked up and got choked by my own intestines. We'd left

Bolivia, but we weren't yet in Peru. What with our rather noisy fanfare, four Peruvian border guards were already arrayed across the end of the bridge, automatic weapons in hand.

It didn't look like a welcoming committee.

CHAPTER TWENTY-SIX

26 hours until flight
9 bottles water
1 ¼ bags food
1 full sub tank + 2 full containers fuel
US$535
2 nasty pills

I swore, making Mike stare, and scrubbed my wet eyes with my now hopelessly filthy shirt. Basically tried to get myself back in the mood for tackling people with nasty weapons.

Which was happening a lot more than I wished.

The Peruvian guards called out in Spanish for us to stop, and Alice slowed to a halt. 'Nice work, Al,' I tried to joke. 'You're learning Spanish.'

'More like, I speak gun.' She laughed, low and nervous. 'Who wants to get out with Eva? Please not me.'

Mike sat back with a flump. 'If you're thinking it's my turn, you're right, but I'm not doing it. Great way to ruin all our chances.'

I took a deep breath. Because it was always my turn.

Brodie caught my eye. 'I'll go.'

My heart stuttered and I wanted to cry. Both useless reactions, so instead I squared my shoulders. We walked forwards until the guards told us to stop. Brodie's hand fumbled out to find mine, and I took it and held on tight.

'*¡Identifíquese!*' barked a middle guard, sporting a greasy smudge across her cheek with a scowl to match.

I didn't know the word, but given the situation we were in, I could easily guess what she wanted. Brodie was already reaching for his passport, so he was on the same page as me. As we handed them over, I repeated my ritual explanation of who we were, and where we were going. I found myself seeking Brodie's fingers again, because unlike the Bolivian side, my speech wasn't making any inroads into the scariness factor in front of us. I held Brodie's hand with a strength directly proportional to the grimness displayed in the eyes studying us.

Two of them moved to flank us and I shuddered closer to Brodie, but they passed by, guns raised and ready.

The shots, when they came, were so loud and close I flinched. They hurt my ears and seemed to tear inside me. I risked a glance behind, then wished I hadn't. The people from the Bolivian side were charging onto the bridge.

A memory flashed through my mind, a stern policeman with kind eyes.

The guns sounded again, still aiming at the sky, thank goodness. The wave crested, hesitated, then began the struggle back towards Bolivia. The guards shot a few more rounds, just to make sure the retreat continued.

I turned away, like a coward. The other two guards were watching Brodie and I with narrowed eyes, and I didn't know how to face them. Tears began to swarm in my eyes. I found myself crushed into Brodie's arms and he was speaking, low and urgent.

'Hold it together, Eva. We can do this, okay?'

I nodded my head against his chest. We had to. There was no other option. Our friends were relying on us. Mess it up and it was clear the sort of reception we'd get back in Bolivia. I breathed in, set my shoulders, nodded to Brodie. And turned back to the Peruvian guards.

They started to question me: Where were we planning to go from here? When was our flight scheduled to leave? What accommodation did we have booked?

I tried to answer as best I could, but some weren't easy answers. Take the last question, for instance. We didn't have any accommodation booked. We probably wouldn't be stopping anywhere. Just reviewing the fact it was past midday and the next day at 3:10pm we had to fly out, and we still had more than twenty hours of driving between us and the airport … well it was dawning on me we were cutting it fine already, and the Nap Seat was going to get a good work out.

If we ever got through this border.

Then they got more specific. What had happened across the river? Why was there blood on my shirt? How come we'd driven over the bridge, quite against protocol?

I got the sense they didn't like my answers. They didn't like us. They didn't like the way we'd set off the people on the other side.

Maybe they didn't want us in their country.

The two of them retreated and talked in low voices to each other, and my stomach started to sink. Their faces looked so uncompromising.

'What's going on?' whispered Brodie.

'I don't know. I think they think we're dangerous. I think they're going to say no.'

I jumped as more shots rang out from the guards behind us, and something flew past us, exploding into flames against the wall of the immigration buildings, making the guards swear and brandish their guns.

I was stuck in a news reel.

Brodie ducked and pulled me to the side. He squeezed my hand. 'Maybe we're dangerous, but I think that'll make them want to get rid of us. And not back where we'll incite a border war.'

I watched the faces with their darting eyes, and all of a sudden I felt hope. Brodie might be right. We might be a problem these guys just wanted to see the back of. The leader of the guards came at us so fast I stumbled, her hands gesturing us back into Trucko. Our passports whistled through the air towards us as we tumbled into our seats. She yelled at us to go, and to my intense relief she was pointing forwards. Into Peru.

'Go, Alice!' I hissed.

'But we haven't had our passports stamped.'

'Just bloody go!'

'But …'

The guard lifted her gun, pointed it right at my head, yelling for us to go. Brodie was yelling at Alice, I was yelling at the world, and then the tyres were squealing. We were on our way.

'Oh man, she was going to shoot you!' moaned Mike. 'Where are my freaking pills?'

'We didn't get our visas! This is so illegal.' Alice's hands gripped the steering wheel.

'That's bottom on our list of problems right now,' Brodie said, squeezing her shoulder. The last buildings whipped past and we were free and my head spun.

'Easy for you!' Alice cried. 'Your passport got done! Mike! Quit it! This is so not the time for your screwed-up addiction!'

Odati grabbed Mike's shaking hands but he elbowed her back into her seat. She swore and I captured one of his flailing arms. 'Mike! Calm down!'

Brodie held up his passport. 'Eva and I got nothing past the Bolivian exit stamp. They just wanted us gone.'

Alice kept accelerating. 'They'll never let us fly out now. That was the stupidest thing we've ever done.'

Mike tried to bite me and something inside me snapped. 'It beats dying, Alice! And hand back his damn pills, would you, because it's going down back here!'

Brodie looked around. 'Whoa. His pills …'

'We weren't going to die!' Alice roared. 'They were police, for God's sake! You should have made them follow the proper procedures. And shut UP about the pills. I'm driving!'

Brodie was searching her pockets anyway. I gritted my teeth, Odati and I holding a writhing Mike. 'Proper procedures don't exist anymore, Alice.'

'They should! They damn-well should!' We all jerked forward as the car slowed down. Alice had her head in her hands, shoulders convulsing, and Brodie gave up his search in order to grab hold of the steering wheel.

Mike screamed something unintelligible and broke free of our hold. Thwack! My vision went all fuzzy. When it cleared, he was doubled over, groaning, and from the look of things I suspected Odati had punched him in the nads.

She leant forward. 'Alice, it's going to be okay. I'd much rather try to explain why we don't have a visa than face what's happening back there, and probably miss our plane. With us out of the picture, they've at least got a chance of calming the situation down.'

We jerked to a stop with a violent engine stall, the beautiful lake glimmering to one side, the road mercifully deserted. Alice fumbled and struggled to open the door, before throwing herself out. I stumbled after her into the tussocks bordering the road. At first she pushed me away, but then she gave up and I hugged her and we both bawled our eyes out.

'This sucks. I'm sorry, Alice,' I whispered.

'I'm sorry, too. This whole thing, sometimes it's more than I know how to deal with.' Her arms tightened around me.

'Me too. We'll deal with it together.'

But then Odati spoke up. 'We have to keep going, guys. You need to get back in. Please. And hand over the pills.'

I drew back from Alice and watched her chuck the pill container to Odati, and I bet I looked as lost as she did. But then I saw what was behind her—great billowing clouds of dirty smoke.

Desaguadero was burning.

'Let's go,' I whispered.

Odati took the driver's seat, looking perkier after her sleep and the drop in altitude. Mike was in the passenger seat, already showing signs of his miraculous drug recovery, studying the guidebook map. No sign of an apology for hitting me over the head, though. Maybe he didn't even know he'd done it. I hated thinking it, but Mike made this whole situation that much harder. I climbed into the rear with Alice and Brodie.

'You want to …?' I gestured towards the empty Nap Seat, and Alice shook her head, wiping her eyes with a dirty hand.

'I couldn't sleep if I tried.'

'Well, I might. Try, that is.'

'Let me dress that wound first.'

I blinked at her. I'd forgotten my side. I'd forgotten my back. It all hurt as soon as I remembered.

It can't have been much more than an hour before that stripping off my shirt had seemed like fun flirtation. Now it was routine, part of survival, and even thinking about wanting to kiss Brodie before felt selfish and wrong. People were dying. Alice handed Brodie my first aid kit and set to with gusto, dousing and dabbing, binding and wrapping, asking Brodie for all this stuff just like some B-grade medical movie. *Saline. Gauze.* You get the picture.

I didn't.

I didn't dare look, I just watched the mystical waters of the lake and tried to imagine it truly was the sea, and we were almost in Lima.

I felt like a mummy by the end. Egyptian to be exact, because the mummification process in Peru didn't involve bandages. So I was one-tenth mummy. And three-tenths naked. Alice didn't request a shirt from Nurse Brodie, but he handed me one anyway, concern creasing his eyes, lips sombre. The shirt was white with a grey pinstripe, buttoned and collared, softened by long use, some fancy crest on the left hand side. It looked like a …

'School shirt,' Brodie said. 'I brought it to keep off bugs in the jungle.'

I pulled on the shirt and buttoned it with slippery fingers. His scent surrounded me. I was exhausted. I could barely manage thanks. I clambered over the seatback and sank. My mind just collapsed in on itself, like it needed to reboot.

Despite it all, despite the terrible cost, we were in Peru.

We should have been celebrating, but it didn't feel like a win at all.

CHAPTER TWENTY-SEVEN

25 hours until flight
8 bottles water
1 bag food
2/3 full sub tank + 2 full containers fuel
US$535
1 ½ nasty pills

It wasn't a long sleep, I could tell that from the height of the sun when I awoke. But it was a good one. My mind had steadied, come to terms with some of what I'd seen and done that morning. It's not like I was comfortable with it, no 'no worries—dead bodies, riots, I'm alright' sort of thing. I think I'd just found out how to not dwell on it so much, so I could keep functioning.

There's a point where the volume of wrong in the world can overwhelm you. And it's then that fear wins. Evil wins, good is lost, and so are you. You can't give in to the darkness that hovers if you want to stay sane. You need to keep smiling, trying, hoping, trusting. Loving. Because that's what makes us human.

That's what I've learnt on this trip.

I studied the same sun the Incans revered so much, beside the same lake they had studied in centuries past, and I determined I was going to survive. Not just me as a body, but me as a person, as an identity. All the bits of myself that made me who I was. I knew I was going to change because of all of this, I couldn't stop that, but I promised myself I would keep true to the things that counted.

The dazed silence in the cab encroached on my awareness. I frowned, sitting up. Soft cotton slid against my skin, heady scent swirled about me, reminding me I was wearing a part of Brodie. I popped up between Alice and Brodie, and surveyed the scene.

Blank stares out windows, Odati focused on the road, Mike twitching the map.

'How long was I asleep?' I asked softly.

I was treated to three sets of concerned eyes, four if you count Odati's quick glance in the rear-view mirror. And I thought most of those eyes could probably do with a healing nap in the back.

'About an hour,' Mike said, after checking his watch. 'But since we set our clocks back an hour when we entered Peru, really you lost no time at all.'

I smiled at him, because it was heartening to imagine I'd just got a free hour of rest. 'Have we been following this lake all the way?'

'Pretty much,' said Alice.

'Wow.' I watched the blue water fly past for a moment—it was hypnotic. 'Well, I feel 100% improved, and I highly recommend our first-class Nap Seat to each and every one of you. Who wants first dibs?'

No one, it seemed.

Mike got me up to date with how far we had to go and how many spare hours we had up our sleeve. Which was about four. And if you believe the guff about needing to be at an international terminal two hours before your flight, I suppose that meant we only had two hours spare. And that meant someone ought to try sleeping, especially one of our three precious drivers.

Odati was looking super-fresh, for sure. But Alice and Brodie looked shot. I squeezed myself between them and hoped sheer discomfort would make one of them decide to have a rest. I didn't achieve the move with grace, kicking one or both of them in the head a few times, but in the end I was perched in the centre seat.

Alice rubbed her eyes and handed me our last packet of cream biscuits. 'You're smiling?'

'Yeah, I've long come to terms with my lack of coordination,' I replied, flicking off the inevitable crumbs as I bit through to the chewy centre.

She tilted her head, then took my hand and squeezed it. 'You're looking much better.'

I shrugged. 'That nap helped me regain a bit of perspective.'

'Perspective …' Brodie yawned. I turned my head to find he was watching me closely through red-rimmed eyes. 'Okay, I need a dose of perspective. Into the back it is.'

He launched himself over the seat with a level of athleticism I could only dream of possessing, murmured a goodnight, and within moments the sounds of steady breathing wafted forward.

I was glad and said as much. If we didn't look after ourselves, no one else was going to do it for us.

Alice looked at me with narrowed eyes. 'Are you suggesting I should get some perspective too?'

I blinked. 'Well, I suppose you could fit back there as well.' I hated the very thought of her curling up alongside Brodie, but if Alice needed to rest, then she should rest.

She shook her head, though, and my shoulders relaxed. 'Nah, I don't need sleep. I need some time in my happy place.'

'Meditation?' I guessed, thinking of her yoga.

She shook her head.

'Laundry?'

'Hairdressing. I love it, it always calms me.'

I stared at her, and she at me, and we both understood what was coming. I surrendered with as much pride as I could.

'No blue,' I begged.

'No blue,' she agreed.

And so I ended up sideways on the seat, having my hair styled with a travel comb and a mini pair of first aid scissors. My heart was thumping and I was nine-tenths hyperventilating, but thankfully very little hair fell. Alice began to mock-question me, a friendly hairdresser catching up on news. The What-cut-would-you-like line. The How's-your-day-been, which was awkward because our day had been shocking. But we got into the swing of it, and I started to enjoy myself.

'So,' she trilled, 'have you heard about So-and-so and the pool-man?'

I laughed. 'I have, I couldn't believe it!'

'Nor could I, I never thought he'd fall like that.'

'Oh, but I heard it from What's-her-face, so it must be true.'

She dropped the mock sing-song voice. 'I've seen it in the way he looks at her, I just wondered if she felt the same.'

I frowned. 'So-and-so?'

'Yeah. How does So-and-so feel about the pool-man?'

I turned to see her expression, and got told off for moving my head. 'Am I So-and-so?' I whispered.

'Maybe. Does she like the pool-man?' Alice whispered back.

I bit my lip. Days ago I'd sworn to fight fear, and yet with Brodie I was still letting it rule me. I pushed my reluctance aside. 'Yeah, So-and-so does like the pool-man. A lot. But there's so much going on at the moment, maybe she's not sure it's the right thing.'

Alice hugged me, jigging with excitement. 'That's so good. Right, I am making this the best damn hairdo the world has ever seen.'

I laughed, happy she was happy, happy I'd shared how I felt in a roundabout way, happy I felt better for sharing. 'But still not blue, right?'

She chuckled. 'No crazier than pink, I promise.'

When she finished, she sighed. 'That was so much fun. Thanks Eva.'

I felt my hair. Twining braids and cascading curls. It wasn't a messy bun. It was so much more. 'Wow. What did you do?'

'I made you all "Victorian lady". Your features are so classic, I think it suits you.' She leaned forward to whisper, 'The pool-man will love it!'

My nerves jangled and I remembered why I've never liked admitting to my friends when I have a crush on someone. Because they always end up telling that person in some embarrassing fashion. Hopeless daydreaming is infinitely better than public rejection.

There would be nowhere to hide in a car full of people.

But I made myself smile. 'Thanks, Alice.'

She gave me a hug.

We were travelling along the edge of Lake Titicaca, passing over rivers so slow and wide you'd swear they were entering the sea. What a shock for them, to find they still had 3,800 metres to go. I settled back with my sketchbook. Some people write in diaries. Not me, I record in images. And I had one helluva day to document.

'We're getting close to Puno,' Mike murmured eventually.

'Can we go around it?' Odati asked, and I was sorry to see Mike shake his head. 'Is it big?'

'Not too big.'

I looked towards the approaching town, crouching on the lakeshore at the base of an imposing dry-grass mountain. It didn't look so bad. No smoke plumes was definitely a good start. Many towns in Bolivia had been fine. Maybe Puno would be as well.

I said as much, and Mike turned around to respond, then did this massive double-take. 'Your hair!'

'Alice …' I looked at her warningly. 'What have you done with my hair?'

Alice smiled. 'You look awesome. I have made magic and brilliance.'

I looked back at Mike. He was staring at me. 'Don't think bad,' he said. 'You look different, but not in a bad way. Nice work, Alice.'

Alice leant in to my ear. 'I told you so. If the pool-man doesn't work out, you could probably try for Mike. You can thank me later.'

I elbowed her away, face broiling, not even bothering to tell her she'd got Mike around the wrong way.

'Okay, people, it's only hair.' Odati had her 'serious' face on. 'We need to prepare for Puno. Eva, can you pass the tyre wrench to Mike?' She looked at me in the rear-view, and squealed. 'Eva! Oh, wow! Alice, you have to do me next!'

I grinned at Odati as I handed the wrench forwards. 'It's only hair …' I teased. Mike laughed out loud.

I rubbed my hands together. They were dirty, a crusty brown flaky kind of dirty.

Blood.

From the wrench.

From the dead man in La Paz.

I shuddered and cleaned them off on my pants as best I could, my smile plummeting. I grabbed a spanner as if it was a lifeline, and reminded everyone to lock their doors.

We were learning. Once almost-dragged-out-the-door-of-your-moving-vehicle, twice shy.

CHAPTER TWENTY-EIGHT

24 hours until flight
8 bottles water
1 bag food
Nearly ½ full sub tank + 2 full containers
US$535
1 ½ nasty pills

Puno was an anticlimax. Whatever passion of anger or despair had rolled through the town, it had evaporated by the time we passed through. So much so that Brodie slept through the entire length of it. It was a pretty town, much like those we'd seen in Bolivia, but with even more of a sense of the shadow of the Incas. Great foundation stones at the bases of grand Spanish churches so seamless, and held together by nothing at all. Mike pointed them out in a whisper as we drove through, and said many had been built using stone taken from Incan buildings.

How those guys cut stone that perfectly was beyond me. I was impressed.

And yet, it hadn't stopped their civilisation falling to the Spanish.

The entire length of the town, I didn't spot a single intact window. They were all shattered or boarded up. And honey-coloured paving stones were conspicuously missing from large stretches of the street we went down. It wasn't hard to put two and two together.

Skinny dogs roamed the empty streets. We passed one barricaded area, intimidating green-camo-clad figures patrolling further in.

Mike's book said 150,000 people lived in Puno.

Where had they all got to?

My heart was yammering like mad the entire time, the spanner handle sweaty in my palm. But lightning didn't strike twice. We made it out of that town with all four wheels inflated. I wanted to dance, would have if there'd been space. We put our makeshift weapons back in the tool bag and laughed at each other, relief like a sugar rush.

Within about twenty minutes it became clear all that adrenaline had had some effect, and a toilet stop was in order.

Now, I love a good toilet.

I even like a pretty appalling toilet when that's all that's on offer.

But with the way all the towns were sending out zombie apocalypse vibes, we unanimously decided the best bet was to dig a hole or two as far from civilisation as we could manage. Odati found a spot off the side of the road where we hoped we wouldn't be immediately visible to any mass murderers taking a drive, and turned off the car. Her hands were shaking.

The absence of the engine noise was palpable. Lake Titicaca glittered to our right. Alice whipped out with a makeshift shovel and a grimace, Mike did the same in the opposite direction, and all the doors and unusual noise managed what the creepy atmosphere of Puno had not.

It woke Brodie.

I was outside, sorting through our shrinking provisions for something different to eat for an afternoon tea that was really also a late lunch and perhaps an early dinner too.

Five tins of sardines.

Three cans of tomatoes.

Half a loaf of super-stale bread.

Six sweetened condensed milks.

I grimaced. Without anything to cook with, and no time to cook anyway, it wasn't looking like the best meal on record.

When I heard Brodie's voice my pulse rate quadrupled, my cheeks turned to flame, and I dropped a can of sardines on my middle toe. I was impatient and yet reluctant to reveal Alice's handiwork, second-guessing what she'd said about him, fighting a powerful urge to climb under Trucko and hide.

Instead I stood up.

Determined to act as normal as possible.

He was talking to Odati, their heads close together, discussing something about Trucko. My nerve evaporated like blood on hot bitumen. I saw Alice returning to the car, so I escaped to relieve myself.

I didn't go far. The mountains around us had a feeling of unreality. Perfect terracing and the occasional alpaca adorned the slopes, and I couldn't shake the idea people could be watching us. I didn't give a rats if someone spotted me peeing behind a bush, but I didn't want them getting ideas about our car, our food, or our miserable stash of money.

And I didn't want to be cut off from my friends.

My nerves had me scanning the surrounding hills, all the while telling myself I was overreacting. Until I saw some movement, just behind a rocky outcrop, not more than fifty metres from where I crouched.

I froze. Even though I *was* listening back in year seven when the health nurse told us it was not good to stop mid-pee, I did anyway.

Whatever it was had ducked down behind the rock. And I figured alpacas don't duck. But people sure do.

I finished my ablutions in a meteoric hurry, eyes on that rock. As I stood, ready to dash to the others and bundle us all into the relative safety of the cruiser, I saw movement again and my fear was like an enormous surge to my brain.

And then a dizzy-hooray spin of the head.

Because it *was* an alpaca. Trotting long-leggedly from behind the rock. Honey-brown face and back. Two white front legs. A shaggy coat that spoke of oncoming winter.

Those characteristic ears were perked right up, as if it were thinking, *What's going on here?*

I wobbled with relief, laughing at myself.

There's something about seeing an alpaca in the Andes that feels right. It turned around, as if to show off its fine, upright form. And its ears perked again, making its neon pink earrings dance.

It was looking back at the rock.

It was looking back as if still thinking, *What's going on here?*

And I was wondering exactly the same thing when my guts froze.

Why would an alpaca dash out from behind a rock, unless something behind that rock scared it?

I was running before I could sort my head out. Running faster than the alpaca had. Back to Trucko, where I found my friends in the process of decanting the first of our two spare fuel containers into the sub-tank. They looked at me with open mouths as I raced up, panting like I'd been running an Olympic sprint.

If I had been, I think I would have placed on the podium.

I didn't bother to hear out their chorus of 'What's wrong?'

'Out there,' I panted, 'behind that rock.' I turned and pointed.

To their credit, they were instantly on guard. No funny comments about it only being an alpaca; sit down Eva, you're maybe a little overwrought.

I think they were feeling it too.

The idea that we weren't alone.

Brodie tipped the fuel container abruptly, splashes of fuel ricocheting everywhere as it poured into the tank. Odati grabbed the tyre wrench. Mike leapt into the back seat, Alice into the driver's seat, ready to get us the hot-foot out of there. I threw the food bags in without care, the sound of cans adding their own tempo to the song of the fuel glugging into the tank. I grabbed a screwdriver, waiting, unwilling to leave Odati and Brodie outside while I huddled within the dubious safety of Trucko.

And I watched that rock.

And just when I thought I had to have been wrong, they came.

CHAPTER TWENTY-NINE

23 hours until flight
8 bottles water
5 tins sardines
3 cans tomatoes
½ loaf stale bread
6 sweetened condensed milks
Nearly full sub tank + 1 full container
US$535
1 ½ nasty pills

I screamed. Odati took one look at them and jumped inside.

'Get in!' I yelled to Brodie. He shook his head, the tell-tale glug-glug of fuel continuing.

'Get into the car!' yelled Odati, and it was only when Mike grabbed my uncooperative arms and dragged me inside that I realised she'd been yelling at me.

Just as my car door shut, the fuel container emptied. In one swift movement Brodie pulled it away and hurled it at the oncoming charge of people. They were zoning in from all directions, including the boy I'd spotted behind the rock. There must have been eight or nine of them, some about our age, one an ancient crone. Male or female, young or old, they carried makeshift weapons and all channelled the same level of desperation.

Alice was trying to start the engine as Brodie launched himself into the passenger seat, yelling, 'Go, go, go!'

But the engine wouldn't catch.

The rear window shattered, crumbled pebbles of safety glass shooting through at us, and a rock too. Suddenly I had Mike collapsed against me, black hair extra shiny, and Odati yelling for us to get down, and cries coming to me from outside that my overstretched brain couldn't interpret.

And the one sound I wanted to hear was the engine roaring into life. Instead it coughed and gave up.

They were on us.

In front they blocked our way forwards. From behind they were arrayed to stop us reversing, and a few were coming closer with knobby sticks and knives at the ready, and faces that told a story tough to read.

It's hard to judge without knowing for sure I wouldn't do the same thing in their situation.

A man appeared outside my window, all worn leather cowboy hat, thick felted jacket and hopeless eyes. He gestured for me to open the door. Which totally was not going to happen. He raised a rock in his weathered fist and readied to throw it.

And the engine still refused to take.

I had the screwdriver in my hand. It suddenly seemed the most important thing to determine whether it was a flat-head or Phillips. As the rock hit the window I shied away, and thanked the stars for laminated glass as it rained all over me like uncut diamonds. His hand came through from the outside, fumbling for the handle, and

I did the only thing I could think of.

I stabbed it.

It's horrifying to see blood well up because of something you've done. On purpose. I pulled back, choking on my heartbeat. The man screamed, at me or the pain or life in general I don't know, but his hand went back to its task and I couldn't let him open that door and take us. I readied myself to stab again.

The car burst into life. Tyres churned against gravel as they searched for purchase, and then we shot forwards so fast the attackers in front barely had time to leap aside. Something rolled back against my foot. Looking down I saw several loose cans among the remains of my window.

I didn't think. It would never feed them all. But it was something.

I picked up the cans and tossed them through the window.

As we accelerated away, a gale roared through Trucko, threatening the stability of my new hair. But it was just hair.

I couldn't comprehend we were safe. I didn't have time to assimilate it either. Because Odati was cradling Mike, and his eyes had a glassy, unfocused look.

CHAPTER THIRTY

23 hours until flight
8 bottles water
4 tins sardines
2 cans tomatoes
½ loaf stale bread
5 sweetened condensed milks
Nearly full sub tank + 1 full container
US$535
1 ½ nasty pills

Alice's unicorn t-shirt was getting its third input of DNA for the day as Odati pressed it against the side of Mike's bleeding head.

Dammit! Where was a legitimate prospective medical student when you needed one? Alice was driving, which left me—the total faker—in charge of fixing Mike's head. I tipped out my entire daypack to find my first aid kit, which wasn't even in there. I found it tucked in the seatback, right in front of my face. But once I found it I froze.

It was synapse-obliteratingly noisy, with the side and rear windows brokenly thud-thud-thudding. It took a moment for me to realise Alice was shouting at me. 'Check his head! Tell me what you see!'

I fumbled Mike's sticky hair aside. A gash ran from near the back of his head to above his left ear. I reported this to Alice, who asked me to check all sorts of things. Indentations or big bumps, pupils, nothing dribbling from his ears. I asked him what day of the week it was, but that didn't work because nobody knew the right answer, so I held up some fingers and he was able to tell me how many and what his name was and who I was, and that we had about twenty-four hours to get to Lima, so I figured he was okay.

At Alice's insistence I cut his hair back around the gash. Mike's do wasn't anywhere near as professional as mine. In fact it looked like a piranha had feasted on his skull. I liberally doused him with saline solution and the whole length of the cut was exposed. Ouch. I had to force myself to look at it. Thank goodness we hadn't managed to eat afternoon tea.

But it wasn't deep, and it didn't seem to be pulling apart, so I packed a fresh gauze on top and wrapped his skull so he looked like the survivor of a plastic surgery malfunction. Alice promised to see if he needed stitches later. Brodie had a sewing kit. Just the thought of it made me want to hurl.

But the crisis was over. Well that particular one anyway.

I sat back with a sigh.

It was incomprehensible to me we'd only started driving from Oruro that morning. It seemed at least a week ago I'd enjoyed a shower and a bed and precious phone messages. I felt empty.

The road was flat, straight and in good condition, and Alice found a driving groove in no way compliant with speed restrictions and kept at it for at least an hour. We passed tiny towns, meeting no interference, though it was clear they were not unscathed. Burnt buildings and smashed-in buses were regular sights along the road. I stared at each of them, but none resembled the bright yellow bus our class had been on. We followed a train line for much of the way, but we didn't see any trains.

The hills around us were tarnished brass, the sky a bitter blue. Now the urgency was gone, my mind began to covet a darkness. The despair in the eyes of the people we'd left behind. That same bleakness inside of me.

Cold.

Drained.

Rumbling?

Of course. Probably plain hungry. Sweet, overly processed biscuits for lunch was never going to be a good move. We needed proper food. I shook myself into action, realising I had Brodie's shirt bunched up around my nose, inhaling the scent of him like a kid with their blankie. I forced myself to search for some of the food I'd scattered in my haste, and I handed out random stuff. Mike got a tin of tomatoes and traded with Odati, who scored sardines. I chucked more sardines forward for Alice. Brodie wasn't keen on fish, so he got bread and traded for some tomato on top. I gave myself the same.

Through dint of creative mix and matching, we all ended up with something resembling a balanced meal, and the condensed milk got passed around until it was empty. I could feel the heaviness lifting.

Odati burped and looked at me. 'What did you give them?'

I didn't think anyone had noticed my desperate charity as we'd sped away. 'I'm not sure. A couple of cans. Whatever was at my feet.'

Odati nodded approval at me. Mike took my hand and squeezed it. Huh. Concussion?

Food makes things seem so much better. All the people we'd met that day who didn't have the option of eating? How would they lift themselves out of the darkness? And I suppose the answer was, maybe they wouldn't. But I hoped they'd find a way. I hoped they'd find in themselves something so potent, they'd gain the strength to continue. Like when we walked in the starlight to Potosí. It's in there, somewhere.

The road grew progressively more winding. Odati was looking awful. She was like our own personal altitude meter, and extremely accurate. We skirted yet another mirrored lake, adorned with alpacas and llamas and fenced by pale hills, and a sign proclaimed us to be 4,413 metres above sea level. Odati retreated to the Nap Seat with her sleeping bag to groan and occasionally throw up out the shattered rear window.

Surprisingly handy that.

The road turned into a twisting dance through the mountains. I have to admit I wasn't feeling all that crash-hot either. Was it travel sickness or altitude sickness, or were the two fighting off against each other in the pit of my stomach to see which might emerge victorious? We went up mountains and back down the other side, each time hoping we'd stay down, only to take another turn and find another rise ahead. Our horn blared at each hairpin bend. Ice spears glittered from the sides of the roads even though it was a sunny afternoon, and the cyclone whipping through Trucko was absolutely frigid. I attempted progressively more innovative methods to tape something over the window, but each time I was defeated by the force of our passage.

So I huddled against Mike and we shivered together under our sleeping bags, feeling like we were stuck on Mount Aconcagua without a tent. I still didn't feel comfortable around Mike, but being near him was far warmer than not.

Despite the cold it was starkly beautiful. And refreshingly empty of people who may, or may not, want to beat us to death. Mountains, mountains, more mountains. And weird-looking rock formations cropping out of the alpine desert. Mike and I passed the time deciding what we thought they resembled.

'Priest in a cowboy hat,' he muttered, pointing to the left.

'Good one. Ooh. Over there: three of the seven dwarves, standing on each other's shoulders.'

'Nice. Which three?'

'Um … Dopey, Happy and … Proudy?'

Mike snorted. 'Even I know there's no … ooh! Kangaroo with a walking stick! On the right.'

At a spot selected to be absolutely clear of ambush risk, Alice pulled over to swap driving with Brodie. She said she wanted to check Mike's head, but she winked at me as she said it. Her scheming saw me end up in the passenger seat, welcoming the warmth Brodie's body had left in the upholstery, and even more aware of his proximity because of that.

'Mike! You're so cold!' Alice's voice came from behind just as Brodie eased Trucko forward again.

'No kidding, it's like a gale-force freezer back here,' he grumbled.

It turned out Alice wasn't putting up with the arctic blast, so we searched for replacement windows.

It hadn't entered my head to stop just to cover the holes. Stopping equalled danger. But since we'd already stopped to swap drivers, it made perfect sense to patch things up. Several first aid kits were raided for tape and the side window was replaced by a shopping bag, the rear by cardboard from the water bottle box. It didn't take long at all, but the difference it made? Amazing.

I could feel warmth stealing back into me.

Alice shuffled forward in her seat. 'Your hair has gone wild,' she said to me. I closed my eyes as she ran fingers through the bits of tangled hair blown free by the buffeting wind. 'Lucky I carry hairspray, just for emergencies like this.'

She pulled out a tiny can and I closed my eyes, barely in time to avoid the mist of spray that enveloped me.

Brodie coughed. 'Man, that stings. No more.'

'Don't need any more,' Alice responded. 'Eva looks fabulous again. Don't you think she looks fabulous, Brodie?'

I sunk back into my chair, staring fixedly at a tear on the knee of my cargoes, wishing Alice would just shut up.

'Wild can be fabulous too, Al,' Brodie said.

There were too many different ways to interpret that. I turned my head to look out the window, hiding my blazing cheeks.

Alice and Mike started a game of cards in the back, because Alice believed Mike shouldn't sleep after a head injury, and noise from the shopping bag window was soon broken by their cries and laughter.

Brodie and I sat in charged silence.

'You warming up?' he eventually asked.

I dared to look at him. Hair sticking everywhere, squinting against the lowering sun, lips pursed as he focused on the road.

I nodded. 'Yeah. I wish we'd start descending, though.' I paused. 'How are you?'

'Surprisingly okay,' he murmured, so low I nearly couldn't make it out.

The horn bugled again and he crept Trucko around a corner, sheer drop to the left. My sigh echoed his. The road kept climbing. I just wanted out of these mountains.

'It was a close one back there,' he said. 'If you hadn't spotted those guys …'

I felt myself blush. Stupid cheeks. 'Wasn't really me. An alpaca spotted them.'

He flashed a lightning grin. 'Maybe we should only have toilet stops when alpacas are around.'

'We could make a sign for the steering wheel.'

'"Only pee around alpacas?"'

I giggled.

We rounded the next bend and before us was the most awe-inspiring and welcome sight in simply forever. A huge, snow-capped mountain was dead ahead, its feet well below us. The road began to descend immediately, and I felt relief assault my limbs.

Brodie whooped. 'That's what I'm wanting to see!'

Alice grabbed me in a bear hug from behind. I found I was grinning so hard my cheeks hurt. It took a few minutes for the euphoria to wear off.

'What is that mountain?' Alice asked. 'It's beautiful.'

'Misty,' said Mike.

I frowned. 'It's pretty clear.'

He almost laughed. 'No, it's Mount Misti. It's just next to Arequipa.'

Arequipa was almost two kilometres lower than our highest point that day. No more altitude. I thought of poor Odati and smiled. We were heading down, down, down and on to the sea. Odati would wake up and wouldn't know herself.

I was feeling better already as we weaved off the side of the *altiplano*.

It was smooth descending. As dusk tinted the vast sky we were driving through woody foothills, and I was filled with hope.

That's why it sucked so much when we hit the roadblock.

CHAPTER THIRTY-ONE

21 hours until flight
8 bottles water
2 tins sardines
1 can tomatoes
¼ loaf stale bread
4 sweetened condensed milks
½ full sub tank + 1 full container
US$535
1 ½ nasty pills

Several trucks, a car and a bus were parked along the road ahead of us, right up to where it curved again, hiding among the shadowed trees that effectively fenced us in on each side. Campfires glittered. No vehicles were moving. None of them even had their engines running.

What the heck was going on?

We slowed to a stop, cautious. Stopping felt dodgy. But a stop where lots of other people were stopped in the middle of nowhere …?

Definition of Super-Dodgy.

Brodie was frowning. Alice looked nonplussed. Mike had his head in his hands.

Odati's face popped up from the Nap Seat, pigtails askew. 'What's up?'

'Don't know,' Brodie murmured.

'Maybe there's been an accident?' I said.

Mike sat up straight. 'It's probably a blockade, I read about them in the guidebook. It's a way for a village to exercise the only power it has—over the road that goes through it.'

'That doesn't sound good,' Odati said.

I had to agree. 'Shall we sit it out for a bit? See what happens?'

Brodie cleared his throat. He turned off the engine and the lights. We sat in the gloom. I took out my sketchbook, intending to record some of what we'd faced through that very long day. But it was almost too much, too raw. So instead I joined the others, just watching. Waiting.

And absolutely nothing happened, except it got darker.

The lights of the campfires sparkled off some sort of reflection on the road. The smell was terrible.

Excrement and rot and a sickly sweet odour.

I kept on looking at the reflections. Like someone had poured buckets of water on the road, letting them drain haphazardly. I hugged myself. I had to know.

I grabbed a torch out of the glove box and leapt out of Trucko. Towards the shining road. Ignoring the calls of alarm from the car. The heavy, mucky smell got stronger as I approached and my heart was yammering in my ears.

I didn't want to be right, but …

I knelt down, studying the stains. It was difficult against the dark bitumen to make out the red, except where it had clotted together.

'Blood?' came Brodie's voice from behind, making me topple

forward in surprise. He grabbed me just before I had to splay both hands on the gore in front of me, pulling me up and away.

I hid from the horror. He held me to him, breath heaving.

This wasn't how things were supposed to be working out.

Tomorrow we were meant to be flying away from this continent, not languishing amid slimy runnels of coagulation.

Odati's voice came from next to us, low and worried. 'What's wrong?'

'There's blood all over the road,' I mumbled into Brodie. Odati was silent for so long I was about to repeat myself.

When she spoke her words were like sunshine after days of suffocating cloud. 'It's probably animal blood. I can smell meat cooking.'

I sagged against Brodie. Of course. Why hadn't I thought of that?

'I know I'm vegetarian and all,' he said, 'but I am so relieved.'

'It's certainly changed my mental picture,' I said, pulling away from him to give Odati a hug. 'Thanks for thinking that one through. My head was in a bad place.'

We walked back to Trucko, where Alice was watching with concern and Mike was single-mindedly tearing the inside cover of his guidebook to shreds. We discussed the options. I found a piece of paper and a pencil and made a comparison chart, which no one else seemed to care about, but it sure made me feel better.

We agreed to send a reconnaissance mission to the source of the blockade. It went without saying I'd be doing the talking. Because talking is only worthwhile if the people you're talking to can understand you. And nobody batted an eyelid when Brodie volunteered to go with me.

'No more than thirty minutes,' Odati instructed. 'If we need to go back, that's all we can spare.'

Trying to break through blockade:

PROS	CONS
• 16 hours' travel if we go ahead (3.5 hrs spare) = much safer, but only if we get through • No obvious murders (been here an hour, heard no screaming)	• 19 to 20 hours' travel if we turn back and go around (= no spare time) (= not good) → If we want to turn back, we need to do it NOW. • Blockade in place for days (blood stains everywhere, lots of vehicles) - unlikely to get through.
=MOVE NOW! Try and talk our way through, if we fail, turn back!	

Our footsteps scrunched in the silence as we walked away. The light of our torch was deceptive, as if all that existed was this one changing circle of brightness. As if we weren't moving, and instead the world was shifting in front of us.

I was nervous as we approached the first group, four men chatting around a fire. They were on edge too. When they noticed our light, two sprang up and pulled out knives. *Here we go again …*

When I called out, they relaxed with the lilt of my obviously foreign accent. We didn't speak to them long. They confirmed it was a blockade. They were truck drivers, they'd been there for four days, it was impossible for them to turn their vehicles around on the narrow road. A group of thugs had come through a few nights back, but apart from that things had been pretty calm.

We mentioned we were going to talk to the blockaders, and the men nodded, wishing us luck in a tone that clearly said they held no hope whatsoever for success this century. Or the next. We said our goodbyes and walked away from their fire-lit circle.

It was cold. Nothing like the *altiplano*, of course. But still … I hugged my arms to myself.

Brodie's arm came to rest around my waist, and suddenly the night wasn't cold at all. It was steaming.

We turned another corner, more fires and drivers off to the side, and a contingent of tourists from a fancy bus up ahead, getting served a fine Peruvian BBQ by the smell of things. My stomach rumbled noisily.

'If you're hungry, I bet we could guilt them into giving you something,' Brodie said.

'Nah, we don't have time for smoky ribs.'

The tour guides watched us as we walked past. But they didn't call out to us, and the one in the middle kept his gun out and at the ready. Pointing like an accusation.

It was obvious when we reached the head of the blockade. Barbed wire twirled across the road, along with a few felled trees. The acrid scent of burning tyres hung in the air, making my nose twitch. And sentries, backlit by the moonlight, wearing ponchos, and carrying rifles.

None of this seemed particularly positive. I reached up to turn off the torch.

CHAPTER THIRTY-TWO

19 hours until flight

1 blockade

6 bottles water

1 tin sardines

3 sweetened condensed milks

½ full sub tank + 1 full container fuel

US$535

1 ½ nasty pills

Blood was thumping in my ears.

Just a look at those rifles and I was on the verge of hyperventilating in the heady air.

Brodie whistled through his teeth. 'Nothing like a challenge, eh?'

A nervous laugh escaped me.

Brodie's lips, always so ready to smile, curved upwards. 'Ready?'

I don't know how long we stood there, statues in the night, before I said it. Before I truly believed it. 'Ready.'

He squeezed my shoulder. 'You're awesome. And I'm right here with you.'

I took an almighty breath, and stepped forward, feeling Brodie move like a protective shadow beside me. I hailed the sentries in Spanish. They didn't offer us refreshments, but they didn't shoot us either, so I took courage from that. I told them our story, the race to catch our plane home. I had it down pat. But I might as well have been mute. It was like they were carved from Incan rock, silent, unmoving.

I changed tack, asking them why they had set up the blockade. What was their grievance? Perhaps we could help?

Silence through which the hum of wind in the grass could be clearly heard.

My heart fell but I refused to show it. I had this image of Miss C waving frantically from a plane window as it took off, me running down the tarmac after it. If we had to turn back, we'd be lucky to see that much.

Then I felt Brodie move, one arm tensed as if ready to fend off an attack. The middle figure stepped forwards.

He stopped, still some paces from us, and introduced himself as Yuval Villca, the leader of the blockade.

'What did he say?' Brodie whispered.

'They're blockading to get the attention of the government in Lima. They're concerned at the lawlessness in this area since the collapse, they want assistance.'

Brodie nodded. 'Doing great, Eva.'

I smiled up at him, then turned back to Yuval. As best I could manage, I spoke of what we'd seen as we travelled here. The burning, the violence, the hunger. 'It's not just here,' I said in Spanish.

Yuval hesitated. 'The cities are worse?'

I nodded. 'Much worse.'

It was so hard, his face a silhouette against the light of the flames beyond. You don't know how much you rely on facial expressions until you can't see them. But I felt like he shrank at my words.

When he spoke next, I experienced an equal mix of sorrow and delight. And guilt at the delight. I must have shown some reaction, because Brodie squeezed my hand. He had one eyebrow raised in clear query.

'Yuval has a son in Lima,' I related in a low voice. 'He hasn't heard any news for a week, he's worried—even more now he's heard what we've seen elsewhere.'

Brodie nodded once, then leaned in quickly. 'Milk the sympathy angle. He wants his son safe, our parents want us safe, too.'

When he pulled away, I nodded, and he gave an encouraging squeeze. And I felt less guilty, because I knew Brodie was thinking the same way I was.

I asked Yuval about his son, who turned out to be in boarding school, the same age as me. Yuval was so proud when he spoke of Esteban. He was studying similar subjects to me at school, so we spoke about them. He liked agriculture. I explained to Yuval that Brodie also liked agriculture and the two nodded at each other, and I felt triumph because with each word we were becoming more human to him.

I had to make my move. I said I was sure his son was thinking of him, because I knew I thought of my parents all the time.

And Yuval's shadow face watched me, silent.

It seemed like he was quiet for longer than it had taken Trucko to start up post-ambush. Then Yuval asked our ages, and when I told him, he was silent again. He asked about our families.

I told him my story. A mum who's an accountant through the week and worked at the local hardware store on the weekend before the downturn lost her that job. A dad, redundant from his teaching job, working whatever he could find. How we have Sunday afternoons together as family time, and have cups of tea watching the chickens peck through the backyard. I was smiling, the image I could conjure was so clear and immediate. I felt I could smell the acacia blossom, hear the delighted clucking of the chooks as they uncovered a delectable bug. I asked Brodie about his family, and translated as he spoke. He had a dad at home, a younger brother and sister still at school. No mention of his mum.

Yuval asked a question, and I translated. 'Do you miss your family?'

Brodie stared at Yuval, eyes glistening in the firelight. 'More than I ever thought possible.'

I swallowed twice before relaying that back. Poor Brodie. Even if we made this flight, it would not take him home.

Yuval spoke to the other two standing guard, so rapidly I couldn't follow—or were they speaking Quechua? Then he was gone, over the barricades in a silent rush, leaving us with only two sentries pointing increasingly uncertain guns our way. I found Brodie's hand and held on tight.

'You wait,' one of them instructed.

Brodie heaved in a breath and let it out in a long hiss, his other hand fiddling with the collar of his shirt. 'This had better work.'

Above us thousands of stars glittered in the sky. Even the fires couldn't mask them. I set my head back, drinking them in. I had done my best and for now the situation was out of my hands.

'Feel free to ask if you want,' Brodie said.

I looked at him, his clear eyes reflecting the heavens. 'About your mum?'

'Yeah. Most people want to know.'

I thought for a while, then shook my head. 'Not if it'll make you feel uncomfortable.'

His lips were pursed, the planes of his face more angular without his usual smile.

My words hung in the air like smoke, sounding blunt in the stretching silence. 'But if you wanted to tell me, you know …'

Yeah, I didn't think I'd helped much. It wasn't show and tell at kindy.

I fidgeted with my nails. Brodie's hand enclosed mine. His fingers played along my own, thumb and forefinger travelling the length of each of mine. I closed my eyes but had to open them again when sensory overload threatened.

'Do you play the guitar?' His face had lost its bleakness as he studied my hand.

I swallowed. 'No.'

'You should try.' He turned my hand over, tracing the underside with fingers so light they were tickly.

'You play really well,' I managed to say.

He softly clapped my hand like a sideways high five. 'Thanks. I haven't had much opportunity lately.'

I felt him shift his weight, he had to be looking at me. I kept my eyes focused on our hands.

'She's dead. My mum. Two years ago. Ovarian cancer.'

I turned to him. 'I'm so sorry, Brodie.'

He shrugged. 'That's why I want to get home. My family. They don't deserve to lose someone again. I want to be there for them.' He studied me, forehead ever-so-slightly creased. Then he smiled. 'Don't look so horrified. You'll make me sorry I told you. It wasn't meant to be a conversation stopper. I just thought you deserved to know.'

I wasn't sure what my mouth was going to say when I opened it. 'I'm glad you told me.'

His lips widened, the smile perking his cheekbones, his eyes studying my face in the pale light. 'Imagine if all this had never occurred. I would never have met you. It makes me almost glad for it all.'

I hoped blushes didn't show up in moonlight. The unreality of where we were, the sheer intimacy of it made me bold. 'Brodie?'

'Yeah?'

Electricity zipped up and down me. 'You said you wanted to be just friends …'

'That was, as I recall, before we kissed. Or do you make a habit of kissing your friends?'

I ducked my head. 'I don't make a habit of kissing anyone.'

He laughed, dipping his head so he could peer at my lowered face. He caught my eye and smiled. My pulse hit the stars and a silly grin spread across my face, matched by his. He pressed a kiss on my hair.

'What do you think he's doing?' he murmured, echoing my growing anxiety in that otherwise perfect moment.

'I don't know.' Our half hour was probably up. 'The others will be worried.'

'Can't help that. We stick together, okay?'

I nodded.

A flurry of movement beyond the barbed wire seduced my eyes, and a figure appeared among the others. I hoped it was Yuval.

CHAPTER THIRTY-THREE

18 hours until flight
1 blockade

Once we were close enough I recognised Yuval from the way he held himself. He wasn't alone, accompanied by two others, both in skirts. I wiped suddenly sweaty hands on my long-suffering pants. Our answer was coming.

He introduced one of the women as his wife. She came forward and I felt Brodie tense beside me. He was making me paranoid. Seriously, even a tiny lady was a threat?

The sad fact was, he was right. Even tiny ladies could carry knives. Or screwdrivers. I quashed my rising fear and stepped towards her. She smiled, reaching out to frame my face in her work-roughened hands. She repeated the process for Brodie, only stopping when he raised a hand to wipe his eyes.

She turned, looking at Yuval. And she nodded.

We were getting through!

Except it wasn't that simple. A nod couldn't clear all the crap blocking the road. But it seemed as if the whole village came out to help, lights and calls flickering through the dark night. My hands were torn and scratched as I hauled aside the wire and branches, but I barely noticed. Time was running out.

I tensed as an arm came around me, but it was Brodie. 'You okay?'

I nodded. 'Just worried about the time.'

He grinned. 'Even those truckies are pitching in now, it shouldn't be long.'

He was right. Yuval approached not long after and explained they'd almost cleared enough for a car to drive through. They'd remove more later, he said, so the trucks and buses would fit through, but their first priority was our flight.

'You go now,' he said. He told us to collect Trucko and drive up on the opposite lane. And he handed me a piece of paper. It was his son Esteban's details.

I looked at him and he shrugged.

'If you get the chance, let Esteban know we are thinking of him,' he said, holding his wife close.

I nodded, though it was damned unlikely we'd have any opportunity to cross paths with his son. His wife smiled at me, and impulsively I hugged them both.

Brodie and I practically pranced back towards the car, the night like velvet around us. I radiated excitement with every step; I couldn't wait to see the relief on my friends' faces.

As we walked past the tourist bus, a voice, male, hailed us. In English. A pinch like recognition, or fear, went through me.

'What's happening up there?'

I tensed. I didn't want this bus to start a stampede. Not until after we'd made it through.

But Brodie answered with the truth. 'They're taking down the blockade.'

The man swore in delight. 'Finally, I'm sick of this place and the good drink's almost all gone. I'll go tell my guides.'

Again I had that feeling I'd heard his voice before. His face was a silhouette with the fires behind, and I fought the urge to shine the torch right at him.

I rushed to interrupt him. 'They still need help, shifting some of the larger stuff. They've asked if we can bring our landcruiser to the front, to use our winch.'

The man nodded, suddenly still. There was something about his stillness I didn't like. I shuddered as soon as he'd left, and the two of us set off again, much faster than before. If just one of the larger vehicles pulled in front of us …

Brodie dipped his mouth to my ear as we walked. 'Smart thinking back there. No wonder I stick with you.'

Some of my unease melted. 'Ha! Because I'm such a good liar?'

'Ooh, now,' he teased. 'Would we call that a good lie?'

We gave the others a fright when we returned, they hustled us into the stuffy warmth with white faces and a heap of questions. I hauled myself up into the passenger seat, while a mildly happier-looking Mike made room for Brodie to tuck himself into the back seat beside him.

I forestalled all questions. 'No time, let's drive. They're opening the blockade, and there'll be the mother of all traffic jams if we don't get through first!'

Odati was at the wheel already and, like it understood the situation, Trucko's motor caught on only the third attempt. We pulled out to the left, and carefully edged our way along the stinking road towards the corner.

I clung to the hope the tourist bus hadn't pulled out already. My heart was doing a mad thumpity thump, and I knew the guys in the back seat were talking and firing questions but I couldn't take anything in. I hoped Brodie was satisfying their hunger for knowledge.

The corner came closer and it seemed we were barely crawling by the time we reached it. The road beyond the corner was revealing itself Oh So Slowly. I wanted to cover my eyes. If a watched kettle never boils, does a watched corner never turn?

Then I saw around it.

The tourist bus was still parked up in the right-hand lane.

I let out the longest breath ever, a whole double-lungful of air I'd been holding long enough to make stars dance in front of my eyes.

Odati looked at me with an amused smile. 'Relieved much?'

'Hell yeah. I just got it in my head that bus was going to go in front of us, and it wouldn't fit through, and we'd be stuck again.'

'What made you think that?'

'This tourist we talked to, there was something about him I didn't like.'

Mike laughed from the back seat. 'Is there anyone you meet and actually like the look of straight away?'

Other laughter joined his. Heat scorched my cheeks but I managed a chuckle. I *was* trending towards being overly suspicious these days.

It didn't take long to reach the blockade line. It was amazing how much had been cleared since Brodie and I left. One set of barbed wire still throttled the road between two shacks, maybe tangled in something. The truckies were attacking it with bolt cutters and verve, and like moths to a flame Brodie and Odati got out to help.

Mike half sat up, until Alice grabbed his arm. 'Not with that head, you don't!' Her expression meant business and Mike settled back in his seat with a lazy smile, like he'd got exactly the outcome he'd wanted.

I moved to get out too, but Alice stopped me. 'I know you and I could clear the whole thing in half the time, but I wouldn't want to spoil their fun. Besides, I'm simply dying to hear what happened between you and Brodie. You two were away a looooong time.'

She had a glint in her blue eyes, one provocative eyebrow daring. But I couldn't think of a situation where I would feel less like talking about whatever it was that might be happening between me and Brodie, than I did right then.

'Ah, I'm going to go thank Yuval and his wife,' I improvised.

Alice sighed. I hopped out, suddenly determined, like an idiot, to catch at least a moment of peace on my own. Totally forgetting our mantra.

We stick together.

Especially in the dark of night, where the flicker of campfires and the flash of torches makes the blackness seem blacker, and shadows slink with the gusting of the wind.

We stick together.

At least, we should.

CHAPTER THIRTY-FOUR

17 hours until flight
0 blockades
1 big mistake

I didn't find my moment of peace. Because someone else found me.

I'd wandered less than twenty metres from the remains of the blockade, beyond a small house to a spot where I could soak in the stars, and be totally alone.

Which is why I jumped when he spoke.

I whirled to look at him. A guy, maybe in his early twenties, goatee, the sort of travel gear you buy from a trendy catalogue when you've some serious disposable cash. Nothing that should ring any alarm bells, but in the flash of fear I'd felt as he spoke, I hadn't even caught what he'd said.

'Pardon?' I asked. My mind was speed-trawling through faces, sure his was one I'd seen before.

'I said, they don't seem to be using the cruiser for anything.'

I smiled nervously, wishing myself back in Trucko. 'No, that's actually *our* car.'

He cocked his head. 'I know it's your car, sweetheart.'

And all at once, I remembered. He was the guy we'd spoken to back at the tourist bus. The one Mike had laughed at me for not trusting. But now I could see his face. And he was also the Golden Boy, from Potosí.

I warned myself not to freak out.

We stick together.

My palms felt slick. The sound of workers clearing the blockade was masked by blood pounding in my ears. I looked around, hoping to see someone nearby, but they were all hauling some last thing off the road.

Why was I suddenly doing things without thinking them through first? This one would have been a cinch.

Go For A Walk In The Dark All Alone:

PROS	**CONS**
• Don't have to be teased by my FRIENDS	• Get accosted by CREEPS
STAY IN THE DAMN CAR!	

We Stick Together.

I made to move back, cleared my throat. 'Um. I have to—'

Golden Boy's hand flashed out to smother my scream. He held my back to him, hand over my mouth, as he whispered in my ear. 'I've been mouldering here for three days, sweetheart. And I don't like having a group of upstart kids jump the queue.' His hands tightened their hold, and I could smell alcohol steaming off his breath. 'Let's see how happy they are when they find they're missing their little friend. Maybe I'll help them search. But that doesn't sound like much fun, does it? So maybe I'll just wave them goodbye as my bus goes past.' He started dragging me further into the dark.

Now, then, was the appropriate time to panic.

I sent an urgent message to my limbs, my mind gathering speed as the shock wore off. I stomped on his foot, but it may as well have been an Incan foundation stone for all the effect I had. He laughed, and half-carried me back behind a slanting brick building. Out of sight of anyone who might look for me.

I tried to scream, but all I heard was a roar of triumph from back at the blockade. I guessed the road was now clear for us to go through.

They would miss me. Very soon, they would start wondering where I was.

I squirmed in his grip. One of his fingers broke through between my lips and I tasted bitter salt. I opened my mouth and chomped down on that foul finger. Hard.

That got a reaction. He swore, swinging me around with his other hand so I smashed against the wall. Weakness roiled with blackness through my body, and I struggled to stand with one leg that didn't remember its purpose in life. A slap across my face made my ears clang, but not enough I couldn't hear him swearing.

I didn't have the mental capacity to be terrified. I steadied myself against the wall, relying on his stranglehold to help me stand while I aimed a kick between his legs, pointing my toes like we'd been taught in self-defence. He crumpled, gasping, and the hand holding my collar fled to cradle his crotch.

I turned and ran blindly, literally blindly, back the way I thought he'd dragged me, using the glow from behind the building as my guide. Saplings whipped my body and fallen leaves bogged my feet. I felt I wasn't running straight, but all I could do was keep running.

I could hear his heavy steps thudding behind me.

And then my already dodgy leg caught on something and I fell. I screamed. I could hear his breathing as he came up behind me.

I tried to scrabble to my feet, but his boot crushed into my back, pressing the air out of my lungs. My mouth was gasping against the dirt and the rocks, choking for air.

'No rules remember, sweetheart,' he crowed.

And he was laughing. Well, for a moment. Then his weight was gone and all I could do was suck in air, hopefully enough that I could scream some more.

Then somewhere through the ringing in my ears, I heard Odati's voice, close by my ear, urging me up, felt her hands tugging at my arms. I made myself crawl into her, and haul in some big breaths of air, and I didn't give a damn that everything smelt of burning tyres and crap, because it didn't smell like Golden Boy. Odati was holding me to her, her hair tickling my face, and I wondered where he'd gone.

'Odati,' I gasped. I had to warn her.

Dirt exploded next to us, and something hit the wall of the house. Someone. Someone hit the wall. The someone got up, panting and swearing and the stink of booze rolled off them. I knew it was Golden Boy. But he wasn't focused on me anymore. He was focused on …?

Brodie. Lit up in the drunken light of a fallen torch.

We stick together.

Golden Boy charged at Brodie, hollering, and got a punch in the guts for his trouble. He collapsed, wheezing. Brodie circled the fallen man, with a hard, snarling focus about him. Golden Boy staggered to his feet and the two of them watched each other.

'What did you do to her?' Brodie's voice was *altiplano* cold.

'Who cares? I'll do the same to you! Queue jumpers!' And he leapt at Brodie again.

It wasn't an even fight. Brodie was better built, lighter on his feet. Sober. He easily evaded Golden Boy, landing a kick that echoed horribly and had the guy back in the dirt, quivering and moaning.

Golden Boy tried to sit up, tried to drag himself backwards, but one leg seemed dead or broken or heaven knows what, but it felt like karma to me.

Brodie started towards the downed man, and the look in his face told me he wasn't going to give him a hand up.

'Brodie!' I called, and he halted, looked at me all sprawled against Odati, and those mobile lips of his worked furiously.

'Don't,' I said. 'Please. Let's just get out of here.'

He shook his head—to clear it? To say no? 'Are you okay?'

I nodded. 'Yeah, I'm fine.' It was a lie. My face was stinging, my shoulder hurt where I'd been flung against the wall, my knee throbbed, and I felt like I wanted to vomit through my grit-fouled teeth. But nothing was worth wasting any more precious time on this loser and my idiot decision to leave the others.

Brodie's eyes narrowed and I feared I'd said that last bit out loud. 'Odati,' he said, 'why don't you take Eva back to the car? I'll be up soon.'

Odati hauled the two of us up and tugged me back towards the road. But I dug in my heels. Golden Boy groaned.

I shook my head, eyes on Brodie. 'No.'

'C'mon Eva, let's just go,' Odati urged.

Brodie's nostrils flared. 'Just go.'

'No. I made a dumb mistake, but I'm not doing it again. We stick together, Brodie.'

He cast a swift look at the figure at his feet, then back to me. His jaw was set.

So was mine. Because Golden Boy was wrong. In this new world, it wasn't that there were no rules. It was just that some of the rules had changed. 'We. Stick. Together. Let's go back. Together. You've taught him a lesson. Any more and you're becoming like him.' I held out my hand. 'Please.'

Brodie put his head in his hands, scrubbing them through his hair, then he shook his head and swore. And stalked back up the slope to me.

I was so relieved I staggered from Odati to hug him. 'Thank you, thank you both.'

His arms crushed around me. I could smell the taint of the fight on him, blood and sweat and anger. 'Let's get out of here,' he said.

'You can't leave me here!' sobbed Golden Boy.

I stiffened, worried at what Brodie might do. But he didn't do anything except speak in a measured tone, devoid of emotion. 'We'll let someone know where you are.'

And he turned and nodded to us to head back to the car. I leant on Odati, my leg still numb and sore all at once. We made it back to the road, where a worried tour guide rushed over. Brodie curtly told him where Golden Boy was, and we limped back to Trucko without a backwards look.

Odati helped me clamber into the passenger seat. The seat I'd exited not that long ago, but too long ago. Odati hauled herself into the driver's seat, giving me a tentative look. I nodded at her and smiled. She smiled back, put the car into gear, and we crawled through the newly cleared road to the cheers of the villagers. It took less than a minute to drive through a village that had kept people at a standstill for days. Out the other end, we endured the stares of everyone who was stuck that side, but I could look forward with hope to being free on the open road again.

Airport, here we come.

CHAPTER THIRTY-FIVE

16 hours until flight
5 bottles water
1 tin sardines
2 sweetened condensed milks
¾ full sub tank + 1 empty container
US$535
1 nasty pill

'So, is everyone okay?' Alice asked, when we'd been driving long enough for the chill of reality to set back in. 'Eva?'

My knee throbbed. I felt stupid. 'I'm fine.'

Odati shot a look my way.

'I might have broken a knuckle on my little finger.' Brodie sounded annoyed.

Alice seemed delighted. I stared into the inky night as discussion turned to metacarpals, punching techniques and boxing hand wraps. In the end Alice couldn't be sure if Brodie's finger was broken or not, but she thought not. She handed Brodie a wet bra in lieu of an ice pack, and told him to hold his hand still. Brodie made some joke that earned him a punch in the arm from Alice, and had Mike snorting.

I didn't hear it. I could have done with a laugh. I really hoped Brodie's finger was fine, because I didn't want another thing to kick myself about.

Then Odati dobbed me in. 'How's your leg, Eva?'

Low blow. Alice draped herself across the centre console, half over me, hands moving up and down my left leg and asking me when it hurt. Which was practically always.

'Ow! Enough!' I finally said.

'We need to know if anything's broken.'

'You'll have something broken if you keep up,' I muttered, only half joking.

Finally she sat back. 'It doesn't look good. You're reacting all the way from your hip to your knee.'

'It's probably just bruising.'

'All the way down the leg? What happened? Get hit by a bus?'

I squeezed the bridge of my nose and took a calming breath. 'No, a wall.'

'What?'

'He threw me against a wall, okay? My shoulder's sore too, if you must know. My left knee hurts the most, first it kneed the wall and then I kicked him in the nads. But other than that, I'm fine.'

The general consensus was I was NOT fine. But Alice had to admit my knee wasn't showing the classic signs of a serious problem. She handed me a wet something, which I rather feared was the same unicorn t-shirt, and made me wrap it around my knee just in case, and the medical examinations were over for the night.

I braced myself, and turned so I could see them all. I instantly regretted it because it twisted my knee—you know, the one I'd just convinced everyone was probably okay. And I took a deep breath.

'I'm sorry, guys. It was stupid of me to walk out alone. I didn't think it through. But I've thought about it ever since, and I reckon we just need to admit this isn't a piece of cake, this drive. I mean, we're all stuck in here and the world's falling apart outside. It doesn't matter a jot how wonderful you guys are, you grate on my nerves sometimes. I needed time out, and that's why I walked away, and I've realised how foolish that was.' I took a breath. 'I think we should all commit to three things. Firstly, we stick together, no matter what. Secondly, we try and be understanding of how we're all feeling. And thirdly, um. I'm sure there was a third thing but I can't remember it. So. Two things then.'

I looked around nervously, trying to judge their reaction. What stuck out was that Alice was crying. Silent tears shining down her cheeks.

'It was me, wasn't it?' she said.

'We don't need to point fingers ...' Brodie began.

Alice shook her head. 'It was me. I knew it as soon as Eva walked out. I was making fun of ... never mind. I'm sorry, Eva. I need to think before I speak.'

I told her she shouldn't worry. In truth her comment *had* been what sent me packing. But all that says is I need to grow up. Because listening to Alice tease me about Brodie would have been significantly better than going for a walk with Golden Boy.

The restraints came off after that, all the questions I'd been avoiding, and I found I didn't mind them so much. Like—What the hell happened?

When I explained the guy who attacked me was the tourist Brodie and I had talked to on the way back to the car—I could see no sensible reason to reveal he was also the Golden Boy from Potosí, it would only hurt Mike to remember that—Alice shot back in her chair, wailing about how they'd teased me about him, too. Brodie patted her on the back and I told her it was nothing. But it was Mike who worked his singular brand of magic.

'Alice, for the love of sanity! SHUT UP! Rule number two—be understanding of how others are feeling. I understand you're feeling guilty. But you need to understand I'm feeling like taking two tabs and throwing myself out the freaking window!'

Alice gulped her way to silence. Odati wobbled onto the shoulder of the road, gravel peppering Trucko's side. I just stared. Waiting for an explosion.

And it came, just not what I expected.

Alice started to laugh. Mike managed to glare at her for several seconds before he lost it too. They dissolved in the back seat, leaning against each other for support. I caught Brodie's eye and shrugged, a smile tugging at the corners of my mouth.

'Wait a minute,' Odati groaned. 'We have to go back! We left Alice and Mike behind and picked up a pair of hyenas instead.'

That set us all off.

Alice finally wiped her eyes and looked at me. 'You got him where it hurts?'

I nodded.

'And how'd he like that?'

'He keeled over backwards, groaning.'

She smiled. 'Good to hear.'

Brodie's lips twitched. 'Remind me to watch myself around you two.'

It wasn't quite right to joke about it. I knew that. But it felt much smarter than crying.

We bypassed Arequipa not long after. Its main plaza is apparently gorgeous, lined with stunning old buildings, but we saw none of that. Not even lights to indicate a city. What we did see was a major right-hand turn, pointing the way we wanted to go. We took it and—hey presto!—no town.

No riots, no shootings, no one following us in dodgy vans. No more broken windows.

Mike celebrated by falling asleep.

I started hoping things were finally going our way.

CHAPTER THIRTY-SIX

15 hours until flight
3 bottles water
1 sweetened condensed milk
½ full sub tank fuel
US$535
1 nasty pill

Alice hit the proverbial wall just after Arequipa. Her eyelids drooping, she clambered into the Nap Seat. Mike slept through, only stirring to spread-eagle across the space Alice vacated.

Odati drove on, scratching itchy red welts that had appeared all over her fingers.

'Chilblains,' Alice told her, from her sleeping bag. 'Keep them warm, O. Soon they'll stop itching, and just hurt.'

Odati snorted. 'Good to know, thanks.'

'You're welcome.'

'She was being sarcastic, you know,' I called back through a yawn.

'I know,' said Alice. 'But I also know sarcasm is a flimsy cover for deep appreciation of my stellar knowledge.'

Odati snorted again.

Soon Alice was asleep, her light snoring adding to the racket from the shopping-bag window. Her fatigue was contagious. I found myself leaning my head against the icy window, trying to keep awake.

Brodie tapped me on the shoulder. 'You should sleep.'

I looked at poor Odati, driving through the dark. 'Nah, I can stay awake.'

'I'm sure you can,' Brodie said, 'but do you need to? Sleep now, and you can sub me out later.'

'As Chief Driver-Inspirer?' I grinned.

He and Odati nodded. He was right, I knew it. But Mike was lying across nine-tenths of the back seat, making it eligible for the World's Most Uncomfortable Sleeping Position Award. I thought about the Nap Seat. 'Do you reckon Alice would mind if I went back with her?'

Odati shrugged. 'She sleeps like the dead.'

I clambered into the back, skirting Mike's bulk as Brodie and I swapped places. I could feel the tingle where Brodie's hands had held my waist as I climbed over into the Nap Seat, careful of Alice's curled-up legs and my aching knee. Brodie sighed as he took the passenger seat, stretching his legs out.

He and Odati promised to wake me when they got weary. I grabbed a spare sleeping bag and hauled it over me, lying gingerly on what had once been the backrest. It wasn't flash. In fact, it was sloping towards Alice and I was likely to end up tangled with her. But did I care? No. I slept.

The near-silence woke me. I was warm, sleepy. It was still dark, and we were still moving, but only slowly. My tummy rumbled. The constant noise from the bag-window had ceased. The reason for my warmth became instantly clear. As predicted, I'd ended up curled tightly against Alice.

That should've been fine, except I must have chosen Brodie's sleeping bag because I could smell patent spicy Brodie-scent all around me. My hormones kicked up a gear or three, and I bit my lip, reminding myself it was NOT Brodie sleeping behind me.

Mike's voice came from the front. 'There's so many of them. Hell of a pile-up. Wonder what happened.'

What was he talking about? Trucko snaked to one side and then back again. I eased myself in readiness to sit up and look out the window. And froze as someone else spoke.

'Let's just hope we get through without the same thing happening to us.'

The speaker was Alice.

And if that was Alice, who the heck was snuggled next to me?

I turned my head, searching in the dark for confirmation of what my body had been chanting to me since I woke. Brodie's long frame fitted against mine from my back to my calves. His arm draped over my waist. Instantly my blood was on fire, waking every inch of me.

Trucko swerved again, then began to pick up speed. Brodie stirred against me. He nuzzled into my neck. His lips were soft and his stubble prickled excitement.

Was he even awake?

And if he wasn't, should I wake him?

Before I could finish thinking the question, Trucko made it redundant, lurching as if we'd hit a pothole. Brodie froze. Definitely awake now, then. The shopping-bag window began to beat time as Trucko sped up.

'Eva?' he whispered, mouth tickling the curve where my neck met my shoulder, shooting sparks up to my scalp.

'Uh-huh.'

'Oh, man. Um … Was I kissing your neck?'

I swallowed. 'Yeah. Yeah you were.'

'Shoot. Sorry. I was asleep, I wouldn't normally just …'

I swivelled around further, ready to tell him he didn't need to worry about it. But instead I spotted his face—his lips—and much closer than I'd anticipated. Words evaporated from my brain. I just stared and my heart thundered and he stared back and all I wanted was for the distance between our lips to vanish.

Alice swore and I started. I'd forgotten where we were. I'd forgotten the others were there. My face felt hot. Brodie looked away, breathing out long and slow.

'What is it?' Odati asked.

'The fuel light,' Alice said. 'It's just turned on.'

Mike cursed. 'This can't be happening. We still have about three hundred k's before the next major town.'

'It's happening alright. Have a look.'

Mike muttered something about redoing his calcs as Brodie's eyes came back to mine. He flashed a rueful grin and sat up, taking his warmth with him.

'Any other towns nearby?' he asked in a louder voice.

I heard Alice swear. 'You're like a sleep ninja, Brodie.'

Mike said, 'One small town, back a bit, no diesel though. We checked. The next town is maybe fifty k's ahead, just as small on the map. Then there's Nazca, three hundred k's away. I don't think we'll make it that far.'

Silence. I guess everyone was going over dead-end options, like I was. The last time I'd run out of fuel we were on the lost side of Coolgardie and we'd had to siphon from a passing 1971 turquoise-blue Torana.

Not much passing traffic around here.

Trucko swerved. 'Sorry. More freaking dead cars,' said Alice.

'Had a few of those?' asked Brodie.

'A whole carpark's worth back there. Some mega-smash. It was messy.'

I gasped, sitting up so suddenly I almost brained myself on Brodie's elbow. 'Any of them look like diesel?'

Trucko swerved again as Alice squealed. 'Guys! Stop popping up like that! Anyone else back there?'

Odati shushed her and turned to me. 'Siphoning? Brilliant! There were a couple of older-looking trucks back there, surely they'd be diesel!'

'Have we got a hose?' I asked.

Odati shook her head. 'But one of those cars must have something.'

I felt Brodie nodding beside me.

But Mike wasn't. 'There must be another way.' He turned to Odati and Alice. 'You saw what it was like back there.'

'You're right, it's bad,' Alice said. 'But I think running out of fuel would be worse.'

'I agree,' Odati said. 'Unless you can see another option?'

Mike sighed, shook his head and hunched over.

It felt wrong. So very wrong. But Alice stopped Trucko, and a three-point turn later we were heading back. Back the way we'd come. Away from our flight. Away from our homes.

CHAPTER THIRTY-SEVEN

12 hours until flight
2 bottles water
1 sweetened condensed milk
1 fuel light on
US$535
1 nasty pill

It took less than five minutes of retracing our steps to meet the main block of abandoned cars. The others had been right. It looked like World War Three had had a vehicle party and been too hungover to clean up. After the fifth car I learnt not to look when our headlights lit their dreadful interiors. I certainly avoided looking through the windows of a minibus with a bullseye shatter pattern in its windscreen. A lot of the vehicles had been involved in a pile-up, a whole group were burned to twisted metal hulks, others looked like they'd been swept to the side of the road to clear the path we were negotiating.

'Up ahead are the trucks,' Alice said.

I could see them now, hopefully both far too ancient to think about having anti-siphon devices. We sidled up to the first and largest one, its front crumpled into the rear of a three-car pile-up.

'Keep the engine running, don't you think? At least for now,' said Odati.

Alice nodded, and I felt relieved. The thrum of Trucko meant escape, security.

No one opened a door. The world beyond our headlights seemed black as a horror film. You know, that point where you're hugging your legs under the rug and pleading with the characters to not get out of the car, you idiots.

Except we had to.

Brodie shifted. 'You guys know how to siphon? I'm happy to help but I've never done it.'

I sighed and took hold of his hand. 'It's basically like you'd think it is, so long as the car isn't newish.'

Pipe, tank, mouth. We could do this.

Alice stayed in the driver's seat, our getaway driver. Mike refused to budge from the back seat, no surprises there. Brodie squeezed my hand as we hopped out of the boot to meet Odati.

The three of us stared at each other in the silvered moonlight, before Brodie shrugged and hoisted himself up onto the bed of the truck, headtorch on. 'There's a heap of stuff up here, surely there's got to be a pipe.'

Odati moved to fiddle with the fuel cap. 'It's key locked.'

I swallowed, placing our empty fuel container at her feet. We needed this fuel. Simple fact. 'I'll check the ignition.'

I had to step up to reach the door, and at first it wouldn't budge, the crash impact must have wedged it.

Oh please, please let the driver have gone out the passenger door.

When the door finally gave, the momentum pushed me back off the step. A stench like old socks and broken fridges swirled around me and I shuddered.

I turned to call one of the others. I didn't want to go up there alone, but Brodie had found a few lengths of hose and a brief flicker of headlights in the distance told me we'd have company if we didn't get this over with soon.

I hauled myself back up until I was level with the cab. Sure enough, the moonlight was glinting off keys in the ignition. I made myself not look at the figure slumped in the seat. I held my breath. A drunken fly buzzed past, disturbed from its sleep. I grabbed the keys but they wouldn't come. Desperation made me yank them, but they still held. *Think, think Eva.* You turned the key to start an engine, did I need to turn these keys to get them back out? I tried one way, they turned but sprang back. I tried the other way.

Relief. The keys jangled into my hand. I muttered a thank you to the unfortunate driver and leaped down, breathing deeply in the fresher air.

'Here.' I handed the keys to Odati.

'Thanks. Faugh, what's that stink?'

I set my jaw. 'Let's just get this done already, there's at least another vehicle coming from Arequipa towards us.'

Brodie shot a look at me, eyebrows raised, probably because I hadn't sounded so waspish since Potosí. I grabbed the hose they'd selected, stuffing it down into the tank as soon as Odati had it open. Thinking of that scorching day out of Coolgardie, I sucked. Not with my lungs, but my mouth.

I got absolutely nothing.

I pulled away, catching my breath, and spat a few times. The hose was ten types of nasty.

'Let me try.' Brodie stepped forward. He got the same outcome.

It should be working. Unless … 'What if the engine kept running until the fuel ran out?'

Odati shook her head. 'No one would leave their engine running.'

'They would if they were dead.'

Brodie broke off, coughing, to stare at me. Odati's eyes widened and she took a step away from the truck. 'Is that the smell? Is someone …?'

I nodded. 'Let's try the next truck.'

We clambered back into Trucko. 'No luck Alice, let's try the next one.'

'Rightio. Someone's coming towards us, you know that? Man, what is that smell?'

I put my head in my hands. Was it clinging to me? Odati's arms came around me as Brodie murmured, 'Not now, Al, okay?'

The next truck was barely a truck, more a giant 4WD, faded red paint and a crumpled side. Brodie insisted on being the one to pull the fuel lever, thankfully he found no sign of a driver. My spirits rose. Maybe there'd be fuel in the tank. But Odati was shaking her head as soon as she pried it open. Inside the fuel cap, in English and Spanish, a sticker proclaimed the vehicle took petrol.

We looked wildly at each other. The flickers of light were stalking nearer.

'Any luck?' Alice called.

'None,' Odati said.

Searching the length of our headlights, I couldn't see any more trucks in the tangle.

My brain stopped for a second. 'Trucko's not a truck.'

Brodie looked at me. 'No, it's not.'

'So why are we only looking for trucks?'

'Because they're more likely to take diesel?'

'What about a minibus?'

We were back in Trucko within seconds. 'Back around, Al. There was a minibus back near the end of this pile-up,' I said.

Alice's eight-point turn hit at least four vehicles and would have failed her in any driving exam. I gave her full points. In no time we were heading back in the correct direction, towards the bullseyed minibus I'd seen before, with the unknown headlights flickering in the rear-view mirror.

Our tyres squealed as we stopped. Odati jumped out first, heading straight for the fuel cap. 'This'll open with a lever. My turn.' She didn't sound enthusiastic, but she was already heading for the front. I thought of the windscreen and shuddered.

I grabbed her hand. 'You don't need to. I can …'

'I know you can. I can too.'

I let her go. 'Of course. Sorry.'

Her feet crunched on the road base as she walked to the driver's door. Brodie kept close behind her. I readied the hose and the container, and tried not to think about what they might find. The fuel door popped open in front of me and wordlessly I checked the text on the other side.

I unscrewed the cap. 'It's diesel!'

Crunch crunch crunch. Odati and Brodie were back beside me as I plunged the hose in, and I tried to ignore the smell hanging around them. I sucked, and immediately I knew it was going to work. I bent the hose to cap it as I took a breath, and then I sucked again. Carefully. I didn't want a midnight feast of diesel.

Once you have the fuel over the highest point, gravity does the job for you. I dumped the hose in the container, and counted. Four seconds later, splashing sounds greeted me.

Arms came around me from both sides. 'It's working!' Odati called back to Trucko. Alice whooped in response.

We filled the container. Kinked the pipe as we emptied it into the tank, then began to fill it again. In the night, in the middle of a desert, surrounded by death, we were siphoning hope.

I guess we forgot about the approaching vehicle. Until its weaving headlights started to flash in fractured beams onto the vehicles around us. Trucko's engine was off. Our headlights too.

'Okay team, what do we do?' Alice whispered.

My guts did a flip. 'Hide?' I felt silly. Strangers gave me even more jitters than they had when I'd first met Brodie. I expected at least a few sniggers.

I got none.

Brodie said, 'I'm with you on that. I don't want to risk meeting anybody in the middle of the night.'

'Yeah, and we need all the fuel we can get. We can't run yet,' said Odati.

'I agree, but we have to move Trucko. We're blocking the way through.' Alice sounded clinical.

I felt like hurling, because there's no use hiding if your vehicle is blocking the damn road. I could see the approaching headlights, and the bulk behind them. Some sort of bus?

Odati paced forwards and then ran back. 'There's space ahead, if we roll Trucko forwards they might be able to get past.'

Alice called back, 'Handbrake is off!'

Brodie and I pushed, hands flat against Trucko's chill metal, feet slipping in the shrapnel left by the pile-up, my knee complaining instantly. Inertia held until Odati joined us and finally the tyres crept forward. A crunch told us we'd gone as far as we could.

Brodie's head whipped back and forth along the roadway. 'That should be enough.'

It had to be.

We hid then, the roar of the approaching engine almost covering the sound of diesel overflowing from the fuel container. Cursing, I crouched between Trucko and the stranded minibus, tubing kinked in my hands, Brodie beside me. Alice slumped as low as she could go in the driver's seat. Odati and Mike lay across the floor in the back. In the distance I heard a screech of protesting metal; the route must be tight for the approaching bus.

I bit my lip, and Brodie's hand appeared, taking the hose for me. His face was half-lit by the moon, smiling. I smiled back.

Headlights flashed again, there was another grinding of metal on metal. The bus was coming directly towards us. Trucko would be in full view for them. My boots were lit up, so were Brodie's. I refused to move an inch. *Let them not see us. Let them presume we're just another dead car in a cemetery of automotive achievements.*

And let there be enough space for them to get past.

The growl of their engine came closer, got louder, took over everything. The stench of diesel stung my eyes. My knee was pulsing pain. Then they were negotiating the turn behind Trucko, and I knew it was almost over.

Almost.

Even at super slow speed, the sound of a car crash is horrendous, especially that close. Trucko seemed to compress, caught between the bus ramming into its back, and the sedan in front. The bus's engine roared as it tried to bully its way through.

Two things happened. Firstly, I caught sight of the side of the bus and recognition hit me hard. Secondly, the sedan in front of Trucko gave way, toppling sideways off the roadway. Without its handbrake on, Trucko sailed silently forwards, rolling down onto the tussock beyond. And it left Brodie and I blinded in the headlights of the bus carrying the one man in the whole of South America with a fabulous reason to hate both our guts.

'Holy crap,' Brodie said.

'Recognise that bus?'

'I was hoping I didn't.'

He stood up. I took a few extra moments to screw the cap onto our full fuel container before standing beside him. I decided to try for a smile, then dropped it because I didn't want to look too happy, considering how Golden Boy and I had last parted. Then, worried I might seem too grim, I changed to a half-smile. I probably succeeded only in looking deranged.

The bus hadn't moved, the headlights still glared so I couldn't see anything but a double halo doused in alien abduction vibes. 'I'll run if you do,' I whispered to Brodie.

He grabbed my hand, but neither of us moved.

The bus's headlights dipped to low-beam, and a figure emerged from the bus. It looked like one of the tour guides.

He came forward, then lowered his gun. 'It *is* you. What are you doing here?'

'Running for our lives. How about you?' Brodie said.

'You're out of fuel?'

Brodie shrugged. 'Always good to have more.'

I elbowed him. 'Try to be nice,' I whispered.

The guide shot a look back at the bus. 'Have you got enough now? Because if Damon sees you, he won't be happy.'

'He's the blonde guy?' I asked, stomach curdling.

The guide nodded. 'You should go.'

I nodded back. 'We're going.'

Brodie dropped the siphon pipe and picked up the full container, oblivious to the spreading puddle of diesel he had set off. 'Thanks,' he said, and we turned to leave. 'Was that nice enough?' he murmured to me as we walked towards Trucko. Relief made me grin.

Then that cutting voice I knew so well came from behind. 'Un-freaking-believable. Look who we have here.'

CHAPTER THIRTY-EIGHT

12 hours until flight
2 bottles water
1 sweetened condensed milk
¼ full sub tank
1 full fuel container, not in Trucko
US$535
1 nasty pill
1 vendetta

Brodie froze next to me at the sound of Golden Boy's voice. 'Take the fuel and get into Trucko. I'll deal with this.' He dumped the container and spun around.

Golden Boy was limping towards us, fast. So, leg not actually broken then. Crap.

'What's he got in his hand?' I whispered.

'Please Eva, don't fight me this time. I don't want you anywhere near him.' Brodie was torn between looking at me and facing the oncoming threat.

And he was right. It was time to trust him. Like he'd trusted me to talk our way through the many challenges we'd faced so far.

So I grabbed the fuel container and started heaving it back to Trucko.

I talk better than I heave. Especially with a sore knee. That thing was heavy and I was getting nowhere fast.

In front of me Trucko chugged as whoever was in the driver's seat tried to get the engine going. Everything stank of diesel. And behind me …

Brodie's voice, hard and calm. 'Leave us alone. This isn't worth a fight.'

'Speak for yourself.'

'Put the gun away, Damon.' That was the guide, and it took every particle of courage inside me to keep dragging that container away from Brodie. Gun?

'Why should I?' snarled Golden Boy. 'I can do what I want. And what I want is to teach your stuck-up girl a lesson.'

I sobbed once, chest shuddering, and stumbled as I reached the shoulder of the road. Both myself and the container slipped down and ended in a heap on the stony desert, every bruise complaining. Gasping, I could no longer clearly hear what was being said behind me, but the tone of the conversation was going down as fast as I just had.

Alice materialised beside me, I could tell it was her by the scent of roses, and she hauled me to my feet. She grabbed the fuel container and the two of us started to carry it together. She was walking backwards, watching what was going on.

'Wait, that's the creep from Potosí?' she muttered. 'I thought he must've been the guy who attacked you at the blockade.'

I grimaced. 'One and the same, Al.'

She stared at me before turning her eyes back. So I guess she saw when Golden Boy jumped at Brodie.

I only heard the gunshot.

She dropped the container and ran towards them. I spun to see Brodie still standing, still alive, still fighting. He held Golden Boy's hand so the gun pointed skywards, the guide had Golden Boy by the neck. Another bullet fired.

And Alice arrived on the scene. From her pocket she grabbed her mini hairspray, giving Golden Boy a faceful of makeover magic. He screamed, dropping the gun to swipe at his eyes, then crumpling as Brodie's knee hit home.

For a second he lay there, silent, and I thought maybe he was dead. Brodie was breathing hard, his frame moving with each gasp.

The guide grabbed a cable tie from his pocket. Before I could think of moving, Golden Boy was on the ground with his hands clinched behind him, his guide holding the discarded gun in his face.

'Are you okay?' the guide asked Brodie.

He didn't answer. Alice did. 'Okay enough. You?'

The guide nodded. 'Smart move with the spray. You people should get going.'

'What about him?'

'I'm tempted to leave him, but I can't.' He toed the form at his feet.

Golden Boy screamed. 'I can't see! You bastards!'

'Will the blindness pass?' the guide asked.

Alice shrugged. 'Eventually.'

They nodded at each other, like maybe they both thought it wouldn't hurt Golden Boy to suffer a bit more. Then she grabbed Brodie and they began to walk towards me. Was Brodie holding his arm awkwardly?

I grabbed the container and started dragging again. Now I was closer to Trucko I could hear the engine finally rumbling, hear voices from inside.

'Go out and help them!' Odati was screaming.

I didn't hear Mike's response.

Odati snarled. 'I'm ready to drive us the heck out of here. You are doing nothing.'

A door creaked and Odati raced towards me. Between us we got the container inside just as Brodie and Alice arrived. Odati jumped into the driver's seat, slamming the door hard enough to shake the entire frame. Alice pushed me into the empty passenger seat, sitting beside Brodie in the back. My chest compressed.

Brodie must be injured.

Odati took off. Trucko's engine roared as it tackled the sandy rises and tussock. The road to our left was still choked with dead cars. We bumped over a dip and Brodie tried unsuccessfully to stifle a gasp.

I swivelled in my seat. 'What happened?'

Alice was tearing away the top of Brodie's shirt, it was dark with blood. This wasn't happening.

'Was he shot?' Odati called back.

'Talk to us, Al!'

'Yes, he's been shot! Now let me do my work.'

I felt as if all the breath had left my body.

Brodie's face tensed as Alice felt around his shoulder. 'I'm still alive, you know, you don't need to talk about me like I'm not here.'

'Brace yourselves!' came Odati's call, and I looked forwards in time to see the shadow of the road, now clear of pile-up, rearing in front of us. Trucko mounted the shoulder and all was silent for a moment before the tyres squealed down onto the bitumen. I was thrown to the left as Odati straightened us out, and then we were speeding down the road once more.

'Steady on, O,' Alice said.

'Sorry. I'm just so damn angry and scared and this is the only thing I can do right now.' But Odati did slow down. Moonlight glinted off streaks down her face.

Watching Brodie grit his teeth as Alice delved with gauze and saline, I've never felt so responsible in my life. I left him. And he got shot. *We Stick Together*. What happened to rule number one?

Alice finally straightened.

'Is he going to be okay?' I asked.

'Yeah, it only grazed the surface. I've cleaned and bandaged it. I'm pretty happy.'

Brodie forced a tight smile. 'Metaphysical high five, Al.'

'Back at ya, buddy.'

I've never understood why people cry when things turn out okay, but that's exactly what I did. Odati's hand came over and gripped my arm, and I found myself crying even harder.

Brodie leant forward and cupped my head with his good hand. I breathed him in.

'I'm fine,' he said. 'We have our fuel. He's not coming after us. You did great.'

'Great? I abandoned you, and you got shot!'

'You got the fuel and we got the best possible outcome.'

'Shot is the "best possible outcome"?'

I felt his lips smile against my skin. 'Better than dead.'

'You. Got. Shot. Brodie.'

'But we got out of there. I know it was hard for you to leave me, but it worked.'

I drew back to look at him. He was smiling, eyes intent on mine.

His smile widened at whatever he saw in my face. His hand stroked down my cheek and he kissed me.

Alice wolf-whistled and we broke apart. I looked at her and grinned a goofy grin. 'I say three cheers for Alice and her hairspray!'

She grinned back. 'When I said I had it for emergencies, I was thinking more the hair variety.'

Brodie went to clap her on the arm and then winced, the

movement aborted.

She nodded at him. 'Yeah. Try not to move it, and stuff like that. You were so brave, Brodie. And a big shout out to O as well, am I right? For helping Eva drag that butt-heavy fuel in.'

Odati's voice was acid. 'And who is the only person we're not thanking here? Because now we're all safe and no one's bleeding to death, I'd like to hear what the heck was going through Mike's brain back there.'

Oh. Yeah. The one person who hadn't said anything or done anything since we'd all piled back in the car. I looked at him, hunched up behind Odati's seat. Shaking.

'Talk to me, Mike,' she said. 'You've been my mate since kindy but if you don't say something right now, we are done.'

Mike could only moan. 'It was him.'

My heart did a double-thump. He'd recognised Golden Boy from whatever happened between them at Potosí. But Odati wouldn't have any idea about that, and she'd have no sympathy.

I had to speak up. 'Golden Boy, he was at Potosí too. I think he was the guy who sold Mike the pills.'

Brodie looked at me, eyes wide. 'What, the one who cornered you at the hostel? If I'd known that …'

I shook my head at him to stop, because at Brodie's words, Mike had curled up further.

I leaned across. 'Hey, Mike. It's okay. We're all friends. And we understand.'

He looked up, mouth harsh. 'How can you say that? That we're all friends?'

'Aren't we?'

He punched Odati's seatback and glared at me. 'How can we be friends? I've been a prick to you the entire time I've known you. That doesn't just go away. Scream at me! Call me names! I left you to struggle out there alone! I let your boyfriend get shot! Don't be so freaking nice! I'm useless and you know it!'

Odati's hands were rigid on the steering wheel, but she kept driving.

Alice reached out. 'You're not useless …'

He swatted her away. 'I'm worse than useless.'

I bit my lip and gambled. 'You're right.'

Mike froze. Brodie made a what-the-frigging-heck face at me.

I ignored him and looked at Mike again. Imagined how bad he must be feeling and smiled my kindest smile. 'Back there, you *were* useless. You're strong, Mike, you could've carried that container by yourself, you could've helped Brodie. But you chose not to. You chose to be useless. And, you know, that's powerful. Because if you don't like being useless, you can *choose* to be useful instead. Is it harder having you here, with your addiction and all? Of course it is. Do we blame you? No. Have you been an asshole to me all through school? Yes. Does that mean we can't both change? No. We can choose to start again. We're in the shit. This whole situation is shit. But we're in it together. And you guys mean so much to me. So please, Mike, see yourself how I see you. Capable, strong, funny. Brilliant with that guide book. Nice when you choose to be. So choose it more often.'

He stared at me. His mouth had lost its hard line. The bandages around his head were dusty, stained with blood. His once-beautiful shirt was filthy and torn at the neck. He looked nothing like the cocky boy from school, the one always ready for a joke at someone else's expense.

I made myself smile. 'And maybe, clean yourself up. What bin did you steal that shirt from, anyway?'

He looked down, then back up at me, brow creased. Then his face relaxed, gave a hint of a smile. 'Actually, your mother lent it to me.'

Exactly what I'd said to him when he'd dissed my shirt in Rio. I grinned and he chuckled, though his eyes were wet.

'Okay, you're on, Eva,' he said. 'Thanks guys, thanks Odati. Sorry … and thanks.' He leant forward to grip Odati's shoulders in front. She was crying again, smiling too. Brodie clapped him on the back, Alice reached over to hug him. And I relaxed back into my chair.

Alice sat back with a sigh. 'I've got to say, I'm never going to doubt Eva's instincts again. That Golden Boy was a hideous piece of work.'

I shrugged. 'I don't know. I might have been right about him, but I was totally wrong about you two when we first met. I'd convinced myself you were scoping out the station and not even travelling to Uyuni.'

Alice and Brodie shared a look. 'Yeah, about that,' said Brodie. 'We weren't actually going to Uyuni. We were just waiting to see which bus came first, and then we spotted you lot and figured you looked like you knew what you were doing so we thought we'd tag along too.'

I stared at them. 'Wait, does that mean I was kind of right?'

Their faces were tight, worried. And suddenly it didn't matter.

I burst out laughing. 'You two are so dodgy. Well, I'm glad you spotted us.'

Brodie grinned and Alice hugged my shoulder, and I turned to watch the road ahead with a smile on my face.

Not long after, we whizzed through a small town at the speed of light, leaving only a cloud of dust. The moon came out in force and glinted silver off *water*. We'd reached the coast! Wheels protested as we took a sharp right. We were on the Pan-American Highway, a massive road that travelled all the way from the tip to the top of the Americas. We'd spanned an entire continent.

We were amazing.

CHAPTER THIRTY-NINE

9 hours until flight
2 bottles water
No food except some oats we found under the driver's seat
1 fuel light on
US$535
½ nasty pill

Sunrise revealed dark circles under bleary eyes, hair standing out at strange angles or escaping plaits, bandages dusty or frayed. It also found us in a bleak desert land that, according to Mike's oracle guidebook, hadn't seen decent rain since the last ice age. A thick sea mist meant everything was cloaked in surreal.

And once again, the fuel light was gleaming. Had been for twenty k's. We'd emptied the last of the siphoned diesel into the tank hours back, under a hazy moon, to the sound of surf against cliffs.

We were approaching Nazca, and if it didn't yield diesel, we would have to do some serious outside-the-box thinking.

And if it did have diesel, I didn't even want to think what the price might be.

I clenched my hands around my sketchbook to stop drumming my fingers in a staccato beat of nervousness. Stony dunes rolled by, interspersed with windblown rags and shards of human bone. For so many centuries people had lived and died here, and the wind and grave-robbers had no respect for the dead. Fine if you're a dinosaur. Apparently acceptable if you were buried hundreds or thousands of years before. Definitely illegal if you died last week. So when does it become okay to dig up someone's bones and display them?

It was enough to make me feel insignificant.

We were nearing fifty k's on empty when Nazca rolled into view. Tawny shacks, many half-finished, blending into an ochre land. We pulled into the service station with pounding hearts, from which blossomed hope. Because not all the bowsers were roped off.

And yes, there was diesel!

But at a listed price that made my head hurt.

Our calculations called for seventy litres. That would get us to Lima with a safety margin in case of a headwind or something. But our cash wasn't stretching that far. I ignored the unhappy grumble from my stomach. There would be time to eat …

On. The. Plane.

The fuel attendant came out wielding a hand gun and a fierce expression, which tempered to something softer when he saw us. Tourists = money, I suppose.

I opened the door and hopped out to talk to him. And promptly fell against the car, gasping. My knee. I couldn't even straighten it. I felt arms around me and sagged into them, grateful for the support. Electric blue danced around my face.

'Your knee?' Alice asked.

I nodded, not trusting my voice, but when she seemed hell-bent on inspecting it right there, I held her arm to stop her. One swallow. Two swallows. Blink. Then speak. 'It's okay, I need to talk to this guy.

My knee's not going anywhere.' I hoped, anyway.

'Here, I can help.' Strong, wiry arms came around to hold me up. Alice let go, and there I was in a semi-embrace with … Mike.

Outside the car.

Helping.

Now that was unexpected. I smiled as I thanked him. Then I set my brain to fuel negotiations.

Not easy. My head was thinking litres and the bowsers were talking gallons, my hands were holding dollars and the attendant wanted Peruvian *soles*. He made it clear he wasn't pumping a drop without seeing our money first. This doused my half-formed thought to get all the fuel we needed and then throw our insufficient money at him and run. And I don't feel bad about thinking that, because the price he was asking was Simply Outrageous.

We danced a fine dance.

I pleaded the case of poor students far from home.

He told us about his pregnant wife and elderly mother.

I tried to sway him with our sorry tale of Elena's robbery, and he told me about being held at gunpoint as his tills and shelves were emptied.

Then I stopped messing around and told him how much fuel we needed and how much we could pay. No bargaining. I was too drained to keep mincing about. Time seemed to freeze. The only way I could tell it was still ticking was through the pain in my knee, pulsing with each second.

He just stared at me.

I turned to the others, defeated. 'Maybe there's another service station?'

But what if there wasn't? We needed fuel. He had fuel. But even if we dredged up every coin and note we could find we still wouldn't have enough. A week before I'd struggled to accept my bank account was no longer, my savings were gone. My parent's nest egg too. But

I was starting to not care. There were bigger problems.

I would happily give all our money away just for the chance to get to our plane. Money won't magically run your engine. You can't eat coins.

My stomach muttered in empty agreement. All we had was a pack of oats we'd discovered under the front seat. Nothing to cook them with, but still … it was food.

It was food.

My pulse quickened. 'Brodie, chuck us those oats, will you?' I asked.

He blinked, cocked his head, then his eyes widened and he spun to the car. He grinned as he tossed them to me.

I held them up for everyone to see. The attendant's eyes latched onto them. 'Do we need these?' I asked my friends.

Odati looked from me to the attendant, who had taken a step towards me like the oats were iron and he was a magnet. 'I'm going to say a definite no to that one.'

Mike shook his head. 'I'd rather be hungry in Lima than full here.'

Alice nodded.

Brodie kept grinning. 'I reckon they'll probably feed us … on the plane!'

'My thoughts entirely,' I said. I whirled to face the attendant, whose face was tight as he stared at the packet in my hand. 'All our money, plus this.'

He smiled, nodded, and relief blossomed like a desert flower after rain. The poor attendant found himself enclosed by a big blue-tressed hug. I hoped his wife, if indeed she wasn't a figure of fiction, wasn't watching because the look on that guy's face as Alice kissed his cheek was priceless.

Odati handed across half our once-precious stash of cash, and the reassuring drone of fuel pumping cut through the mist. Now we'd agreed on a deal, we became co-conspirators. The attendant got Odati to hold the fuel gun while he held the real one, sharp eyes searching through the haze of the surrounding streets.

The sound of the fuel pump wasn't so reassuring when I understood other people might hear it too. We may as well have hooked up a loudspeaker to let all the potential thugs in the area know we possessed both money and a working vehicle, and how about you stop by and rob us of both? A free ice cream to the first ten assailants.

Odati was thinking along the same lines, except probably not fantasising about ice creams. 'Anyone need the toilet, do it now,' she instructed. 'Go in pairs or threes, and get back quickly.'

Mike looked at me. 'Do you need to go? I can help you.'

'Um … Thanks Mike, but I'd prefer one of the girls. Squat toilet, you know? With a bung knee? It's going to be bad enough without having a bloke holding me up.'

Mike nodded. 'Sure, sure.' He looked at the ground, face pinched, while Alice and Brodie made frustrated gestures at me.

I swallowed. 'But maybe you could help me walk over there? Thanks for offering.'

I saw Brodie duck his head as he smiled.

It doesn't need to be said, but when your knee is knackered and it can't bend, squat toilets lose all appeal. Especially with your friend holding you up. Thankfully, Alice's toilet-side manner was impeccable. Braced against the uncertain bacteria-laden walls, arms around my waist to support my busted knee, looking at nothing as my pee foamed into the stinking pan.

The fuelling was close to done when we hobbled back to Trucko. Brodie and Odati made a dash for the loo. I found the growing fear from the attendant was contagious. I watched dust swirl around alleys and rooftops with trepidation.

Then the drone of the pump turned to a gurgle. The pumps

revved up a notch and cut out. Silence. The attendant's face fell.

The fuel had run out. I glanced at the meter, we were still two gallons short of how much we'd agreed to receive. Two gallons short of how much we'd need to make it to Lima. Goodbye safety margin.

But I didn't have time to stress about that particular problem, because Brodie and Odati were running towards us, yelling.

And not far behind them ran another problem. Well, three to be exact, and they didn't exude friendly vibes. We tumbled back into Trucko, the attendant somehow crushed in next to me, reversing with a squeal of tyres. The fuel line, nozzle still securely attached to Trucko, snapped off at the bowser and flicked around behind. I watched as it took out one of our attackers.

Odati roared in reverse halfway up the street before pulling a hand brake turn so Trucko was facing the way we wanted to go, and all us occupants of the back seat became a painful human ball against one side. Then she slammed her foot on the accelerator and aimed north.

'Wait!' I cried.

'No way!'

'But the fuel guy's here!'

Her foot lifted and the engine lurched with shock before she slammed the accelerator once more. Behind us, two figures still ran. We zoomed away, not stopping for several blocks. Then I asked the attendant where he wanted to be let out. My brow creased as he stammered out his answer, and when I relayed it, silence echoed.

'We can do that,' Brodie finally said. And the rest of us agreed.

That's how we ended up heading north on the PanAm Highway after a slight diversion past a concrete dwelling on a gritty side street. We had three extra passengers. The attendant, his very, very pregnant wife, and his elderly mother. I had to grin. He hadn't been playing me with a sob story after all.

Half an hour later we dropped them off at his mother-in-law's house, with the rest of the money we owed for the fuel, as well as the precious oats. My stomach grumbled half-heartedly to see it go, but this was about survival. About getting home.

We never even learnt their names, but even accounting for the extra two kilometres we drove to drop them off, I was glad we helped them. As we waved them goodbye, our main tank showed two-thirds full. And that had to be enough. If we drove carefully.

If nothing went wrong …

Mike said the PanAm Highway was often called the most boring road in South America. I could only agree. The land was desolate, dry, draining. The strange sea mist cleared to a vibrant blue sky and the day became stifling. In the back of the car we tore down the plastic bag window, just to feel like we weren't drowning in our own sweat.

Alice tried to fix up my knee. She wrapped it tight and rested it high, to reduce the swelling. And we sat as the monotonous desert streaked past. My pencil flew across paper recording some of the faces we'd met and the more picturesque places we'd seen on the way here.

Until Brodie, our one-armed driver at the time, broke the silence.

'Hey, there's a plane!' he said.

CHAPTER FORTY

4 ½ hours until flight
1 bottle water
No food
1/3 full main tank
US$5
½ nasty pill

Of course, aeroplanes didn't use to be all that exciting.

Mike shrugged. 'There's been heaps of …'

But his confidence vanished as he, along with the rest of us, probably began to appreciate how long it had been since we'd seen one. When you're racing to catch a plane, it's not a good feeling to know there haven't been a heck of a lot of them flying lately. I had to stretch my mind to remember.

'Potosí,' I said. 'The last time I saw a plane was Potosí, waiting for the bus.'

'That's, like, five days ago. Surely we've seen some since?' Odati asked.

Silence. We craned our necks to watch as it soared just above us.

'Looks like a military plane,' Odati said.

It was that strange semi-grey colour that's supposed to help with camouflage, but to me it just seemed to stick out more. It was big and bulky, maybe a cargo plane? My knowledge of military aircraft was significantly less than many other subjects.

Mike tried to smile. 'At least they're keeping the airspace safe for our flight this arvo!'

Brodie spoke as Trucko slowed right down, the accelerator temporarily forgotten. 'There's another ... oh no ...'

I shrank back at the sudden dread in his voice. And I saw it too. The second plane. Except it wasn't a plane.

It was too small.

The wrong shape.

And it was flying right at the military plane. And it was flying too close.

I didn't want to watch, but my eyes were frozen in place.

The impact was shockingly beautiful, colours blossoming out to encompass a much larger area than the plane had previously inhabited. Oranges and reds and yellows, and then the black, black smoke.

Then the noise rolled past us in a wave of violence, making this ludicrous fireworks display far too real. I felt sick. Mike *was* sick, his head out the open window, body heaving, as the bits and pieces of what had once been an aeroplane and people and hope started gracefully falling like too-brief meteorites.

Nothing was left of it large enough to gouge a furrow in the hillside next to us. Instead sections and parts, both metallic and horrifyingly not, rained down on the pale desert and bounced across the road.

Then Brodie's foot hit the floor, Odati screaming at him to drive. Other sounds began to return as the memory of the blast faded from my ears. Panicked cries from Alice, torn from her sleep in the Nap Seat. Retching from Mike. And an ongoing 'No, no, no,' which could have come from any of us.

Brodie drove like he couldn't get away fast enough, which only served to make me wonder who had shot down that plane, and where they were now. Not a nice thing to be wondering.

Trucko was just about the only thing moving. I did not want to become target practice.

If there was all-out war, then I didn't want to become involved. Surely it wasn't my war. I didn't want to be its statistic.

Mike slumped forward, shuddering. I had to tear my mind from the blast and put the shreds of my brain back together. How long since he had last taken his pills? I'd lost track. It was hard enough to comprehend we'd left the relative safety of Oruro only the day before. The shock and fear of a disintegrating La Paz had been exactly twenty-four hours ago. Up until then, I'd hoped society might hold up to the changes the collapse had forced on it.

But bowling up the PanAm with the shock of a downed aircraft resonating, I knew there would be backlash. There already was backlash. How many centuries have we humans relied on money to keep our processes ticking along? How long has wealth been synonymous with high status?

And now it was evaporating into the dry desert sands.

Then Mike started going troppo in the seat next to me. At least it was something I could deal with. His long frame was taut like at any moment it could snap. He looked up, and I saw his eyes. This wasn't Mike anymore. He was holding on to himself somehow, but the fight was obvious. He was crying, had scratched bloody welts down his face, only barely missing an eye.

And the only way to help him was to give him what was killing him.

'Pills!' I muttered, giving myself an order as my other hand reached for Alice's pocket, where we kept them.

But when I tipped the container, only one tiny half fell out.

The end of them.

Shit.

I grabbed Mike's face, forcing his lips open, grinding the pill against his teeth and into his gums with my forefinger. His eyes have always been dark and deep, but now they were totally black, trapped, malevolent.

The tension in him slowly dissipated and the brown began to return, his pupils retracting to a more normal size, his breathing becoming shaky rather than heaving. I felt able to take my hand away from his mouth, where I'd been holding it to make sure he didn't spit the pill out or something. Alice thrust a water bottle at him, and he swallowed a few gulps.

Mike's voice was soft, eyes half-closed. 'I'm so sorry.'

'It's okay.'

Brodie shot a look at Mike in the rear-view. 'How much did you give him?'

I think Brodie wanted confirmation Mike wasn't about to explode. But it reminded me of the empty container. 'A half.' I glanced at Alice, who nodded.

She knew. Not just A Half. The Last Half.

It wasn't a nice feeling. But we'd be on the flight in a few short hours. We'd be able to get help for Mike, to get him safely over his addiction. We'd be okay.

Brodie's shoulder was troubling him, so he ended up between Mike and I, and Alice took a turn driving. I stared out the window, too keyed up even to try sketching. Instead I wrote a mental list:

Bad Things
1) Running out of time to catch plane
2) A plane just got shot down—will ours?
3) Ran out of Mike's pills—he's going to have to go cold turkey ... not going to be pleasant

I had this nagging feeling there was something extra bad that I'd forgotten to add. Yeah, I know, like the other three weren't bad enough.

Mike finally broke the tableau, picked up his guidebook and flicked to some of the map pages. He took out a pencil and began scribbling notes and calculations. The drug swung him from demon to nice-guy pretty quickly. I still wasn't used to it. I hoped I'd never need to get used to it.

Finally he spoke. 'We're going to make it in time.'

'Are you sure?' Odati asked.

Mike nodded. 'Yeah, based on how far we've travelled since Nazca, we're going to be there about 2pm.'

An uncertain silence followed. The flight was 3:10. It sounded too good to be true.

'Anyone else not particularly thrilled with the idea of getting on a plane anymore?' Odati asked.

I shuddered and felt the pressure of Brodie's hand on my knee.

Mike's eyes glowed as he leaned forward. 'Watching that plane being shot down is the best thing that could've happened to us, can't you see?' He shushed our horrified reactions. 'I don't mean it was a good thing to happen, but at least we *witnessed* it. We know the risk now. We get on our plane this afternoon, and we tell Miss C what happened, and they can adjust our flight path, head straight out over the water.'

His words succeeded in reminding me we would be back with Miss C in mere hours. And of course, he was right. Relief felt like cola at an Uyuni bar, buzzing as it went down.

Tumult. Realisation. Even joy. We were going to make it!

CHAPTER FORTY-ONE

3 ½ hours until flight
Below 1/3 main tank
US$5
No water
No food
No pills

I felt off-kilter. I forced myself to stay awake, to be there for Alice as the others fell asleep. Point out the occasional bird, an ancient carving in a hillside. Anything.

Not that running into someone was going to be an issue out there. But running off the highway was certainly on the agenda.

I became aware of being watched after a while, and turned to find Brodie's blackened eyes studying me.

'You okay?' I asked him.

He smiled. 'Yeah. Great sleep.'

'Does it hurt much?' I reached up to touch his nose, where the swelling remained around the bridge.

He grinned. 'Only when I touch it.'

I pulled my hand back and felt a blush rise to my cheeks.

He chuckled. 'Knee hurt much?'

'Only when I move it.'

His smile widened and I grinned back. We sat next to each other, holding hands. And I managed to escape my unease. Alice and Brodie swapped places about 1pm, when the dream of Lima seemed just ahead of us, and Mike slept on, oblivious. I started to bite my fingernails.

When Trucko's clock displayed 1:16pm, Brodie said something you never want to hear when you're racing for the most important flight of your life.

'Uh oh.'

Steel fingers gripped my stomach. 'Uh oh, what?'

'Fuel light just turned on.'

Ah. Yes. That was it. What had been gnawing at me. The fourth Bad Thing to add to my list.

Two gallons of diesel never received in Nazca + extra distance driven to drop off the attendant x extra speed escaping downed plane = Big Problem.

The flurry of reaction woke Odati and Mike. Some questions we didn't know the answers to, like how many kilometres could we drive with the fuel light on? At least fifty, we knew that much. Some we could answer ourselves, like how many kilometres did we still have to go? It wasn't long before a road sign flashed past.

'Sixty-five to Lima,' I breathed.

'Where's the airport?' asked Brodie.

I didn't know. It could be somewhere close, maybe right near us. Or it could be on the other side of the city. I crossed my fingers.

Mike and his guidebook swapped spaces with Odati in the front.

As we slipped into the streets of Lima, Alice took my hand. It was evident peace had fled the capital.

Burnt-out cars, broken windows, dug-up streets. We passed a drunken blue neon sign: *CAMBIO*. Now crippled and lifeless, it advertised a money changing service. Desks were tossed out on the street, grimy paper still flickered where it was trapped beneath bricks and shards of glass.

The streets were silent, lit with the cheery mid-afternoon sunshine. Our tyres crunched over the stinking detritus of an overturned bin. The sound of our engine reverberated down the street, making shattered windows shimmer and refract glittering rainbows. Mangy cats slipped into the shadows as we passed.

We went around corners without sounding the horn.

Odati spotted the twitch of a curtain on the third floor of a building we passed. Our first sign of human life. Brodie reckoned he saw a figure flit across the road in our wake. If people inhabited those streets, they were anxious to stay hidden. Was that because they feared us? Or feared something much worse that was loose out here? My stomach filled with twitching alpaca ears.

We were weaving down an avenue when a blast went off somewhere to our right. Distant. Eerie. Resonant. The gentle patter of gunfire followed.

None of us so much as flinched.

'Another half a k and we should see a turnoff for the airport,' Mike said.

Alice looked at him. 'How much longer, do you think?'

'Can't be more than three-quarters of an hour.'

All at once we were twisting arms to check watches and bending heads to read the front dial. It was 1:40pm. Our flight was leaving in one and a half hours. And we were going to be on it.

If we found our way to the airport.

If the fuel held out.

If no one shot us.

If...

So many ifs.

But what if we actually made it? What if?

'I hope they open the airline lounge,' I said. 'I could do with a cup of tea.'

'And an apple danish,' Odati said. I looked across at her, and we grinned.

Alice grabbed both our hands. 'Screw that! I'm heading straight to the bar!'

An army checkpoint materialised in front of us, and we gagged on our laughter.

It was formidable.

It meant business.

Cold eyes watched as we approached, six weapons trained on us.

'We get through here, we're safe.' Brodie's jaw was set firm.

I wanted to agree, because surely this checkpoint marked the end of lawlessness, but the words wouldn't form. All I could think about was the glaring lack of entry stamps in our passports.

We were illegal. And judgement was coming.

CHAPTER FORTY-TWO

80 minutes until flight
1 fuel light on
5 passports without entry stamps
US$5

Passports were handed my way in the loaded silence. Brodie brought Trucko to a standstill in front of the barrier and I bit my lip and rolled down the window.

The soldier who approached us was young, eyes so sharp I couldn't look at them. Like smiling at an Andean ridgeline, with about as much likelihood of getting a smile back. My hands shook as I passed him our documents.

He looked at the passports, studying a few, barely seeming to open others. Five times he looked up, comparing photos with our bedraggled reality. And each time I fooled myself that he'd thawed somewhat.

Ice Man told us to wait, and walked away to talk with an imposing officer behind the barrier who reminded me of my old gym teacher, Mr Balio.

I caught Brodie's raised eyebrows. 'He says we have to wait. I was just thinking, there aren't many other options.'

Brodie smiled, then turned back to tapping out a frenetic tune on the steering wheel with his good arm. I fought the lead lump that was settling in my guts. The two army guys reviewed our passports and talked at length. I ruthlessly stamped down on the urge to tell them we had a flight to catch. But still, we did have a flight to catch.

Aeons later they turned, and both walked towards us. Ice Man was carrying our passports, while Mr Balio's body double was smiling.

And it was a nice smile. My heart fluttered back into life.

Mr Balio spoke in perfect English. 'Welcome Odati Richards, Mike Cho and Eva Somerville. We have been expecting you. I am glad you have made it. We have little time, so I will not hold you any longer. You are free to go through. Good luck.'

Relief.

Absolute relief.

After everything we'd been through, we were safe. The levels of adrenaline in Trucko dropped perceptibly.

Ice Man handed back our passports and I gripped them, already starting to stumble through a grateful speech when my throat contracted.

The bundle in my hands wasn't large enough.

I stared down. Only three passports. All dark blue. Alice's hand came across, trying to find the missing maroon bindings.

'What about us?' she asked.

Mr Balio responded. 'You other two are not on our list. You have no entry notations for Peru. We will have to investigate further before we allow you into the safe zone.'

His English was faultless, but I didn't understand him. 'But, none of us have …'

'Eva! Stop it!' Brodie was glaring at me from the front, and my arguments dribbled into confusion.

'What's happening?' asked Mike.

'They're not letting us through, are they?' Alice whispered.

Odati smothered Alice in a sideways hug. 'This is bull!'

'It is,' Brodie said, 'but it's real. And you three have a plane to catch.'

'So do you!' Odati cried.

He shook his head. 'We were only ever hoping, from the moment we spotted you at that Potosí bus station. It's your plane. And you need to go *now* to catch it.'

His lips were pressed tight, and I don't know if he was avoiding looking at me, but it sure seemed like that. I was fighting a battle not to cry, trying to imagine what it would feel like to leave Brodie and Alice behind.

I had that uncomfortable about-to-hurl kind of sensation.

Mike was giving an encore of the failed Chilean border bid, head buried in his hands, shoulders shaking the passenger seat. The maelstrom kept swirling around him, but I don't think it was anything to what he was dealing with inside.

Brodie opened his door and got out.

Odati opened her door and got out.

Like this was a normal driver changeover. Even though Brodie wasn't making any move to climb into the back. As if dumping them was standard procedure.

Alice was a vision as she followed Odati out. Black regrowth shaky at her roots, cheeks red and blotchy. Face set.

I needed to think. I couldn't think. I shuffled across to be closer to them. This couldn't be it.

Brodie and Odati embraced, Alice dragged bags out from under the Nap Seat with fierce concentration. The strings of Brodie's guitar thrummed indignantly as they caught on some chair appendage on the way out.

I blinked. 'No!'

Odati winced and climbed into the driver's seat. 'It sucks but it makes sense. We can help Brodie and Al once we're safely through.'

I shook my head. 'This makes no sense at all!'

She bit her lip. 'What choice do we have?'

Everything crystallised and my brain started functioning again. 'The same choice we've always had. Rule Number One: We Stick Together. We don't leave them.' I looked at Alice. 'We stick together.'

She smiled. 'You're so sweet, but sometimes you're a dill. Rule Number One is out the door, Eva. You need to catch your plane.'

Images flashed through my mind. My parents. My bedroom. The sleepy hammock in the old plum tree out the back.

All I had to do was abandon my friends.

I shook my head again. 'No. We stick together.'

Brodie's eyes latched onto mine. 'If you miss your plane because of us, I would simply hate myself.'

'I'm not suggesting anyone miss the plane. I'm saying let's all catch it *together*. We haven't even tried to convince them to let you through. We don't try, we can't win.'

He leant in through the window, eyes fierce. 'You don't try, you can't screw your own approval. Just go, Eva. Please. Odati, just drive.'

I shook my head. Odati was staring, mouth twisted in what I guessed was sympathy, otherwise she'd eaten something bad for lunch. Except we didn't eat lunch.

So …

I ached for a sheet of paper and some time, because I desperately wanted to list out the PROS and CONS for this one. But I didn't have time. I made my decision anyway. 'No. We stick together.'

But Odati slammed the driver's door shut, crunched the car into gear, shaking me into reality.

'What are you doing?' I asked.

'Leaving, like they want us to.'

Panic clawed at me and I slid back across the seat to the side where the army guys were still watching us. I opened the door. 'No! If *we* can get through, why not them?'

I swung my legs around, determined to get out of the car. I focused on Mr Balio. 'Please. There must be something you can do.'

His face twitched into impassivity, the way the real Mr Balio's used to when I was trying to convince him I shouldn't have to play hockey in the rain. I hopped down from the car with the solid intention of talking to him face-to-face, but found myself swooning into his arms instead. My knee!

It wasn't exactly the composed approach I'd intended.

CHAPTER FORTY-THREE

70 minutes until flight
1 fuel light on
3 passports accepted
2 passports rejected
US$5

Yeah, I'd forgotten my leg was busted. But my knee certainly remembered.

As I crumpled, I heard cries of alarm from behind me, muffled by a ring of chagrined apologies passing between myself and Mr Balio, a chorus of blushing. He deftly manoeuvred so he was supporting me rather than the two of us quasi-embracing.

'You are hurt?' he asked.

I nodded. 'I was kind of kidnapped at a blockade back near Arequipa … it's a long story. But that guy you're refusing entry to, he saved me. And when I was being dragged out of the car by a rioting mob at the border, the girl with the blue hair did everything she could to protect me. Please, sir, I'm begging you. Let them through.'

His eyes were closer than I would normally be comfortable

with, but I took advantage of that, holding his gaze.

His dropped. 'They don't have entry permits.'

I opened my mouth and closed it again, Brodie's words ringing in my ears. If I spoke now, we could all be marooned in the danger zone. I couldn't say it, and I hated myself for my silence.

So Mike's voice surprised me with its tranquillity. 'Neither do we.'

Several things happened at once.

Behind me, Brodie swore so loudly several soldiers took a step in our direction. The arm supporting my waist tightened as Mr Balio flashed a querying glance at the Ice Man soldier, whose cool composure had shattered.

And Odati gasped, 'Mike! No!'

I heard the dull creak of the passenger door opening, and Mike was there beside me, facing back towards Trucko, one hand on my arm. 'Eva's right. We stick together. I'd be dead without you lot. More times than any of you could ever manage. I owe you all. I'm not leaving anyone behind.'

He caught my eye, a totally different Mike to the one from school. Serious. Vulnerable. I nodded at him.

Behind Mike, Ice Man was twitching fingers in my direction. I knew what he wanted. Our passports.

The game was over.

The old one anyway.

I dredged up a smile for Mr Balio. 'Sir, what Mike is saying is the truth. When we crossed the border, our mere presence caused a riot, and your border guards chose to let us through straight away. Their decision saved our lives.'

He looked unaffected.

I pressed on. 'It's not our fault we don't have permits. Please don't punish us for being victims of this collapse.'

He bridled. 'There is no collapse …'

'Then why are you guarding a safe zone?'

'We are experiencing temporary security issues.'

He didn't even look like he believed what he was saying. I shrugged. 'I hope you're right, but I've seen enough dead people these last two days. We're kids, sir. We're foreign students. I'm the only one who speaks any Spanish. We have no money, no one to protect us. No one except you.'

He winced, looking past me. I hoped he was looking at the others. I hoped we looked suitably bedraggled. I remembered us all looking pretty awesome and tough, but I was hoping to an outsider with no idea of what we'd been through, we would just seem bedraggled.

I pressed on into his silence. 'Our teacher obviously trusted you. She asked you to look out for us. And you have. Please. Just let us through. We want to go home.'

Was he wavering? He needed something to push him over the edge. Onto our side.

I asked Mike to pass me my daypack. Not much in that fraying bag of mine. My only tools. My best weapons.

I grabbed out my sketchbook and a beautiful 4B that spread like a satin sheet. I didn't bother with the coloured pencils. I didn't need colour in my stand-off with Mr Balio's doppelganger. With faces it's all about expression, perfect use of lines to waken the paper. With faces, colour is irrelevant.

I drew. As quickly as I could while still imbuing soul into the people I created. Mum on the edge of a smile, like when she's about to win a trick at cards. Dad the way he stares out the window, waiting for inspiration, except I made him stare out of the paper. My pencil flowed with love and longing.

I stabbed it down with emphasis. 'These are my parents, sir. I want to go home to them. We all do.'

Mr Balio looked at me again, so long I was wondering whether if I blinked I'd lose the game, and we'd be tossed back onto the dangerous streets outside.

Then he nodded.

'You can go through.'

Mike and I got halfway through a whoop of joy before Mr Balio raised his free hand. 'But only you Australians. We've been asked to help you and help we will. The others will have to wait until we can contact their consulate.'

I choked on my premature joy. Full circle completed. Begin again. It hurt.

'You have phone coverage here?'

Mr Balio worked his lips before shaking his head. 'Not often.'

'Is the British Embassy still operating in Lima? You'll talk in person?'

A reluctant shake. 'No, there was … it was … No. No it's not open anymore.'

He knew it and I knew he knew it, but I asked anyway. 'So how will you contact anyone about Brodie and Alice?'

'They will have to wait.'

'Well then we'll all have to wait. We're sticking together, sir. We won't abandon them now.' And I raced out a simple portrait, all five of us, arm in arm. The work of moments, but each line told more than any line I'd drawn before.

He hesitated, confliction running laps around his face. 'That's your choice.'

'And I've made it. Have you made yours, sir? Do you want to explain to two governments, to our parents, why you sent us back into a war zone?'

As if on cue, a bomb went off a few streets away. Mr Balio didn't take his eyes off me. Gunshots echoed too loud for comfort, and I could sense change around me.

'Please, sir.'

Army uniforms whipped around, orders snapped back and forth. Trucko's doors creaked and slammed. And I willed Mr Balio to see it from our side.

He shook his head, as if fighting a battle inside as well as out, then he pinned me with his eyes. 'Who let you through at the border?'

I hung my head, I couldn't remember her name. I couldn't even remember if I'd ever learnt it.

But inspiration hit, and I fumbled with my sketchbook, flipping back a few pages. Back to my memories of the border crossing. And there she was, a single sketch in a ring of memories. The look on Alice's face as she gripped the steering wheel. Brodie's strong hand on my arm. The Bolivian officer who was so kind.

I pointed to the stern Peruvian guard in the centre of the page. 'Her. She let us through.'

Finally Mr Balio gave in. 'I know her. Okay.' He paused, and I didn't dare breathe. 'Okay, okay. You can all go through. Go now. Go quickly.'

Another massive explosion sent hungry shrapnel flying in search of a meal. But wild joy was racing through me. I was dizzy with it. More reports echoed off the broken buildings around us. Mr Balio nodded at me and then was gone into the melee. I was left swaying on my feet.

The sound of fighting was everywhere. Dust. Cries. Guns. Ice Man screaming at us, 'GO!'

Shouting.

Brodie yelling at us to get in the car.

I gripped Mike's arms. He shot one final glance at the battle going down and then practically threw me into the back seat.

Go! Go! Go!

CHAPTER FORTY-FOUR

60 minutes until flight
1 fuel light blinking

Trucko squealed into motion, tearing through the barricade, now unmanned as the fight in the street behind intensified. The passenger door Mike never got around to shutting swung in a wide arc before clipping a pole and slamming shut with an echoing violence.

So much time wasted at that army checkpoint.

But how could it be wasted when we were all still together?

Hours could have passed at the checkpoint, or barely minutes. My memories felt like random pictures grouped together. I whipped my head around to check Trucko's seats. We were all there. All five. Still together. Hard to comprehend.

Alice was next to me, tears trailing dirty cheeks. She smiled and her arms came around me and we squeezed each other tight.

'We're through!' she whispered.

I drew back to look out the window at white high-rises whipping past. Odati was driving us fast down a six-lane highway. Green parklands, trampled flowerbeds, a definite reduction in deconstructed vehicles. 'Lima looks nice …'

And then I saw something else. A plane, taking off. Serene in the cloudless blue sky. And it was like my stomach had been crushed under a pile of broken bricks.

I yelped.

'What? What's going on?' Odati yelled.

'Plane,' Mike said, frowning at his watch. He twisted to show us. 'Man. Does that say 2:05? Or 3:05?'

Our plane was leaving at 3:10. He was shaking so hard it was difficult to read his watch.

Alice looked at the dash. '2:05. It's 2:05. We're okay.'

I settled back in my seat, head dizzy like I was trying to sing on the altiplano. 'We're okay,' I repeated.

Mike lent his forehead against the seat back and laughed. 'We're okay.'

I giggled, edge of hysteria and all that. I didn't care. It felt good.

'We're not okay yet.' Brodie's sharp tone brought me back to myself.

I stiffened. I knew we weren't. But we were a Trucko-load more okay than we'd been before we crossed the barricade.

Alice touched my arm. 'Brodie's got a point. We need to keep focused until we're on that plane.'

I nodded. I stared at the beautiful buildings passing us by, but I couldn't catch the euphoria I'd enjoyed before.

Mike was concentrating on his guidebook. 'We can't be much more than two k's from the airport, and there's still thirty minutes. I think we'll make it!'

I'm not badly superstitious, but that felt to me like asking for trouble. Not long after, the engine gave a laboured chug. Odati frowned. Trucko gasped to a stop. Ahead of us was a glimpse of the entry ticket machines for the airport carpark. It was not a place I would choose to park.

'What's up?' Brodie asked.

Odati swivelled round. 'We're out of fuel.'

Silence.

Our fuel light had been on for so long, we'd grown accustomed to its glow.

Mike shook his head. 'No freaking way. We run there!' He jumped out of Trucko in a graceful leap and pointed straight ahead. 'There's the tower! We can still make this.'

Alice tumbled out after him, dragging bags along with her. Hers was on and buckled as she touched the ground. 'Let's run like our lives depend on it!'

No one mentioned that maybe they did.

It was a riot of backpacks and urgent voices. Two kilometres, Mike had said. Probably less now. And less than half an hour until take-off. I opened my door, swung out my good leg in readiness to take the leap. I mean, I wasn't really up for running but after everything we'd been through, I was going to give it my best shot.

Except Brodie was there. Eyes more grey than blue. 'Give me your hand. Ouch, not there.' He lifted me into a fireman's carry and turned to run.

'I have your backpack, Brodie,' Mike called, running past with his battered daypack on his front and Brodie's monster pack on his back.

'What about your guitar?' I protested to Brodie.

'Stuff the guitar!' he said. I hugged him tighter with my arm.

'Let's go people!' Odati yelled, dashing past.

We were off. A ludicrous, jogging assemblage of shapes that didn't even seem to be human. Not that I saw much of it. What I did see was lots of Brodie's shoulder. The fireman's carry was not as comfortable as I'd imagined. And since I'd always imagined it would be quite uncomfortable that's saying something.

I heard a whoop from Alice and risked a sideways look to see the unmanned ticket booths whipping past. We were technically inside the airport.

The pace had noticeably slowed. Puffing and rhythmic gasping breaths rattled through the air around me. Everyone's feet seemed silent on the smooth bitumen in comparison to the breathing. Brodie was heating up, but he wasn't labouring too hard. Three cheers for rugby training.

I caught glimpses of Mike behind me, face red. Then I saw something else.

'Trolley!' My cry came out strangled but I managed to point with my free arm. Brodie's steps faltered, then kept going. Just as I was figuring no one had heard me, he stopped and I found myself twirled into a baggage cart. With barely a moment's pause he was running again, pushing me in front of him. Odati was loping ahead of us and when I looked behind, Mike was pushing Alice and two backpacks in the trolley I'd seen first. He looked beat. Alice looked colourful. Forget the full rainbow, she was just red and blue.

Brodie just ran. 'We … gotta … stop it!' he panted.

Turning to face forwards again, I immediately saw what we had to stop. Over a chain-link fence with one huge gate padlocked shut and covered in multiple warnings about not entering …

Our plane.

The boarding steps were pulled up to it. I could see a lone figure standing at the top. I yelled, waving my hands. But over the roar of the engines I had no chance. The figure came down the steps and disconnected them. The airline doors shut. The stairs began to roll away.

Odati smoothly changed the trajectory of her run, and headed towards the fence. She flew at the wire, climbing it like an army recruit with a grenade in their lunchbox. She vaulted the top and scaled halfway down the other side before dropping to the ground. She was off running again immediately. Towards the departing steps.

Brodie pulled up at the gate, breathing in heavy gasps. I gripped the slick metal of the trolley and watched Odati and just plain *hoped*.

The figure pulling the steps stopped short. The guards at the terminal doors put up their hackles, guns appearing in brawny arms.

My heart stopped, and then leapt back into action at triple pace.

Breaking into a secure zone in an airport in a militarised zone in a country in the middle of upheaval in a world reeling from the total reshuffling of economic theory was probably not a smart thing to do. Especially if you couldn't speak the language to tell them why you'd done it.

But it was a very brave thing.

The guards were well trained. I didn't get halfway through yelling *'¡Somos estudiantes!'* before they fired.

My heart stopped.

And Odati fell, in a slow arc, onto the tarmac.

They surrounded her, ordering her to take off her backpack, but she was beyond understanding even if they'd been speaking English. She lay there, clutching her leg, fingers fluttering like a moth flown too close to the flame.

'No!' Mike's cart hit the fence with such force Alice almost ricocheted into the wire.

I kept screaming we were foreign students. The plane crept away and I barely noticed. I certainly didn't care. Because it was Odati on the ground out there with guns pointing at her from all angles and her blood dripping onto the bitumen.

One of the guards noticed us and paced over, alarmingly composed, frustratingly slow. I clung to the fence as the words bubbled out of me. We were students. Odati was just a student. Just a student who wanted to go home. Our teacher was on that plane. That's why she jumped the fence.

Please.

But the message didn't seem to be getting through, and the other guards were still shouting at Odati. So I shouted at her too, screaming over the rising roar of the plane.

'Your daypack! Take it off! Take off the bag!'

Finally her arms extricated themselves from backpack straps.

Finally, the guards shut up so only the scream of the plane engine could be heard. Hot tears burned my cheeks.

'*Somos estudiantes. Por favor.*'

And we seemed to pass a test. They started to listen to me. A couple of them gave Odati first aid. The lady who'd been pushing the boarding steps called the plane up on the radio.

It slowed down.

And stopped.

Silence. The whine of wind through the security fence. I closed my eyes and made myself breathe.

After everything, despite injuries and cobblestoned hurdles, we had made it. I imagined Miss C and Sarah looking out the windows and seeing us. And I imagined them crying as hard as I was.

I was glad on so many levels that it was over, because I had nothing left to give.

The lady-of-the-steps came over to the fence, and I blinked hard, focused on what she was saying.

'Where are you from?' she asked in Spanish, and I repeated my spiel once more.

She frowned at me. 'What is your business in Peru?'

'We're here to catch this plane home.' I gestured at the now stationary plane. It was much smaller than I'd expected.

Her frown deepened like she couldn't understand me. Then she spoke and it was my turn to frown. She repeated what she'd said and I understood it as perfectly as I had the first time. Nothing was wrong with my language skills. I swore in Spanish just to prove it.

'What?' Brodie asked.

I tore my disbelieving eyes away from Odati's contorted form.

I opened my mouth but nothing came out. I tried again. 'It's not our plane.'

'What?' Three voices at once.

'It's not our plane. This plane's taking medical supplies to towns in the north.'

Their faces changed to horrified comprehension. With clarity I saw how very, very achingly tired they looked. Brodie buried his face in his hands for a moment before searching the tarmac for any other planes. Mike sunk to his haunches.

Alice looked at me. 'What's going to happen now? Will we be arrested? Will Odati?'

I shrugged, feeling everything green inside me wither to sooty greys and dusty browns.

I turned back to the guard and the steps-lady on the other side, but failed miserably at forming a question. No other planes were moving out there. Where was ours? Where was Miss C? Sarah?

Brodie reached out to touch my shoulder, alerting me to the guards now surrounding us. They made it clear we were to go with them. I staggered as Brodie turned my cart around. I don't know how any of the others managed to find the strength to walk.

They took us to a room, standard luridly uncomfortable airport chairs around a table. It didn't seem like an interrogation chamber. Mike supported me into a seat. They offered us weak tea and stale biscuits, mouth-watering after Trucko-rations. They found us someone who spoke English. He seemed kind. He and two airport officials spoke rapidly in Spanish, but the words flowed over me. Maybe our flight had only been delayed until the next morning. I could barely care. I only wanted to know how Odati was.

The interpreter finally told us she was fine, if you could call being under arrest and having a bullet dug out of your thigh fine.

I couldn't.

The hands on the clock on the wall ticked around and by the time they reached 4pm we knew two things.

We weren't flying anywhere that day.

Odati was going to be okay.

I didn't have any tears left.

CHAPTER FORTY-FIVE

No flight
No food
No money
No fuel
No pills

The interpreter asked if we had anyone we could stay with in Lima? Anyone we knew? We weren't allowed to stay in the airport. Security protocol or some such bull.

'Surely it's just a night or two!' I pleaded.

He shook his head. 'There are no further evacuation flights scheduled. But we will advise you if that changes.'

I've never felt so lost. I needed to not be responsible for myself or anyone else any more. I badly wanted to hug someone, someone who could pat my back and tell me it was going to be okay and they were looking after me. I was more needing my mum, but even a flight attendant, or Miss C, would be great.

I cried out. 'Miss Cooper! Our teacher! She was going to be on the same flight as us, she must still be here too …'

The man shook his head. 'All the other Australians flew out today.'

A biscuit/tea sludge rose in my throat and I swallowed painfully. 'No. We were here at 3:10 and they didn't take off.' My hands searched my pockets for proof of the flight time, but the scrap of paper I found wasn't the note from Miss C.

The interpreter winced. 'The flight was moved forward. I can confirm the rest of your class were on it. I'm so sorry.'

Alice leant into me and I put my arm around her.

Mike was watching us. 'That plane just after the barricade?'

No wonder it felt wrong, watching it leave …

The man cleared his throat. 'Is there somewhere else, someone else you can stay with? If you have someone, we might consider releasing your friend into your care rather than pressing charges.'

I badly wanted Odati with us rather than alone in some cell. Now more than ever, we had to stick together. But we didn't know a single person to quote as our contact.

My fist was still gripping the crumpled paper I'd mistaken for Miss C's note. But it wasn't hers. An unfamiliar hand, the letters more angular than I was used to seeing.

I gasped, making Alice jump. 'Yes! Yes, we have someone we can stay with.'

The others stared at me like I was mad, but maybe that brilliant kind of mad that can work miracles. I didn't bother trying to explain. I read out the details on the paper for the man to annotate our file with.

Esteban Villca. Student. Collegio de Salvación.

I passed the paper over so he could copy the address.

'How do you know Señor Villca?' he asked.

And I thought of that blockade near Arequipa and smiled. 'We're friends of his parents.'

The man nodded.

CHAPTER FORTY-SIX

No pills
All 5 of us still alive

As soon as the door shut I was engulfed in a three-way hug.

Someone who looked like a doctor came in later and talked to us, well, Alice mainly, handing her a roughly scrawled list.

How often to bathe a gunshot wound.

How often to change the bandage.

What painkillers to use.

What antibiotics she'd need.

I didn't have any time to feel scared before Odati was wheeled in on a flimsy airport wheelchair. Her skin looked blanched but she was smiling. I wasn't sure whether hugging her was going to cause her more pain, but I couldn't get up anyway. The others made up for my static nature.

We were together again.

The next day we could figure out what the heck we were going to do. But in that moment, all we needed to focus on was getting somewhere safe where we could start to recover.

The immigration guys drove us in an airport van to Esteban's boarding school. On the way we passed Trucko, tired but proud on the side of the road. It was already jacked up and missing all four tyres. I thought about Brodie's prized guitar, but they wouldn't let us stop. They kept their guns out and their eyes sharp.

So perhaps Safe Zone was something of an aspirational title.

It didn't take long for the van to turn into a driveway leading to a collection of imposing looking three-storey buildings. Some were beautiful and old with towers in the corners, others utilitarian red brick. Moths filled my stomach, fluttered up my throat. I held Odati's hand like it was the sole path to convincing this school to take us in.

We were met by armed guards, scarcely older than us. Students, though we didn't know that at the time. When they heard Esteban's name, they nodded and I smothered a sigh of relief. He was, at least, still alive by the look of things.

Their principal came out then, a formidable looking woman by the name of Sister Gracia. And standing a respectful distance behind her was a boy, he had to be Esteban, eyes curious as he studied us perfect strangers claiming his friendship. I handed Yuval's note to the Sister, and she passed it on to the boy. He took one look and then he nodded.

He must have recognised the writing.

Sister Gracia took us in like injured kittens. We were assigned beds, had showers, and ate beans and rice tasting better than anything else we'd ever eaten in the history of eating. That evening we gathered with Esteban and the other students in one of the common rooms, slouching into comfortable chairs. We spoke about his parents, about his town. He soaked up everything we had to say. His English wasn't perfect but it worked.

It was hard to stay awkward when we were warm and relatively safe and everyone was so friendly. Odati was cocooned on a sofa with about eight attentive boys hovering around her.

We weren't flying home.

But our classmates were. Miss C was.

And we had found somewhere safe enough to wait. I didn't have much to complain about.

The couch dipped next to me and I turned to see Brodie sitting down, all cleaned up and tidy like I'd never seen him be before. He bit his lip. 'Hey.'

'Hey.'

He took my hand, tracing my fingers with his, so gently and deliberately I was transported back to before Lima, when I'd thought we'd had something. Did we still? He was so close to me I could smell his soap and the hairs on my arms stood on end.

'So, I've had a shower …' His lips quirked and fell again. Was he nervous? 'And I've eaten. And I've a real actual bed waiting for me tonight …'

I felt my cheeks heat and his eyes widened.

'I am not …' he faltered. 'That was not a proposition. What I'm trying to say is, I'm feeling safe. And I suddenly thought about how I'd be feeling if Alice and I were still on the wrong side of that army checkpoint.' He watched me steadily.

'And?'

'And I'm really grateful you wouldn't leave us.' He gripped my hand. 'Thank you.'

I looked at his fingers entwined with mine. 'You're welcome.'

He leant his head against mine. 'It was a good day when you stomped past me at a bus station.'

I smiled. 'It was. Missed a bus, caught a boy.'

He was smiling too. 'Think you've caught me, do you?'

My cheeks blazed.

He buried his face in my hair so I could feel his warm breath, then kissed my cheekbone. 'I don't mind being caught,' he murmured.

Our lips brushed together. 'Nor I.'

We kissed then, and I didn't care that we were in the middle of a crowded room. Someone wolf-whistled, and we broke apart to see Alice grinning at us.

I rested my head on his good shoulder. Soft conversations swirled around us.

'You're not sad about missing your flight?' he asked.

I took a moment to think about it. 'Yes and no. It would've been great to be going home. But I know Sarah and Miss C and the others are and that somehow makes me feel better. And here's not so bad.'

His arm tightened around me. 'Not so bad at all.'

It was Alice who helped me to my bunk. She pretended she was taking me because I was tired, but she was asleep within moments of hitting the mattress. Odati was already curled up on a bunk in the corner of the room, painkiller-ed to the max. I sunk backwards with a sigh.

Could it only have been a week before that Odati, Mike and I were left behind? How much could change in a week. In the world. In the way we all saw each other. In the way I looked at life.

Out in the common room, someone started playing a guitar and I knew the song immediately. Brodie's ballad that had so surprised me when I first heard it. My skin prickled. Brodie must have found a guitar.

The intricate beauty of his voice lulled me to sleep as I imagined his fingers flying over the strings.

CHAPTER FORTY-SEVEN

I'm happy here. I feel like I can truly help people, be of use. I have Mike's real smile and Alice's skyrocketing confidence, Odati's hugs and Brodie's support. We're safe and well-fed at Esteban's school.

Alice volunteers with the ambulance crews and the rest of us help in the school gardens, growing food for the school and the surrounding neighbourhood. Brodie is in his element. There aren't any goats, but he reckons alpaca cheese could be the next big thing. Mike's not completely free of his addiction yet, but one of the doctors has put him on a program that will get him there soon. And safely. He's asked me to teach him to draw.

I'm still worried at what's going to happen. At night when I hear explosions I think of the thin line of defence that keeps this inner city safe, and I try not to picture what would happen should it fail. Every time Alice is on call, I barely sleep until she's safe back with us.

We didn't make it onto our plane.

We're grounded.

But I think we're adapting. I think the wings that sustain us are in our minds.

I hope everyone's okay. When I get homesick I imagine Mum and Dad out the back with Sarah, hearing about all we did before that bus drove off without me. The acacia will start flowering soon, and I picture them under its cheery yellow mantle and I know the bees will be there in droves like they were last year and the year before. Even though the news, when we get it, tells me Australia is as volatile as here, I picture them safe.

And once I pop this massive email in the outbox, I'll be able to imagine you reading it, and you'll know everything we faced from the moment that yellow bus left us behind. I don't know how long it will take to crawl to your inboxes, but I have confidence it will make it. Eventually.

And so will I one day. And Brodie, Odati and Mike. Maybe not Alice, I think more holds her here than beckons her home. But we'll all make it to where we want to be. Because we've stuck together.

It's become like second nature to do this, "now" is the 8th May at midday.

I love you guys.

Xx Eva

ACKNOWLEDGEMENTS

I wrote the majority of the first draft for this book during NaNoWriMo 2015, so let's start with three cheers for NaNoWriMo and a long-distance hug to the best of NaNo buddies, Pierr Morgan. You rock!

Many people gave critique and important feedback on this manuscript, helping it become what it is. A special shout-out to the SCBWI Australia West peeps. The energy that forms when groups of children's book writers and illustrators get together is epic. And to everyone I've worked with at Rhiza Edge, but especially Rochelle and Sara: you are wizards. Thank you!

To the rest of the Faux Four—Cristy Burne, Nadia L. King and Shirley Marr—you ladies make writing fun and I'm so glad we found each other. An extra special thanks goes to Cristy—fab sister and awesome beta reader. My manuscripts are always longer than yours. I owe you.

Writing means a lot of time at a laptop, and even more time with your head in the clouds. So my final and most heartfelt thanks goes to Andrew and J. For your love, support, enthusiasm, adventures, and cups of tea. You two are the best!

Printed by Libri Plureos GmbH in Hamburg, Germany